MAKING SKELETONS DANCE

PETER MACSOVSZKY

Making Skeletons Dance

TRANSLATED BY
JOHN MINAHANE

Seagull
BOOKS

LONDON NEW YORK CALCUTTA

Slovenské
literárne
centrum

This book has received a subsidy
from SLOLIA Committee,
the Centre for Information on
Literature in Bratislava, Slovakia

The Slovak List

SERIES EDITOR: Julia Sherwood

Seagull Books, 2024

First published in Slovak as *Mykať kostlivcami*
Drewo a srd, 2010
Copyright © Peter Macsovszky, 2024

First published in English translation by Seagull Books, 2024
English translation © John Minahane, 2024

ISBN 978 1 8030 9 414 4

British Library Cataloguing-in-Publication Data
A catalogue record for this book is available from the British Library.

Typeset by Seagull Books, Calcutta, India
Printed and bound by WordsWorth India, New Delhi, India

A row of keys hung from a shelf above it on which some short stout candles flickered and poured out pools of soft tallow. They cast their uncertain light on a skull with green sequins for eyes and a circlet of gilt marigolds for a crown. Above this, on the wall, whole skeletons danced and cavorted, rustling in the draught from the door, for they were cut out of paper.

Anita Desai, *The Zigzag Way*
(2004)

Telling the reader that any possible resemblance to real persons is coincidental would be pointless.

CONTENTS

Making Skeletons Dance

1. There's somebody

whose refuge is a pub like this, neither filthy nor spotless, but the sort of place where a passer-by does not stay too long. Battered, creaky chairs, dust-coated wooden panelling, a slot machine. For somebody, refuge means a bar counter, subdued conversation, light music, worldly-wise glances from bronzed faces. For someone, again, it's a woman willing to hear the cycled effusions of pain, morning and evening. Hear them, tend to them, cultivate them and protect them. Fantasies of alleged wrongs and menaces. For Simon Blef, whom no misery is tormenting today and therefore claims no caring, refuge means this Amsterdam pub, neither filthy nor spotless, scrunched at the corner of Gravenstraat and Nieuwezijds Voorburgwal. From here Simon Blef gazes at the world, observes passers-by, how they borrow and steal gestures, in a way that is both unique and custom worn. Not quite half an hour ago he was boring through the crowds that came hurtling out from the platforms of Centraal Station and wondering whether to go left and find some quiet boozer in the red-light district side streets, or go right and cast anchor as ever in this unprepossessing drinking shop, which basically serves as an entrance hall for a hotel and restaurant on the first floor.

Simon has picked his spot by the window so he can see the doings not only on the street but also by the bar counter. Encompassing with one's gaze the largest possible segment of the world currently served up: then he feels in a place of refuge.

Indifferently he tracks the translocation of torsos, their jostling, swishing, hesitancy, and then a renewed repelling decisiveness. Voices, hair, eyes, chests. Some shift this way, others that. Footsteps squelch, figures hunch, limbs seesaw. Shoe soles stick and unstick themselves from the dark-grey paving stones strewn with squashed-out bits of chewing gum, spittle blobs, remnants of ice cream, sandwiches and fruit. Plans, itineraries, turbulence in stomachs. Bodies prevaricating, bodies galloping, bodies embodying something. Announcing something, concealing something. Out-thrust inquisitive jawbones, nervous eyeballs. These this way, those that way. Bags of dreams, bladders of words. Bladders of phlegm.

Some push bicycles, more have wives dragging them. Certain wives grip umbrellas or guidebooks, while a number are shoving prams. Howls come out of those, babble from others, a rustling sound from still others. But Simon, behind this glass, hears nothing, only gazes; analyses nothing, only props up his jaw. And contentedly breathes, blows on his tot of Holland gin. And torsos flow. Flow here, flow there, limbs in the current.

And he gazes, gazes at the bristly bricks of Nieuwe Kerk, gazes at those especially, at that sullen gothic temple which someone denied a belfry. Truly, no belfry. Not like Oude Kerk in the red-light quarter: that market stall of God can boast of a sturdy rearing spire that may be seen across the roofs and canals, the barges and bicycles, across the hordes of scruffs leering in front of the display windows with the pink-lighted benefactresses; it can pride itself on a smartly tapering helmet, not like its younger sibling where, you'd never believe it, the rulers of Holland take their oaths of office. The black bricks of Nieuwe Kerk. A delight to gaze at, gape at for hours on end, which Simon alone knows.

Some of those fluent torsos stop and look hither too, at Simon, into this brown twilight; they gape through the greasy windows, curious whether there mightn't be a space for them here—two or three chairs, a table, a slot by the bar; they gape just for a moment, without deeper interest, then they pass on to the window opposite which is all laid out with women's party shoes. The torsos shift over there and afterwards move on further, gaping at the summer shoes, the white, the pink and the blue, they examine the merchandise, they examine the sales assistant and her customers within, working out what's the point of them, what they've got on and what they have on their minds, they gape at them, just for a moment, before being washed on further, to another shop, to another bar, or they betake themselves straight to Spui Square for a beer in the smoke-dusky Cafe De Zwart.

Simon diverts his attention to the bar counter and the jovial barmaid. Scraps of foreign languages filter to him from the handful of men sitting on the high chairs; sometimes he seems to be hearing American, then again Spanish—the foreigners guffaw, they arrive and depart, some descend to the cellar to relieve themselves in the cramped toilet smelling of suds and then clamber back up the breakneck stairs, and order another beer or another short.

Like sailors on dry land hit by a rainstorm, Simon muses. And now we're drying off, we're in an interlude. We're waiting for a favourable wind in our skulls. Simon taps his forehead and grimaces. A favourable wind. Holland gin, old, yellow and strong, first stings you and burns you, then starts to warm you up and finally gives regular heating. The little stoker in the steamship's bowels. And a beer for company. Two golden liquids. By their light, the soaked sailor immediately picks up courage: to murmur under his moustache or scribble something in his notebook.

Simon Blef, notorious recorder.

Favourable wind, blow away these thoughts and blow in something . . . something . . .

The golden light of the beer and the golden light of oude jenever. These two lights have a mutual understanding. They stand facing, one in a quarter-litre measure, the other in a sovereignly moulded brandy glass. They comprehend each other, whispering something; Simon bends closer, but so far, he cannot distinguish even a word of their dispute. So he cranes forward and again looks for the hostess, whose round face might have been cut from a painting by Franz Hals. And he sees, in her movements he sees, in the motions of her fat he sees very well, that this woman is not, quite definitely not, this woman does not belong to the clan of soaked sailors: the sea did not cast her up on a port lashed by rainstorms; she is waiting for nothing, her fat is not waiting for a favourable wind. She—Simon mentally names her Jooske—is no castaway, she need not wait for a merciful boat, an ark that will take her on deck, dry her off and feed her; not for one second does she await such a ship, she has never awaited it, for she herself is the ship that must be waited for, and she will arrive, she will sail up alongside, tilt the bottle and rescue the mariner's throat.

2. Running into the pub comes

a blond youngster, who straightaway starts clawing, grappling his way up onto one of the dry-swabbed barstools. He leans against the counter, stretches his neck, looking for a barman, for anyone, for movement irrespective.

This young fellow doesn't yet know dismay, not yet. He doesn't yet know he could slide and how he could slide off that rickety bar seat, topple and go thwack on the floor in a pool of beer or melted ice, or the puddle between one spit blob and another.

Atoms, oh, atoms! Child's molecules, child's sweat, boyish breath, putrid socks, sticky fingers, dried chocolate behind the nails. Shit-stained underwear; stink of sprayed urine. The monkey hormone of youth. Chemistry of unrestraint. Bruises on the knees, the elbows. Falling milk teeth. Snots and spits. Laughter and chatter. And yet again those sticky fingers. Does anything more repulsive currently exist on earth than a small boy's sticky fingers? Simon imagines how those sticky fingers with dried chocolate behind the nails leaf through a freshly printed book and destroy it. What a good thing it is that all

those years, which so many remember so lovingly, how good it is that
those sticky-fingered and kids'-sweat-smelly-socked years, those years
of unbridled howling and screeching in the schoolyard, years of casual
shoves and elbow jabs, sweaty bread and oranges in plastic bags, what
a good thing that all those and similar years are gone forever, those
years of stomach upset, parental slaps and Physical Education masters'
cruel jests. What a good thing that Simon now can just sit as he is,
pour yellow liquid into himself and indifferently watch the muck-
daubed crush on the streets. And what a bad thing that he will never,
ever, have one hundred per cent protection against a brat warren like
this, which by voice, stink and motion instantly hurls him into the
hullabaloo of school!

They'll break up eventually, all those wells, canals and piping
that distribute hormonal rabies and nourishments through the body,
they'll all dissolve; all those networks of soft engineering will dissolve.
All the glands and veins, all the bladders and reservoirs, eyeballs and
hollows. The atoms will split like hazelnut shells. Eventually, even
this child will begin to lose the elasticity of muscles and mind; first
he will lose flexibility of mind, and afterwards his fixed ideas will fet-
ter his muscles, sucking away their power, and the muscles will
shrink, they'll surrender, the child will begin to shuffle, one day he'll
discover that he's seventy years old, and yet still that child who's
climbing up on the bar counter. And then he'll no longer be bothered
that at any moment he's going to die; all that'll worry him is that in
seventy years he has not moved anywhere (and where indeed should
he have moved to?) and now he must die as a child. What an idea!
Simon immediately starts to come to life. And afterwards, those worms
that chew the ancient's body will dissolve, they'll disintegrate, and
something smaller, something much smaller and more wretched will

bear off their scraps to their version of a den, to a further safety, to the safety of further ruin. And there in that ruin, in that workshop and forge, those miniature scraps will be reassembled, and from their combination once more something greater will grow, once more only some miserable chirping thing. Simon reaches for the tot of Holland gin.

Mariner, he records words like that.

One day he would like to write a novel. About sailors, because they are permitted to drink, to drink deep. When he reads about sailors, or more precisely about writers who have hired out their services on long voyages through the world's seas, he has a feeling of doing something beneficial for his health. Not just anyone, after all, may sail the oceans; the mariner must be a strapping lad, he has to have muscles like steel, use strong language and be able to handle a lot of drink. A sailor cannot sit around with namby-pamby creatures who imagine they're writers, but in reality are scared to live. A sailor— that is, above all, an opportunity to become a writer. The sailor travels much and experiences much while doing so, he involves himself in all sorts of things and gets himself out of all possible scrapes, he dodges the Grim Reaper's scythe, and afterwards he will either write or not write about that. *Either*. Precisely this *either or* makes an impression on Blef. The sailor may freely decide; he may spurn the opportunity of *immortalizing* experiences such as the namby-pamby writers do not encounter even in dreams. Simon would like to have the body of a sailor, he would gladly *reside* in some sailor, but needless to say, only somewhat circumspectly, so that it doesn't do much damage. To him, not to the sailor. When he looks at the barflies by the counter, there are one or two that he'd tip to be sailors. Except what could they be doing here, in the city centre? And what is *he* doing here, dreaming as much as he does about the society of sturdy fellows? Why doesn't he take himself off to the port; why isn't he searching there for his pub, for his life's opportunity? He ought to make his way there without delay; but the fact is, he's never met a genuine sailor in his life. And indeed, he still hasn't taken part in a sea voyage. Though he enjoys looking at the sea's crashing breakers, on no account would he entrust himself to the care of the marine element. That's why he's such a feeble swimmer. Splashing about close to the shore, that's fine, but to lie flat on his back in the water—not to be considered. Secretly, however, he thinks of how he would love to humble the water. Joyfully would he walk upon it, such a deed would express his delight in setting physical laws at nought. If he was able to walk on water, if he did not need to fear *Nature* (that Nature whose regularities all kowtow to, as if life on a planet with such physical regularities as these was the first prize in some transcendental lottery), he would then even have the courage to become a sailor. Except that today (because once again we have here certain regularities of Nature considered to be *natural*) it is not only exaggerated caution that impedes him in this, but by now also age. At this age and with such enfeebled musculature, no one would give him employment on any deck. So then, he must content himself simply with novels about sailors. Except that those infuse him with a further discontent: from their pages he senses salt, fish, sea wind, the unattainable horizon of steely good health. Yes, if there's something that excites him in sailing novels, it's that physical condition which he's never going to achieve. But if at some time he engaged himself in writing a novel, he would not rake over his own state of health in the story; he wouldn't distribute his valetudinarian fears and handicaps among the various characters. He'd write about the sea, about a sailor's pensiveness, about a writer who had for a while become a sailor. He'd *roll out* the theme, as they say. Of course, first he'd compress, but afterwards he'd roll out. Motif after motif, detail after detail. He'd write about a sailor, so that the sailor in his novel might with a tranquil conscience drink. Because what could be more dismal than a novel where a writer is drinking? The sailor would sit in a hostelry like this one, or even smack bang right here, in this pub, at the corner of Gravenstraat and Nieuwezijds Voorburgwal, he'd gape at the street, and he'd drink. None of that philosophizing about novels and questions of being. *Questions of being?* Simon's sailor would roar. *You've the sea out there, go live some life! Afterwards you can blether.*

Bursting into the barroom after the boy came a burly, self-assured woman, her massive thighs squeezed into faded jeans, her white blouse loose, fanning, rakish: breasts of the indestructible peasant female. Breasts undulating over the doleful potato fields. Beyond doubt: a mother. A woman, a hunk, a tigress breezing along in power-saving mode; the name Hanneke or Marjon would suit her. Sheepishly she smiles at the barman pulling half-litres, at that emboldened, moistened, red-cheeked philanthropist who had surfaced from the devil-knows-where, maybe from a secret dungeon under the counter, and asks for a lemonade for the boy. The woman, who indeed is probably not called Marjon, doubtless has bounded out of a car parked somewhere nearby. A specimen northerner, the kind that never feels the cold, never, even if she were to stroll through the town in this outfit during a blizzard. Clacking her car keys, a single mother. Or is the successful daddy, after all, hunched in the stowed-aside car? In the front passenger seat, the mother-in-law's seat? Daddy, Daddy, veins, lungs, masculine stink. I too have one, somewhere, Simon thinks, somewhere I too have got it.

Along Gravenstraat now comes a trio of teenyboppers, draped like so many ragpickers, as if some punk's entire wardrobe had fallen on top of them. One of them is spitting, not furtively but methodically, swishy, squelchy spittle. Her girlfriends are enjoying themselves. Coarse badinage brimming up from the throats of a new, sexless generation. Why sexless? These are certainly not lacking the sexual organ, certainly they possess it shaved and tattooed all round with stupid symbols. Between their legs they carry sexual parts that have seen and tried everything already, except tenderness and consideration. If the vaginas of these schoolgirls could speak, their utterances would be in a vulgar voice such as comes from the gullets of drunks in the mean suburbs. Teenyboppers. No, no! These are matured, full-bodied bullfrogs. But in here there's safety, they won't come in here. Throughout the week they are sucking energy drinks; imbibing alcohol comes on the agenda only on Friday or Saturday evenings.

Daddy. So, has he remained sitting in the car? That fragile creature. Because only a fragile man can survive beside Marjon. Or conversely, Marjon can survive only by the side of a fragile man. A regular Boer, if she was giving too much lip, would hit her a decent wallop. So then, is the fragile one now crouching in the seat and impatiently rustling a newspaper? *NRC Handelsblad* or, so as not to overburden one's brain, *Het Parool*? Rustling, because they can never be opened neatly. Or has he got out and is standing now in front of the vehicle? And smoking? Does he dare? Is he smoking impatiently, or with relish? These people certainly have such things well organized in that household of theirs, in a cosy little house somewhere in the garden quarter of this not-too-large but also not-too-small city, at an agreeable distance from the canal, comfortably close to the main town, under the broad grey heavens, under the stormy sky of Cuyp or van Ruisdael, under a sky that seems as if at any moment it must fall down and crush the little cows in the fields, the peasants in the byres, the cyclists on the brick-red cycle tracks. They have their life, this Marjon and her mannikin, definitely they've got a just and well-balanced distribution and scheduling: when she cooks, after work he goes to pick up the child from school; when she goes to get the child, he cooks. He's an indifferent cook—but that doesn't bother anyone: the important thing is that what lies on the plate looks like food, like a colourful, articulated, at least slightly alluring mass of aliment. Simon instantly imagines a square plate—which he can't bear to eat from—and upon it: four or five peas, a drop of some brown sauce, arugula, or briefly a stem or leaf of something green and exotic, some harmless nettle that's transported here from the Mediterranean; potatoes, one or two, beans, everything without memorable taste; a recipe from a supermarket flyer, on quick and healthy cooking. Here, on the plain lands under a van Ruisdael sky.

Simon prefers van Ruisdael—probably from a wilful streak, since where Dutch painting is concerned, everyone goes for Rembrandt and van Gogh. And Mondriaan. In America with only one 'a'. Simon, then, has found his way to van Ruisdael. Not too well known, but not unknown either. And it has to be acknowledged that no one paints rainclouds like van Ruisdael. As if only rainclouds mattered. Here yes, here *only* the rainclouds matter. Whether we can make use of them, or we just let them freely drift in the sky. Some blow-in from abroad would like best to take this sky away with him; he doesn't know how to arrest it, to immortalize it. A camera won't help. Van Ruisdael managed it, but how, how did he contrive that? Simon ruminated, thinking of the *View of Haarlem*: the stunningly high sky, rainclouds malevolent only to those who do not understand this country, and below, almost on the bottom margin of the painting is petite Haarlem, with the little cathedral and the even smaller houses around it; in the foreground a belt of fields suddenly illuminated by sunbeams, which have found a fissure between the luxuriant clouds. Miniature figures in the fields, as if they were listening. This woman would fit into place among them, this putative Marjon. No sportswoman, she.

So then what? A scientist? A teacher? No, more likely to be a secretary. For example, in an educational institute. In an office, the cramped kind. But not cramping her. People like that are unaware that there's something not right about the office. Long manicured nails. Coarse voice. Seemingly self-assured belly laugh, toss of the mane. She too, when she was young, used to behave like those ripe-grown bullfrogs on the street. Afterwards she tamed down. Seemingly. She ceased to be bored. Or she ceased to amuse herself. Her forebears, no doubt about it, used to worship Wotan and then later, some centuries on, textile-factory looms. Her neck, her noise, her expansiveness, testify to nothing but that. Her gallop.

Now she is smiling sheepishly at the bartender, the red-cheeked one, straight into his muddy, rainy gaze; she pays for the lemonade, and with that she prods the boy out of doors. But how she strides! As if she were walking across clods on sodden fields. No one had thrown boards across the miry puddles. And in mists, but now no longer in a van Ruisdael painting but in the recent past of this tumultuous woman: windmill silhouettes, not far off the thickset belfry of the village church; wafting in on the wind is the wail of an abandoned cow.

And again, the daddy. By no means fragile. Thoughtful, sporting build. He'd like to see his wife on a clay court, but it seems he's already reconciled himself to her sedentariness, to her couch, with the depressions in it and on her orange thighs. Ultimately, even that sedentariness of hers has a certain grace, the charm of the full-grown pussycat. Far from it, this is the genuine granddaughter of frivolous but not immoral sailors' wives. Who a few generations later banged on the table and roared: Enough! Enough of waiting, enough of the long boring evenings, let's amuse ourselves! And to this day they're amusing themselves. Marjon, she's the very embodiment of such vigorous table banging—she truly will not prance round a tennis court or wheeze in a fitness centre: she has the right to weariness, to lounging, to her nails and her yeasty allures. She keeps the house in tip-top shape, dust doesn't even manage to alight on the furniture, she is industrious and provident also. So then, Daddy works, for example, Simon makes a big effort of imagination—in research? In a marketing department? A well-proportioned figure, sunburnt in fact; really now, where did he get that delicate hue of brown? An exotic ancestor? Surinam? Indonesia? Let him be called Geert. Simon somehow doesn't believe that this good-looking and inquisitive man isn't cheating on his wife. He doesn't believe it. But how might that unknown adulteress look? Maybe again like this Marjon? For indeed, she's still not to be cast aside: she sparkles, she smacks, she pounds, she sails. But not for long now. Not for long. And maybe there isn't any Geert waiting for her out there, maybe she's not bringing up the boy with a Geert, but— with a Gerda.

Yes indeed, with some Gerda that she joined in a partnership after a number of unsatisfactory relationships with men. Actually, both of them had gone through such relationships, from one to the next. Marjon had brought a child from some marriage. More probable, however, was that by agreement with Gerda, Marjon underwent artificial insemination. Both of them were longing for a child. After so many years of caring for abused dogs, brought in from the southern European lands. Even today they have three, and from time to time they put up another, until some passably kind and loving master is found. To the three dogs they have added three cats from the animal shelter. The cats, however, apparently were insufficient to remove negative energies from the household, because Gerda still, after years, had a suspicion that her former partner was using black magic to manipulate her from a distance. It had cost Marjon no small effort to knock these obsessive ideas out of Gerda's sconce. After four years' cohabitation they finally got married. The ceremony took place in the town hall; for bridal gowns they had brown medieval costumes sewn, inspired probably by the times of Robin Hood. Just preceding them was the marriage of a gay couple, who had decided on a more restrained outfit: white monkey suits with jaunty white top hats.

No, Simon decides, Marjon is not running around with any Gerda: she is no lesbian, surely she has a comely and submissive husband. Simon accordingly will not continue to nurture fantasies about the cohabitation of two women; he would rather return to his daydreams about the sailor novel.

Outside, in front of the pub, on Gravenstraat, two bewildered Japanese women extract a map from a small rucksack. People, cells, people, the weave of outlined streets. A tram's rumbling, molecules of the metal wheel, in the tram once again cells. Eyes flashing hither, eyelashes twitching at the smoke-blacked walls of Nieuwe Kerk, then back to the map, to the molecules of paper. They squint at the sky, with foreboding. Will it rain, or will this drizzle cease?

3. Blef's Blef

Him? Now? Here? He comes to mind? Into the picture? Into the scene? The scene of a sailor groping in memory? Here, to the wooden, spittle-streaked, creaky floor of an Amsterdam pub? So then, Blef's Blef. Blef, progenitor of the Simon Blef here seated, and Blef, progeny of a Blef deceased? One Blef in the midst?

Blef, blether, blasphemy. Ultimately this will remain of him, the old one, if anything at all. They will remember this of him: his clowning, masks, tricks, physical prowess, operetta arias and walking on his hands. Even that is something. Blarney, bluff, blunder. Beneficent builder of blunders. Actually, they were spellbinding, those blunderings of his, women found them charming, men provocative; to the more educated they seemed banal, while they gave inspiration to well-versed debaters in local salons: how to make the library's cultural activities more effective, how to improve the condition of the women's football team, what themes the philosophical circle might occupy itself with (Sartre and de Beauvoir?). He'll come up with a solution: Anton Blef. Philosopher. Always he declared himself a philosopher. Though having studied only librarianship. Originally, he hadn't wanted even that. He longed for a career as a gym master. It occurs to Simon that had the country where his father was born possessed a sea, maybe he'd have become a sailor. Anton Blef, seafarer. At the end of the day, he had found his path to the waters of ship modelling.

Babble, bobble, bubble.

Simon turns over a leaf in his notebook.

Occupy himself with Blef, then. OK, but not for long. Not for long.

Occupy himself with that man, old Blef, with his bewitching, bragging babble right here, in this tavern, in this (further) tavern chapter.

Because (they say) to make a trinity is best? Because even blessing begins: in the name of the Father. Next in line comes the Son, while the Holy Ghost remains somewhere at the end, out in the garage repairing the fifth wheel. Clinking of a spanner.

Jooske, aha, Jooske! Dear Jooske! Here! Here! One more round, *rondje*, let the heat be stoked properly in the boiler house of faint-hearted recollection! Properly; let the fiery fluid smite the bowels!

Simon quickly receives what he has demanded, and even with an added bonus: a buxom smile and an almost manly clap on the back. He hurriedly wipes his brow (embarrassment?) and has a sip of the beer. First the beer, then the gin.

And Blef the elder—wouldn't somewhere else do better for remembering him? This spittoon on Gravenstraat, after all, doesn't have much space for dispensing; this street is too short, too narrow, for the parade of events bound up in memory; one digresses in here to think about other things. To drag spectres in here? Those that are neither ludicrous nor horrific? Wouldn't some noisy shebeen with a pong of vomit be better, somewhere in the boisterous vicinity of Oude Kerk, in the labyrinth of red and pink windows? Such a dive, oh yes indeed, it would be a more suitable rolling mill for thought; there a person would reckon differently with the (heroic) deeds of the fathers!

The fathers! Fathers of deeds! Fatherhood, *fatherly* feelings, masculine *tenderness*, tears of emotion over the fragile little body of the offspring: blé-blé-blé . . . Some fathers this side, the others that side. Some drag wives, others wheel prams. Prams? And in the prams are future fathers, future appendages of wives, future carers for sickly mothers and sickly wives, future fathers of fathers and fathers of deeds!

The empire of Simon's father is not extensive, merely variegated. Certain of its nooks bring to mind a scrapheap, while others bear a striking resemblance to warehouses of unusable toys. Mountains and forests extend to the east, and brooks, waterfalls and bridges. Seeing it *in extenso*, with a manly, sovereignly proprietorial, proprietorially contented and complacent view (or rather prospect?) of the jewels of this small kingdom, old Blef's eyes turn moist. This, precisely this he calls his beautiful home, his loveliest corner, the hands on whose palms he always might (could, wished to) weep. To the west of the empire, hence on the hospitable lowlands, the traveller is welcomed by villages with the granite facades of former cultural centres, single-nave churches and their humble, somewhat dumpy belfries, robust blue frescoes, bashful specimens of folk baroque, ruins of castles and mansions' cracked plasterwork, and swimming baths' wooden cubicles. But here already we're in the south, that is to say the south of the empire: football boots, tennis shoes, goals, points, seconds, rusty buses, sportsmen's dressing rooms, showers, sportswomen's sweat, half-abandoned village football pitches, cows grazing on their margins, nothing for weak natures, nothing for Simon or a small person or one who comes later. The father's empire has never suffered from an insufficiency of women. It has fresh and fading women, feisty and humble, seasoned and unpractised, meritorious and potentially so, budding and blooming. And the north? What's to the north of the empire? No one's thought of that. But in the empire there was (is) also this: catechism illustrations, where a naughty altar boy (future father) had sketched obscene details; home-made binoculars; then a Communist Party card, a service weapon, an accordion, a guitar, a career, photographs, two children from a second marriage, photos, promotion, conspiracy theories, years in the diplomatic service, photos, cameras, a trip to the Sahara, then more photographs, a Cambodian princess and a group singing of French chansons in a bus trudging through the Mongolian steppe, photos, political downfall, a second divorce, a pack of thirty dogs guarding a strategic object, seminars on bioenergetic healing, photos, a country cottage (damp and elongated), a jovial neighbour in a tracksuit (a hole in the tracksuit, and another in the father's). Swallowed up in his father's empire there was also a piano, one entire sturdy piano, Simon's mother's piano; the empire swallowed it like a thing of nothing, more easily than a snake does a mouse.

Piano, *piano*, Simon repeated to himself. Keys, molecules, veneer. He'd heard all sorts of things about it from his mother and grandmother, but the mysterious fact was that he remembered only one little story, an invention of his Uncle Tomi, his mother's brother. Allegedly that piano (a grand? Simon, as he'd always imagined it, wished it to be a grand; hitherto he had not asked his mother whether it really was a grand, and also black; maybe she'd told him several times that yes, haven't I told you, it was a grand, or no, no, it was just an ordinary small piano, but Simon had no memory of this, he knew only that now he could scarcely bear the thought of a piano, a little piano shoved against the wall, like in Westerns, he couldn't imagine, or didn't wish to imagine such a retiring, delicate, self-immersed, insulted-seeming piece of furniture) had been bought along with two angels. Statues? Did they buy it together with statues of angels? Simon then barely ten, asked again. No, they weren't statues, said the uncle, then a stripling of about sixteen, a well-known liar and ruffian. But normal live angels, about half a metre tall. Nothing ornamental, don't think that. They helped in transporting the piano, and they shifted it whenever there was spring cleaning at home. You'd want to see how they toiled! They were sweating like little pigs. Draught angels. (It couldn't be a small piano then, for how would they drag it? It would kill them. Quite different with the winged version: the wings have legs and the legs have wheels.) For the most part, they rested. Where? Always in a different place, said the uncle knowingly, and with sadistic indifference scrutinized Simon's face. Simon believed him for a moment. In the end, why not, why couldn't someone purchase two live angels with a piano? Not to believe in angels, after all, would have meant (for Simon) renouncing his entire Catholic upbringing, all the beautiful stories and spiritually charged illustrations of the saints, the whole dimension of mystery, expectation and miracle, all those cosy evenings illuminated by haloes and the consoling speeches with which his grandmother regaled Simon (the second one, not that other one, not his mother's mother and mother of Uncle Tomi, but the second, more important, kinder one, his father's mother, the mother of old Blef). Simon believed, and his belief lasted as far as the kitchen, where he asked (his granny, the mother's mother) what truth there was in all this, whether live angels really had appeared in the house and whether they had pulled behind them (ropes in hand; and panting?) the piano. Granny rolled her eyes, actually she didn't, she did not roll them, she was not a woman of eloquent gestures; chronically she was overcome by weariness, a languor of mysterious origin, an exhaustion stemming from people or from the white wine that she hid in her bedroom in the heavy, shiny wardrobe (of red spruce?) behind her folded bridal garments, and which she kept sipping in small doses. In brief, she stammered something, she hadn't expected such a question, actually she hadn't been counting on any questions the livelong day, she'd given no consideration to questions and answers, she was ceaselessly in the grip of a communicative lethargy (no common kind; hers was, as it were, metaphysical), so she mumbled something, probably a question, a question for a question, she was able only for a question, something like: 'What're you talking about? (and with this 'What're you talking about?' Simon now, in the pub on Gravenstraat, imagined eyes rolling), and immediately she blurted out that no angels had ever been seen in that house, not even porcelain ones.

And what if, despite all? What if nonetheless some were here, swishing their incomprehensible wings? Alive and finely shaped? And merry? Playful, running about and leaping on the fake Persian carpets amid the glass cases with the real ones, the crystal vases and cups of Meissen porcelain that no one had ever used? And: do angels have a skeleton? Ribs, collarbone, skull, thighbone, joints, pelvis? To be sure, they need not be composed of cells, molecules, or any kind of soft, breathing, ruffled and warm matter; simply, whether they have skeletons or not, that is what Simon would like to know. Whether they have skeletons, whether those corporeal repositories of theirs are of ether or indeed of astral substance, or if they don't have a skeleton to stiffen them. Because then how can they survive in the colliding currents of air?

The piano disappeared, plunged into the unappealing lake of the past. No one stole it and no one chopped it up to make winter fuel: Simon's parents, a marital couple who could no longer stand sharing a domicile alternately with the bride's parents and with the groom's, required their own space, an apartment, a humble two-room high-rise apartment, for example, in those apartment houses that had lately (at that time lately) sprung up by the railway bank (evidently the sounds of trains, the scraping of brakes, announcements through amplifiers, clattering in the depot and the smell of oil and rust, had afterwards stimulated vagrant inclinations in Simon), and Simon's mother, who had not played for years, decided to sell the piano. And four years later the piano rolled away to the father's empire. He didn't even need angels for his transport. He waved a wing and made a splash in the mournful lake of the past.

Since the inexhaustible libido of old Blef (who was not even thirty then) drew him to another woman in the capital city, the divorce was just a formality. Simon's mother later declared that financial distress made her sell the apartment and find cheaper accommodation. The piano was thus exchanged for an apartment, the apartment fell victim to the divorce; nonetheless the divorce, and everything that followed from it, pertained to the father's empire.

A magnificent piece, she recalled. Steinway. Or Petrof. I no longer remember. What's certain is that at most there were two others in the town. Today they'd be valued at a fortune, she mused. But I wouldn't sell it. Would you play it? Simon asked. With your sixty-five-year-old fingers? That you tapped a typewriter's keyboard with for thirty years?

And what would you play? Something by Satie? Satie? And who's he? Or Beethoven's Moonlight? Debussy's Arabesque No. 1? But you don't have to bury me right away just because I don't want to play. My mind is still functioning. See how many crosswords I solve in a week. Well? Now you're silent, what?

4. He cannot sit here to eternity,

before too long he must shell himself out of this half-light, crawl forth
from this retro-romancing, unstick his arse, stretch out his shoe, his
foot in it, the joints and hairy tufts, into the street; compose the chest,
set hair, ears, eyebrows to the wind, which is sinuously sliding in over
the clattering trams on Nieuwezijds Voorburgwal. Attach himself to
something. To those who so single-mindedly stride in this direction,
only immediately to reconsider and head off in the direction over
there. Or join the parish of those who a moment ago were still heading
that way, but at the halfway stage (between what and what?) pulled
up short, muttered something under their moustaches, stopped,
screeched, and set off back in the opposite direction, along
Gravenstraat, devil-knows-where. Or they were motionless for a
moment, something captivated them, or nothing captivated them,
they stopped just like that, stayed put, had an awareness of how pleasant this was, or alternatively, how unpleasant it was, how disquieting,
how audacious, to stop still like that in such a flow of torsos. And
squint at anything that glimmered in the vicinity.

And again those fingers. Memory fashions ludicrous things: fingers, those sixty-five-year-old, those that maybe have never played demanding pieces, only the perennial etudes, preludes and sonatas, the small-town repertoire. Again just those fingers, their sixty-five-year-old hysteria. Not panic, sixty-five doesn't have that, while for twenty or sixteen it's a constant. The panic of a sixteen-year-old girl has the sixty-five-year-old fingers in its power. And with it, the Sunday forenoons replete with instant esoteric aphorisms and fragments of tabloid adventures. Was it for this, for such minor moods and brain squalls, that Simon came here? So that he could grope in something that is commonly groped in by those whom years ago he'd left behind in his so-called native country, which might long ago have had a sea if it gathered the tears of its hypochondriac and selfish citizens?

With uncertain lettering he scribbled in his notebook: *sea of hypochondriac tears*. There, in that country, of which its inhabitants avow that although it is small, it is the most beautiful country in the world, not to mention the fact that the most beautiful girls are born there: in that country whoever does not complain, whoever does not lament, whoever does not backbite, whoever does not dig pits for others and pitch logs at competitors' legs, is of no account, isn't even a human being but a non-human insentient being, robot, machine, thing. And here? Here, under van Ruisdael's sky, is it likely that people do not weep, do not slander one another and destroy one another's careers? But assuredly, certainly the same thing happens here; simply that Simon still doesn't understand the local language, gestures and attitudes well enough to identify dirty practices straight away. The conclusion he draws from this is: the more fully you know a language (for example, the so-called mother tongue), the more you will reveal the *nuances* of human malevolence. Profound knowledge of a language therefore means a profound knowledge of human evil. For Simon, as long as this country strikes him as at least somewhat foreign, he will feel freer here than in the land where it seemed he was abused in both the mother tongue and the administrative language. Only an idiot can cherish tenderness for his *native* language. Only an idiot, a dangerous idiot can love the language in which you most precisely understand hatred and insults.

He took a sip of beer. His grey, sleepless face fused with the surrounding furniture, with the wood panelling of the walls, the grubby glass, the grey and cluttered wall of Nieuwe Kerk on the opposite side of the street. The room seemed submerged in a kind of lilac steam, a sticky mist composed of self-pity and utterly futile memories, which a person can make nothing of even decades later.

After the beer, a slug of jenever. Just then he wanted to write something, but his pen fell on the floor, and when he bent for it, fever flooded his head. And his father's empire was back in a blink. Back it came, bouncing once again into this pub, actually it had never exited, it had just hopped aside, gone down the winding stairs to the cellar, to the toilet with the metal doors, down to squeeze the earthworm.

Simon finally grasped his pen, straightened up, but his father's empire did not budge from its place. That empire of itinerant attractions flared up again in full lilac-hued parade, the empire of a Grand Pasha (the harem, its contingents, White slaves, hired janissaries, the politic and yet transparent diplomacy of Ottoman officials), a sultanate of sporting achievements, a Cambodian princess, espionage tasks, a dizzying political career, a theory of possible Turkish origin (old Blef in his youth had looked like a fiery Arab, in old age like a Persian-carpet salesman), and grotesque talks with the sly foxes from the Holy See. An empire daftly hammered together from private (and notably banana) colonies, so far flung that neither the sun or the moon (for a few years) ever set on them. The empire, then, was back; in Simon's memory it stretched forth once again, an empire resided in, lived and moved in by one of his grandfathers also, father of old Blef, a handsome man with a thick white mane and the black brows of an ageing Chaplin. Old Blef's old Blef was, however, taller in stature than the real Chaplin; he never wore scuffed shoes or moustaches, and all that bound him to modern times was the profession of engine driving. And this Chaplin, Anton Blef declared, surely must have had a woman at every railway station; he was after all handsome, dashing, supple and muscular. In vain did he go to Mass and confession, you won't get rid of libido, throw it out the door and it'll come back through the window, and if not by the window, then it'll crawl through a crack in the wall or from under the secretaire, or by that same door where you flung it out, old Blef philosophized. In short, even if you literally shat on it, even then you won't rid yourself of it, it'll peck its way out through the cellar or crawl down from the ceiling, hop right into your head and deny you sleep; it won't let you eat, or even shit. To old Blef's Blef, the admiration and lures of women could not have been and indeed were not indifferent, Anton Blef pronounced; his own philandering triumphs were not sufficient for him, constantly he needed to give a historical basis to his charm and his right to a hunter's appetite, via the story of his father, an enthusiastic lover of folk songs and popular hymns. My father, said old Blef, so adored folk songs that he wrote them down in a notebook, indeed he began to go to the railway singing club or mixed choir, or just a male choir, I can't be sure now; old Blef didn't know, he never took pains with details, at any given time his only aim was to entertain the listener. Driven by this purpose, he did not hesitate to disparage his own mother, Simon's adored grandmother (the second one, needless to say, not she who sheltered bottles of white wine in the wardrobe); he did not hesitate to ridicule her, and from time to time in company he brought out a tale about her jealousy, how secretly, under the mask of night, she followed her husband right under the windows of the building where the singing group was meeting and waited there, with a whetted kitchen knife in her bosom, hee-hee, till those nightingales had sung themselves hoarse. My mother with a knife, just imagine it! Whether she desired to kill her husband or the (probably non-existent) seductress, was not known. Simon's father however claimed that it was the adulteress, yes, definitely she wanted to waste her; what a farce! What temperament! He guffawed in his attractive baritone, polished by time. Concealed in his guffaw was admiration and a certain condescending respect for a simple woman; that was undoubtedly part of the ritual, instrumentally inserted in his homage to family. Each time Simon imagined a puddle of blood, wheezing breath, Granny in fetters, farewell, *sursum corda*, farewell, the Catholic paradise and the garish postcard of St Peter's Square that Father Daniel had sent from Rome. Ah, Father Daniel, old Blef might at any time recall him in a merry company: he was a nice, well-educated man, what he liked best was to educate altar boys; yes, I think he was a bit of a poof, no doubt about that, but he was the considerate kind of fairy, he didn't hurt anyone, he'd just stroke a forelock and kiss cheeks, platonically. I went to him for Latin.

Or was old Blef's mother perhaps planning to kill her husband, taking no account whatever of the seductress? Had her hatred become concentrated above all upon men? On the empire of coin-clinkers? Because deep down she was governed by the *spirit* of female solidarity?

But why was she planning to perform her deed under the windows of the station building; why after the singing session, why in public? Was it all one to her by then? Had the chalice simply brimmed over? Simon imagined the engine driver's funeral: a noisy knot of his engine-driving colleagues, stokers, ticket collectors, dispatchers, sheet-metal workers, the station master in uniform, two cleaners, the lady that takes the money at a hatch in the station toilet, cashiers, accountants (who were singing group members?), the buffet server, the old woman who used to sell faded flowers near the station pub; and then Granny in handcuffs, a priest, the blade of the bloody knife, a poppy-seed tart such as only Granny knew how to bake, that God-fearing, self-sacrificing and beneficent woman, apple tart, according to old Blef she didn't have a clue about sex, curdled noodles, one could therefore presume, by the number of children she gave birth to, that in all her life she suffered her husband to approach her three times, Grenadier March (the adored food of Simon's father), only three times and then with stringent provisions for modesty (a white nightdress with a hole at the level of the pudenda), for in truth she was not tormented by any sexual appetite, the male body repelled her, actually she despised men, with a mystical awe she thrust far from her the festivities of the flesh, so that her husband, the handsome engine driver with the thick brows of an ageing Chaplin, who during one of the World War air raids had not hesitated to leap from a speeding locomotive right into the cornfields, had to seek relief elsewhere, and maybe he didn't have to, maybe he sought nothing, he was too fatigued, maybe old Blef just invented all that and would carry on fabulating, so that even when on the verge of the grave he might adorn his libido with a patina of family history.

What hour is it? How many hours by now have set up in sequence? Or: how many of them have escaped? How many black rods have slipped by? What do the numbers say, as they incessantly slide down a blind tunnel or fall into some pipe, a vacuum cleaner's suction or other indifferent pipe? Something, some monster, some gigantic buzzing biomorphic mechanism is permanently hoovering data from this world; sometimes it sucks them up more slowly, at other times faster, the main thing is that it's hoovering, cleaning up. Or not, it doesn't hoover, doesn't clean, the data remain in their places. And the numbers spin and spin. They spin something very simple and yet ungraspable; they rove and they weave a saga of disappearance, they keep spinning on these little places of theirs, they do not budge, they do not vanish anywhere.

5. Not infrequently here,

to the boozer on the corner of Gravenstraat and Nieuwezijds Voorburgwal, a cat comes visiting. Actually two. Now one, now the other, they never seem to come together. One of them is probably a tomcat. A big tom so pudgy that he can no longer leap up on a chair, on some customer's thighs. From time to time, when Simon appears in these parts, he steals over and pleadingly eyes him. Pleadingly, or with cold, derisive interest.

(Pleadingly, as if he wanted to sneak into Simon's jottings.)

(He doesn't need to wheedle, no need whatsoever, truly it is not difficult to sneak in, not at all taxing to appear in Simon's jottings and leap from line to line.)

The big tom doesn't look like he's begging for a titbit. Simon, not without a certain pride, entertains the thought that this obese animal with moulting fur has imprinted him permanently on memory, has appropriated him in his shaggy empire. From Jooske he knows that the tom is called Mikey.

While Mikey appears mostly during rainy days, the second and considerably smaller cat comes to survey the visitors only when the sun shines. Jooske, who maybe is not called Jooske at all, said that she's called Indie. Jooske brings her home—Simon would like to see the bag. Maybe she just shoves her into the car. Mikey, however, evidently remains; he slithers down to the souterrain, doubtless he's got a den there. It's no longer worthwhile for him to drag himself off somewhere, that has long been decided, so he's living out his days in this pub.

Indie by preference dozes on the high barstools with their perforated fabric of claret-coloured barchent. That barchent transports Simon to his native country. The yellowed cultural centres, the punctured upholstery on office sofas and armchairs, the reek of railway restaurants, the smoke and ash of licensed night bars and eyes on the tights of the faded secretaries and culture agents; the twenty-year memory of a desperate effort to break free of universal dullness and commonness. And here suddenly, in Amsterdam, barchent returns, coarse and soft, smelling of nicotine, charred grease, chops in batter.

Each time, whenever Indie appears on the scene, Simon coaxes her to him, to his lap. Now too, though it isn't by any means sunny out of doors, Indie has dragged herself out of her hidey-hole and is bustling about Simon's feet. Simon looks inquisitively into her pale green eyes and Indie, with the same unconcealed curiosity as if she were seeing him for the first time, gazes at Simon, notorious recorder. Simon is convinced that what is looking at him from Indie is not Indie but *something* else. Indie, the cat's body, is only a costume; hidden within is some alien mechanism, system, machinery, and the body of Indie is only a *holder*, like a camera case. Otherwise, how could it be that only the cold curiosity of a researcher was reflected in Indie's eyes? Douglas Adams wrote somewhere that mice let people make experiments on them because it is their opportunity to gather information about people. The virus of toxoplasmosis is transmitted from cats to mice, which determines that the mice go to meet their certain death. But, Simon cogitates, what if the mice invented toxoplasmosis and are using the cat as a farm for its production, for the narcotic needs of mice? Indie's gaze gleams relentlessly, precisely as the gaze of any given pub record-taker, shamelessly parasitizing either on foreground activity or on visions jostling through the lilac mist of a tipsy memory.

6. He searches for

the clock face. To make tracks, or to stay. Again, the warmth floods him, the flux of indifference; he'd rather not go anywhere now. This condition was well known to him: it would not last for long, just a few minutes, and once again he'd be seized by restlessness. Then he'd want to go somewhere immediately, but he wouldn't find the publican, he'd have no one to pay. He'd look out the window and his gaze would collide with inquisitive faces that are trying to decipher whether they may still find places in this pub. They peep awhile, then they continue. Their dallying continues, their loitering continues. The babble in the bar continues, gurgling in the radiator, clinking in the kitchen. Simon too continues, he searches for the clock face. How much is left of that day; how long can he still sit lounging, as he puts it himself, *creatively* lounging?

The earthworm calls to be heard. Wrinkly one, chilly one. Until now it was nicely settled in the heat, screwed in. Nothing disturbed it, no gurgle from the radiator or cold draught from the door. Most of the lower vertebrates and the majority of birds do not have an

earthworm. Alternatively, some birds have an earthworm sometimes—when they carry it in their beaks. And if they fly with it, the
earthworm flies. Among mammals, the tubular bodies form an earthworm. Certain mammals have an earthworm containing a special
bone. Among humans, only men have the earthworm, but without
the special bone. They use it to excrete fluid waste, in which useless
molecules depart from the body. Simon's bladder is now agitating the
earthworm, depriving it of afternoon sleep. It can look forward to
cold fingers, to gurgling in the subterranean parts, but the bladder
doesn't give a shit. All the more, though, Simon does. Simon does
give a shit. He takes the shit, ignoring challenges from the bladder,
spinning one deferment after another, cosily pouring into himself further tots of the firewater. Adjournment drags after adjournment. The
earthworm, however, cannot see as far as Simon.

Each time he casts anchor in this pub, Simon has the feeling he's
taking part in some kind of test. The first shot is a taster, the second
is to confirm an opinion. A turn-about comes with the third or fourth
glass. The body is no longer testing the liquid; rather, the liquid tests
the body, the body's percipience: whether despite progressive inebri-
ation and the spreading lilac mist, it retains a memory of the taste of
that first mouthful. The opinions of taste buds, gullet, bowel, stomach
change continuously during consumption, they sway, collide, square
off, cooperate, sometimes inclining to a more favourable verdict, at
other times bristling with anger, overwhelmed by righteous abhor-
rence. But memory, that's no namby-pamby thing, it behaves like an
adventurer in the tropics: brandishing the machete, it cuts and slashes,
carving a pathway through fearsome thickets of lilac mist back to the
taste of the second gin glass. Hacking out a road places certain
demands on the mariner, but precisely because of the lilac-toned

intoxication, a miracle occurs: time spills out, changes to axle grease, to a temporary emulsion on the way to the past and the future. The brain soaking itself in a royal bath of narcotic liquors is actually a very comfortable, humane, carefully upholstered time machine. Just sit, and then go pell-mell with the wind.

The mouth, ah, the mouth! That too asks for its quantum of reflection. But now, now it's the earthworm that calls to be heard. Fat, placid, largely phlegmatic, that's to say, philosophically apathetic, at the rear end grafted onto this delicate, spoiled-rotten trunk. It calls for a hearing, but not actually verbal, for what kind of mouth has it got? How wretched an opening is that? An outlet! Outlet, which has a teardrop already on the slicer; a tear and a whole army of yellow tears to follow it, which the urinary bladder, choleric that it is, now prepares to shed. Outlet, little mouth, all that's missing now is a tongue. In that little mouth, in the little mouth of that unhappily imprisoned half-reptile, a tongue—sexual life would look differently then, Simon mused.

He could not hold out any longer. No, truly he could not last longer, action required, action, quickly defer the postponement and defer even thinking about postponing and rise and go, go, walk and descend to the sightless, dripping underworld. Down the metal spiral staircase to a narrow, dusky corridor, there to unloose and there to expel steam, squeeze the worm, arrange it, *pis en plassen*, wave it afterwards, make the dragon nod in a sign of relief and farewell and go back up and pay, or stay. Pay or stay, continue or continue. Because whether one stays or goes, both actions will be merely continuation and neither continuation will be a solution. And every solution will be only a variant of a preceding variant. Variant of continuation.

Simon pulls himself together, bangs his belly against the table, plunks back into the chair. He rises, but again hits the obstruction. Again with his belly, and again thuds on the chair. The gin glass wobbles, Simon is not giving up, he has no retreat, with the worm one cannot bargain, the worm is not the friend but the master of man, a master kitted out like a servant; with such there's no joking, machination and traps are threatened, and ultimately disgrace. To relieve the bladder somehow, to go and give relief, to rise and to act. Simon grasps the table, the wooden legs creak. The gin glass wobbles again. A drop from it splashes onto the beer mat. The bartender stares at Simon, who sends him an awkward smile, lowering his eyes; a blush suffuses him, he steps forward. The bartender's cloudy gaze suddenly shifts to the two Japanese tourists who have just entered the pub. On his way to the toilet Simon still manages to jolt one of the barstools which is sticking out from its row. However, he masters that narrow staircase corkscrewing down to the souterrain without a stubbed toe or a single curse.

7. In the underground

three graffitied doors gleam dully: one leads to the men's toilet, a second to the women's, and the third (ajar) to a sort of storeroom: bottles, vegetable crates, a jar, a rag, a broom. Simon kicks the Gents' door (not wanting to touch it with his hands) and plunges into darkness, because the glimmering light from the corridor doesn't penetrate here, to the darkness reeking of sweaty pelvises and armpits, pungent urine, disinfectants, liquid soap and perfumes for men.

Somewhere something gurgles, and for a fraction of a second it brings to Simon's mind a mountain stream, but immediately the darkness sneaks in a memory of one of the chimneys of a ghastly mansion somewhere in San Francisco (the shrilling of seagulls intruding from the nearby port in October): he begins to feel the tiled wall (he hadn't wanted to touch it), searching for the switch, thinking of the microbes suctioning up to his fingers, and how they arrange things with such-like underground toilets in this city upon the water.

He gropes a bit, and actually props his right hand on the wall over the pissoir (hadn't wanted to touch it), while with his left he clumsily fumbles in his fly, and meanwhile it occurs to him how strange it is to piss in a pissoir in a toilet below water level. If the walls in this place were of glass, the canal dwellers (supposing there are some still), namely, the water sprites, fish, assorted aquatic vermin, might roll their cold eyes on the urinating guests. And the pissing guests while pissing might look all round them and gape at rust-eaten bicycles. And that same researcher's interest would gleam in the cold eyes of the fish as in the eyes of all of this world's notorious recorders.

Simon finally finds and grasps the earthworm. Inclining his head, he thrusts out his belly and pleasurably shuts his eyes. No researcher's interest. The gurgle suffices.

8. When he surfaces

from the glimmering underworld, the pub community has added further noisy fellows to its wealth. Americans: the identifying marks are there. T-shirts rolled up, waists bared. Slapping shoulders and thighs, pounding the counter. Cock-a-doodling, whooping, deafening laughter, and no one rebukes them. Jooske smiles obliviously, facing away from the action, immersed in cigarette smoke.

The Japanese tourists are patiently ruminating a question. They fall silent, they wait. The bartender is explaining something to them with a smile, to which the Japanese nod ardently. Maybe they've even understood what the bronzed face behind the beer pull has babbled. They keep mute, smile, and again they have a question. Sharply the American voices skip across, skip over and skip off, they bounce off the ceiling and the floor and straight back again from the door that's inscribed *Telefoon*. And once more off the ceiling and the glasses on the bar counter. Shivering and clinking. It wouldn't take much more to make Simon flee. But he knows he's responding too squeamishly:

for a long time he's been on his own, but today, this evening, his solitude comes to an end.

The Japanese and their question. The bartender leans both arms on the counter and uninterruptedly flickers his heavy eyelids at the tourists. Americans, with their gestures and manias: each of them is a companion known to the wide world. They come in droves and droves, some of them funny and others funnier still. Bulging fishy eyes—admittedly they've got none of that researcher's interest. But at least they've got life in them. France is more French thanks to American brats, and Paris more Parisian, and Europe too is more European, thanks to France. But this is Amsterdam, and those fellows are behaving as if they were in Paris; they're making a Paris of Europe, although who knows whether Amsterdam, with all those blacks, South Sea pirates and herbalists from the Middle Empire has much to do with Europe. This is Amsterdam, a far more mysterious and unpolished place than Paris; this is Amsterdam, of which an Algerian race driver wrote that its canals are like the circles in Dante's *Inferno*. Circles, *circles*. The time of the circles had not yet come.

This is Gravenstraat, my Gravenstraat, Simon muses, I have discovered this street, and I discovered it only and exclusively for myself and for Estrella, I'm the only one who knows it, I alone am familiar with its filth, I alone know why Jooske smiles, what old fat Mikey is mewing about, where Indie likes best to roll about. All of you, clear off.

Americans. The spice of Europe. Of the Europe that long ago evaporated, smouldered out; they've minced her, portioned her, froze her and crushed the frozen meat, and now they're warming her up again in microwaves and carrying her to the table for the hearty gourmands.

Delicatessen, yeah, really these Americans are like Europe's delicatessen; one can only envy them their faith that this is Europe, the genuine Europe, the piquant spice of America. When Simon was in Philadelphia, a little old Jewish woman turned to him at a supper and spoke as follows: Tell me, lad, do those people in Europe still hate one another so much? Oh far from it, Simon said, everything's different now.

Everything's different now, on the continent of masterfully simulated junkshops.

Simon listens to the Americans.

9. And to his amusement

he ascertains that they're not all brats of the brat pack: in fact, two of the three are women and the third is Norwegian. Now, one of those girls, with the look of a farmer, big broad shoulders and squaddie's haircut, said something extraordinarily important, because her friend, sitting between her and the silent Norseman, launched into intensive explanations, happily not very shrill. This one didn't look like a farmer discharged from the army. Her hair was a bit longer: a black fringe, with a gold streak cutting across it, hung halfway down her nose; her eyes were painted like Marilyn Manson or some other Gothic rock-star. There was something she was elucidating with great verve, and obviously whatever it was would rouse one's burning passion; she flung her arms about, threw leg over leg, first the left over the right and then right over left; her red tennis shoes were already a bit dust-coated or smeared; she'd probably arrived in the city just a few hours ago, and already the grease of the streets had stuck itself on those tennis shoes whose white leather uppers were inscribed with red felt pen: SATAN.

Analis, the Goth girl is called Analis; how fitting, how tasteless, Simon thinks. Who knows how it's written? Do you spell it just ordinarily: Analis? Or: Anna Liz? Or: Anne Lise? Doubtless it's written quite differently, but Simon Blef records it in his notebook: Analis. As he hears it, so he renders what he in fact hears is *Eneliz*, but Analis is more beautiful, so he inscribes it Analis. Even though it could be: Annalies.

For the moment, Analis and her companion take no notice of the Norseman and the Norseman seems content, doesn't fret, doesn't flare, simply continues caressing the beer glass in front of him. And Analis just explains and explains, eyes rolling, fingers stretched, spread out, and she's talking about . . . about . . . about art, yes, she's babbling something about art. Analis is studying here, in Amsterdam, the pub learns, but she's not staying here, she stays with her grandparents in Amersfoort, otherwise she's from California, her mother is Dutch, and so Analis is hoping that quite soon she'll be able to put down some roots here, though as yet she doesn't speak Dutch, but already she's attending a cheap evening course (Volksuniversiteit), she feels good here, Europe is Europe, after all. The girl who looks like a farmer nods and burps.

Analis continues:

'I'm not starting from scratch, of course, I graduated from art school already, but you know what I mean, Europe is Europe, and everything's different here, there's freedom here, atmosphere, higher demands; they understand my things better in Europe, my art, though I can't complain, no actually, they did, how can I put it, they did grasp my works at home too, in California, I was able to get in galleries, OK smaller ones, but still galleries, if you've got connections it can be done, yes, even in "the art world" '—Analis scratched the inverted commas in the air—'that's how it goes, and I exhibited in Japan too, OK, not exactly in Tokyo, but even Fukuoka's not to be sneezed at, I've got a very good Japanese friend and he knows the gallery owners there, it's really funny how they devoured me in Japan, the Japanese think that whatever comes from America, it can't be shit, but what was really funny was that afterwards in California too they began to respect me, because they thought, if somebody manages to exhibit in Japan, well she can't be a total waste of time, that's how it functions, really, but that condition of things doesn't satisfy me, I won't genuinely learn from all that if the things I'm doing are worthwhile.'

Analis pauses briefly, takes a sip of her beer, looks round at the unspeaking Norwegian, smiles at him, turns to the prospective farmer, who also sips her beer, and continues her explanation. The Norwegian sips his beer and carries on stroking the damp glass.

From a further torrent of words Simon distinguishes the verbal collocation handmade paper. He shifts his chair, the better to hear. And he learns: Analis accomplishes her artistic ideas on handcrafted paper, she makes it herself, she learnt this first of all at home, in California, and afterwards in Japan, she hasn't yet mastered all the knacks, but she believes she'll be able to return to Japan and pick up more tricks. It won't be easy, assuredly not, traditional paper manufacture is something like a religion in Japan, in the whole country it's kept alive by maybe five great masters who scarcely let anyone into their presence, they will hardly speak to anyone, but she believes that thanks to her Japanese friend she will eventually find her way to such a master, that she'll be able to spend at least a few days, or in the best case two weeks, in his presence; the master is said to live in a remote place, somewhere in the mountains, in all probability in a monastery, without even a regular road going there, in wintertime when it snows that's it, isolation's complete (Simon to his notebook: monastery? mountain to the north? Lake to the south? To the west? Roads? And east? What's east? River? River! Protection complete!), it's impossible to get there and it's equally impossible to get out of there, who knows if they even have electricity, if they have hot water, clean towels, definitely it won't be simple accommodation, but she's no milksop, she isn't finicky, she'll stock up with towels and soap, if there's pressure she can take it, from early childhood she has travelled in exotic lands, her parents were microbiologists, often they would go to the tropics and take her with them. And what's that master called, the future farmer asks. Washi? Have I remembered that correctly? Is he called Washi? No, no, Analis says, washi is the name of the paper, the master is called Ichibe-san or something like that, she doesn't know exactly, she'll find out later. They say he inspires great respect, because he makes paper, she must repeat that in Japan it's regarded almost as a matter of religion and such a master, such an old master who knows ancient techniques is actually untouchable, they think of him as a saint, one isn't allowed to brush against him even with the end of one's sleeve, one isn't allowed to look him in the eye and under no circumstances to address him; in his presence you may move only with lowered gaze, ask no question, make no objection, say nothing, only remain dumb and learn, learn and learn!

'Eighty,' said the bartender, and his red eyes blinked.

'Eighteen?' The Japanese gaped at him uncomprehendingly.

'Eighty, not eighteen,' the bartender repeated.

'For one night?' the Japanese asked.

Simon forgets all the time that there's a hotel on the first floor of this pub. One enters there through an inconspicuous door, still more inconspicuous than the one that has a plaque inscribed *Telefoon*. Who knows whether the hotel goes on further to another floor, or whether it occupies only one storey as in Cairo, where it is usual that a hotel takes up only one or two floors of some high building, grey and dingy, which might be under construction or it could be abandoned, no one can tell.

10. 'I've been drawing from way back,'

Analis said. 'Mum and Dad say I was painting when I was six. Maybe I started even earlier. Really, I don't know when.'

'So you were just like Alexandra Nechita,' said the farmer, laughing; it turns out that she answers to the name Lois.

'No, not at all,' Analis said, raising her voice, 'that's not it, I'm not some syrupy little follower of Picasso, cubism or recycled cubism doesn't grab me, I was painting totally differently, with a lot more sense of detail, of natural detail, my parents were microbiologists after all, I was puttering about at their ankles all the time, I spent my childhood between pipettes and chemical compounds, you understand me, you know what I mean, between test tubes and microscopes, actually I used to help them, maybe that's where I picked up my phobia about viral infections, it's a phobia which, actually, I have to thank for a great deal and I extract quite a lot of motifs from it, you know this, I've shown you those drawings of female figures, with necks, backs, shoulder blades, calves being gradually overgrown with moss and the tiny foliage of climbing plants, so that's a metaphor for an unknown disease, changing into a different living organism, I know what you're going to say, yes, Kafka had that too, this motif and maybe also the genuine fear, and maybe not, maybe he was just having a good laugh, Milena thought that too if you ask me, but this is not about Kafka, Jonas here (Analis nodded at the Norseman) thinks I'm obsessed with Beardsley, but he's wrong, Beardsley doesn't attract me at all. Jonas is marvellous, I regard him almost as my brother, at first we couldn't stand each other, he came to the States on some student programme, and my parents didn't take to him at first either, but afterwards, everything changed after that, in fact we see him as another member of the family, now we're discovering a bit of the Netherlands, but in summer we're going to his place, they say Bryggen's a magical region, although Jonas doesn't live in Bergen, but Bryggen can't be missed, I'm looking forward to the port, the sea birds, I adore sea birds, the black feathers, but not because I'm some sort of melancholic, no, I think I'm not like that, I've got plenty of natural vitality, but I love it when art has balls, you know, when it's deep and dark and ravenous, and well, the movement of sea birds captured with black Indian ink on handmade paper . . . But maybe,' Analis continued, 'maybe there's a memory of Rome, of Bernini, of his Daphne, who is gradually changing into a tree, her body has buds and leaves sprouting from it, maybe that's been etched into my subconscious somehow, my parents took me to Italy when I was seven years old, we used to walk around Rome from morning till night, afterwards we went to some big park where there was a building crammed with sculptures, then later, when I began to take an interest in art history, I learnt it was the Villa Borghese, I'm going to go back there some time, in short, the Villa Borghese and Bernini's *Apollo and Daphne* there. Back then I used to think the Italians were perverts, they always took me in their arms and kissed me and hugged me and they'd say *bella, che bella*, and my parents too were appalled at first, but afterwards they realized that it's just an innocent delight in children, Mediterranean cordiality, Mediterranean weakness for children.'

11. He ceases

to notice her, ceases to keep his ears cocked; his gaze strays to the inscriptions over the bar counter. Six boards in all, of which four black and two green. On the blackboards, smooth chalked writing about food. The first says: *Appelgebak met koffie en slagroom.* The second: *Uitsmijter ham kaas.* The third: *Kroketten met friet.* The fourth: *Bitterballen.* On the green boards, the inscription *Corner House.*

Ah, so that's what this dump is called, Corner House. I must write that down immediately. How often have I come here, and still I don't know what it's called!

Above the bar counter, shining once again, is the unwearying round face, Jooske! *Jooske is terug*! But what's this? Jooske wearing glasses! Small rectangular glasses in a black frame. This way, Jooske looks like an experienced woman. Like a well-read woman. Or if not well read, at least the kind of woman who knows by now that she doesn't have to read. Who really knows only one thing, that being the most important, namely, *how things go.* An experienced, prudent, calm and also energetic woman. Who does not stop lying for one single moment. She lies with her squinting look. She squints at her devastated colleague, squints at Analis, squints at Simon. A little souvenir of deceit is despatched to each one.

Squinting, she says: *Both of us know what's going on here.*

And her eyes say this also: *Ah, how great it is to see you here again!*

She squints and pours. To Simon it seems as if she wanted to say: *Don't be afraid, I have a good memory, I haven't forgotten anything, to be sure I remember you, why wouldn't I? After all, you're unique!*

When she passes by Simon, once again she slaps him lightly on the shoulder. And Simon blurts out: 'Nog een keer, graag!'

'Jazeker,' Jooske declares obligingly.

And Jooske squints again, Jooske, dependable shipmate and steersman on these choppy waters. The idyll is splintered by the shrill sound of Simon's mobile. Grabbing it, he sees on the display: Mother. So then, sixty-five-year-old fingers without a piano have once again pressed a keyboard at the other end of Europe, not right at the end but close to it, out there where the aboriginal inhabitants still exchange greetings with the foxes at twilight at the margins of the bigger towns, and where very little extra would have been needed (or would be needed now) for Asia to begin right there—the Turkish version of Asia, vegetables, ice cream and bath. Fingers, still nimble, still not quivery, but now maybe not so graceful, have successfully pressed the correct numbers in the correct order, and Simon is able to hear and nod agreement.

12. Do you know who's died?

his mother chirrups in an agitated voice. No idea, Simon answers patiently and cautiously sighs. But his mother has ears like a lynx: What're you sighing for? Is something bothering you? You're hiding something from me, right? You're not doing well over there, are you? Simon: Mammy, nothing's bothering me! Really! So, who's dead? Well, actually it's the boss . . . my former boss! Enthusiasm seemed to be lacking in his mother's voice, there was rather a tremulous surprise. Yes? Simon says wonderingly, and remarks: I thought he was long below ground. Not at all! his mother says. And are you glad? Simon asks. Glad? Look, how do you mean, am I glad? Oh, glad as in glad, I mean you couldn't stand him for twenty-five years. Well, yes, I couldn't stand him, but only a little. A little? And is that possible? Simon wonders. Not stand someone a little, is that possible? He asks again, tacking on the comment: only you women know how to do such things, not stand someone a little bit, partially hate, what? Really, believe me, it wasn't such a serious hatred, his mother says. But it seemed quite dramatic, Simon observed. I remember countless things. Every day, every morning freshly and from the beginning you hated your work, your office, in summer it was stifling, day after day your sweaty, greasy, fat and gossiping colleagues disgusted you, with the farts they left after them in the toilet, and your boss above all, his stink, his cigarettes, his obscene remarks, and the way he would shamelessly rub his balls with his right hand as if something was biting him there, yes, often you told me you suspected he had fleas, lice, crabs, who knows what kind of vermin. You couldn't stand your life, you threatened that one day you'd slam the door on it all, pack up and travel to somewhere, you didn't as yet know where, maybe the Riviera and maybe the Canary Islands, but off you'd go, you were fed up to the teeth, but even so, you eventually did nothing, you stayed where you were, you kept on going to work, you put up with your boss' double-meaning comments, you went in there and you navvied, you used to say you were navvying, though no one could imagine what it looked like when a secretary was navvying, but let that be, we believed you, we grasped you, such a life can only be hated. Well, so what? You can't understand that! OK, so finally that monster died, Simon interrupts her. You shouldn't talk like that. Even he was only a human being. Right, he was, Simon agrees, adding: That's the worst part of it. Imagine, his mother would not be deflected from her theme, he was only seventy-one years old! How only? Simon wondered. What I meant to say was, he was the same age as your Uncle Albert, who's still a dapper lad. Definitely, Simon says, but seventy is an age when people commonly die, or am I wrong? Are you burying me again? His mother says. Not burying, I'm just pointing out to you that if this was the Middle Ages, then not just your boss, Uncle Albert and you would no longer be living, but even me, people then used to die a lot earlier, and here we are amazed that someone at the age of seventy gets sick and dies? What kind of world is that? You're callous, his mother comments. And will you go to his funeral? Simon asks. I don't know, I suppose so. Imagine it, he was only as old as Albert, and the last year he just lay helplessly in bed, they had to feed him like that, he couldn't even hold a spoon, soup dribbled out of his mouth, he jabbered some gibberish and probably fouled underneath him, who knows if they gave him nappies or how they managed that, you remember his daughter, the cripple, she had one leg somehow twisted, when she was walking she'd drag it behind her, the parents gave her everything, she studied to be an interpreter, English and Spanish, she even went out to Mexico, clever girl, you have to admit they did the very best for her, who knows how she suffered, poor thing, when she saw her father tied down to the bed, helpless, incapable, skin and bone, a regular skeleton, not that I know how he looked in his last days, I'm just imagining, life is shit. Simon, that's why I'm always telling you that you have to live here and now, you must live for today, enjoy it with whole heart. The shit? Simon queried. You don't understand this, his mother snapped at him. Listen, Mammy, have you been drinking? The instrument was silent for a few seconds. Hallo, do you hear me? Have you been drinking? What's it to you? his mother breathed. I haven't been drinking! I just had beer, one, two, can't say how many, drinking beer is no crime anyhow, and even if it was, we only live once, you know, just once, life is shit, so I haven't been drinking. Why do you think I've been drinking? Because you repeat yourself, Simon said firmly, you're all over the shop. Really? And how about you, sonny? Don't you worry, my lad, I can hear perfectly well how you're slurring, you've difficulty speaking, your voice jumps up and down, how you mulch words, I hear music in the background, a racket, talking, bottles clinking, you're sitting in some boozer again, have you found regular work yet? Stay dumb, you don't have to answer, I know very well you haven't even looked for it, you haven't moved a finger, say nothing and tell me instead about your language course, are you attending regularly? You can manage talking in the shop, on the street, on the train, you understand the evening news on TV, have you got to know some influential people? All that doesn't happen so fast, Simon says. You think starting life in a foreign country is that simple? But you know what, we'd better end this. OK, his mother agreed, that's all I wanted, that he died, he was the same age as Albert, take care, ciao.

13. Simon flings the mobile

on the table and tilts the rest of the gin into him. Then he tucks the instrument into his bag. Albert, what's Albert got to do with that? Simon's Uncle Albert: he doesn't talk much, he'd rather spend his life in some shack on the edge of a fishpond. His wife was old Blef's sister, which meant he had married into the genuine dragon-seed offshoot of the Blef kindred. Long years after her divorce, Simon's mother still kept up relations with her former in-laws, from time to time they'd meet, debate, reminisce, browse fashion magazines and eventually the two women would quarrel over something. Albert mostly remained mute, Simon's mother despite her sister-in-law's displeasure used to thrust a bottle of chilled beer into his hand, each time the same ritual repeated itself, whole decades long. Each time, Albert copped it from his wife for accepting the bottle of beer, and afterwards Simon's mother would spend days recovering from their repugnant scenes. Gizela, Albert's wife, never arrived at awareness that she was ruled by her passions. She would explode unexpectedly, at any time, without the slightest motive, in rain or in shine. But her fits of anger passed quickly, to be followed either by remorseful tears or euphoria.

Albert, breathe on me, while I'm talking to you!

Ah, Gizela.

I know you've been drinking, no pulling the wool over my eyes.

But Gizela, don't be silly. You know very well that I'm coming from work.

From work supposedly, that's familiar. I followed you with the spy-glass from the balcony, I saw everything. I saw you stumbling over the bridge. You stopped at the kiosk by the Red Bridge, didn't you?

Gizka, well, so what? I've told you, I didn't drink anything.

Indeed, you did. And not just one beer.

I honestly don't know how I'm to explain this to you. Gizela, you're out of order.

Albert! Breathe on me. And march to the shower!

And Albert made himself scarce. Regularly, he made himself scarce. Not only to the shower. Much more frequently, to the allotment district on the other bank of the river, where he had secret supplies of alcohol. Fishpond close by, a stone's throw, what more did he need? He fled from Gizela, but without her he wouldn't be able to live. He could not imagine how it would be if Gizela didn't fill the apartment with her electricity. At the end of the day, even capriciousness is a form of com-munication. What kind of mysterious entity was using Gizela in this way, for the purpose of communicating with Albert: this was not some-thing that Albert pondered. He didn't believe in hidden entities, although he had seen spectres of all sorts on the shore of the fishpond at night.

When he was little, Simon had not understood that when Auntie Gizela flew in a rage, that didn't mean she had adequate reason. In her presence he chose rather to behave bashfully, although that didn't help, as bashfulness annoyed her too. When she had one of those days, Simon didn't know if he should like Auntie Gizela, or how to classify her, but he was pleased when she sometimes took him to the hospital where she worked as a laboratory assistant. He liked the enigmatic snapshots of glowing misty skulls, chests, pelvises, thighbones, muscles and capillaries, exposed to the air current over the bathtub. Gizela, like all the Blefs, had a certain artistic talent, and when she didn't have patients, in the nurses' room she'd amuse little Simon by drawing and cutting out skeletons, which Simon stuck in books to serve as bookmarks. From time to time he pulled out his paper skeletons, caught them by the skull and gently blew on them and watched how their limbs and ribs danced. Gizela, then, preferred to draw skeletons, while her father, old Blef's Blef, made drawings for Simon in notebooks and memo pads of hefty locomotives that the rust had long ago devoured. Of Gizela's paper skeletons, perhaps the most firmly fixed in Simon's memory was one that she had coloured, for whatever reason, with blue and yellow pastel. Simon kept this skeleton for a long time, but later on, evidently after one of the numerous moves accompanying the stormy life of Simon's mother, the skeleton disappeared forever. Afterwards Simon still remembered that Auntie Gizela had given him a gift of an orange skeleton made of plastic, the kind drivers hang on their rearview mirrors.

That orange skeleton, Simon remembers and looks at the departing Analis, had eyes too, black eyes, actually just two black balls. And a hat too, lemon yellow. Where could you find such a skeleton today?

Simon looks at the reflection of light in the gin.

Analis. So you're going, dear Analis. You're doing the right thing. This establishment is not for artistic souls. Seek in Jordaan. Or head right for De Pijp. Over there, the ravens that are getting ready to fly out of your head will certainly be appreciated by others, and not only your own small retinue.

Explosive laughter. Jooske behind the counter can no longer contain herself. Red-flushed face, the ample bosom quaking, straggly-black hair. Frans Hals: *Gypsy Girl*. For three hundred years she's been laughing, through the mouths of women like this, *heel Nederland*. Sometimes unbearably. When a robust woman like this begins to roar with laughter, fears take hold of Simon. He's afraid of that windmill gesticulation. Jooske, however, even if she's massive, nonetheless remains a woman— probably because she has more resemblance to Hals' *beauties*, the women of the *old* world. She doesn't change into a golem.

14. And it's beginning

to drizzle. The pedestrians on Gravenstraat hunch and make beelines, their footsteps pick up tempo, grow denser. Under the grey walls of Nieuwe Kerk and the weeping shop windows umbrellas blossom. Some immediately fade away, others hesitate, linger. A buzz of cyclists, somnambulistic zigzagging: one has lips pressed tight with tension, another shyly grins, but all of them impel, sweep along, their metal horses to left and right, juggling, balancing, braking, foot propelling on wet pavements, trying to tighten their hoods as they ride.

Simon fishes crumpled banknotes from his pocket. He doesn't trust wallets. Sometimes he carries one, but it's empty. To fool the pickpockets.

He'll make tracks, like Analis. He'll go to release the ravens. Into the rain. He won't wait for a more propitious wind, he won't wait till the weather has second thoughts. He won't tarry, because he's not very much of a *mariner*. Without regret he'll get going, step out into the street. This anyhow isn't serious rain, no one takes any notice of it, no one notices most of the rain, in this country at least.

Simon turns to the beer counter and he sees: Jooske is listening abstractedly to some man, not a customer though, because he too is standing behind the counter and speaking almost in a half-whisper. Evidently the boss of the business, or something like that. A foreigner, no burly Dutchman but a diminutive speculator, a merchant from Persia.

Jooske is listening to him with lowered eyes, nodding, thinking of something else, wiping a glass.

Whether she really is wiping something, and whether it's glass: Simon cannot see from this angle, it's what he imagines.

Another Persian profile enters the pub.

Curved nose, piercing dark eyes, thick grey locks, olive skin. The image of old Blef! Father's empire, again on the scene.

Old Blef had declared more than once, and more than one woman certainly had believed him, that he came from an oriental family. Probably from the Near East. That although his father (Blef senior to old Blef) was no Arab or Turk, or indeed his grandfather, that is to say, old Blef's Blef's Blef was not a Turk or Persian, and even on his mother's side there was no known desert or nomadic origin, but even so. All kinds of things might have happened three hundred years ago when the Turks had overrun his native town. And when I say all kinds, Anton Blef would announce, raising his index finger eloquently, I mean all kinds, literally. So if some of those genes were transmitted to me over centuries and mark my external appearance, it's no great surprise. Therefore, today I look like an ageing trader in Persian carpets. But it's also possible, Simon, that we're of Jewish origin. And that would entitle us, you and me, to study the Kabbala. You know, Father Daniel, that mildly fairy-ish Franciscan, said to me once: Anton, you know you've the look of a Sephardic Jew. I don't know if he wanted to flatter me with this remark or express revulsion, but I do know that when a Sephardic Jew grows old, he begins to cultivate the impression that at this stage he should devote himself solely to the Kabbala.

Hm. Baruch Spinoza never managed to grow old, Simon reflects, so he never even began to devote himself to the Kabbala. Or he experienced just as much of that as he had to. Was able to. Managed to. Precisely like that, or *had to*? Connecting Simon with Spinoza, here comes the rain, which last year at roughly the same time of day caught him by the synagogue. And then, Spinoza's house in Den Haag. The windows look almost exactly into the street opposite. Simon and Estrella noticed that the street is uncannily quiet, no vehicles pass along it, pedestrians move conspicuously slowly, and no women appear among them. Illumination came to them suddenly, when they saw the red lamps. Thereafter Simon had gone into that street a number of times, actually only to demonstrate to some visitor the bizarre atmosphere, the dreaminess and lassitude which distinguished that place from the clamorous prostitutes' quarter in Amsterdam. By one of the display windows, once he actually heard his mother tongue, here, the tongue in which the human person can be most humiliated. He looked in the direction and saw a girl nearly two metres tall with dyed hair. The girl noticed Simon but did not return his shy, apologetic smile. She merely assessed him and turned back to her friend. Simon strode on further, back to Spinoza's house. Spinoza would have had something to study here. If he hadn't studied this side of life a long time ago, theoretically at least. The Netherlands enabled this Portuguese Jew to live in seclusion and devote himself to his thoughts. Seemingly it had allowed him that. Seemingly it had shown that it tolerated any opinion whatever, or if not, at least it could behave decently. But in 1672, in the Hague, something happened that must have shaken Spinoza decisively. Not far from the house where he lived his quiet life, an infuriated mob flung itself on the grand pensionary Johannes de Witt and his brother, falsely accused of treachery to the state, and literally tore them to pieces. On the way to the gallows, the brothers were battered and stabbed; afterwards their bodies were stripped and hanged head downwards. Subsequently they were quartered, and bits of them were put on sale and devoured raw, for general merriment. Simon looks at the dark wall of Nieuwe Kerk. At any moment it may break out again. But since what prevails today is a unity of disunity, the people would not now hurl themselves, in concord and solidarity, upon one man, but each would turn against the next. Spittle, blood, urine, bits of flesh. Cries of pain, scarcely distinguishable from laughter.

Jooske is smiling mechanically. One Persian, two Persians. The Persian who was hitherto standing behind the beer counter now moves out from it to embrace his countryman. Kisses, kisses. Then they both take out cigarettes and with unhurried steps go out, in front of the pub. To smoke in the rain.

Persians? Nothing uncommon in this mercantile city, see-sawing as it does between two identities: Western neurosis and Eastern languor. Like Rembrandt, between asceticism and hedonism. Rembrandt, if he hadn't been lazy, would have certainly fled to Persia. Whether he would have felt *at home* there is, of course, another question. Perhaps he saw himself in the role of a well-nourished Persian merchant, wallowing on thick carpets, in the company of curvaceous beauties. Choice edibles, it goes without saying, to hand. But what luxury will it be, if he doesn't have remorse? Without remorse no hedonism will ever be complete, every wine will sour. So that behind the brocade curtains at Belshazzar's feast, translucently shining through, there are Mennonite sermons, heretical speculations, and the shoemaker Böhme's dusky flame. And meanwhile, hovering over the canals, a babel of boatmen, merchants, servants, bearers of burdens. Merchandise from the Orient illuminates the brown facades of bourgeois palaces. Chests full of pearls, coins, gold chains, bangles. Aroma of fragrant oils and incenses; scents of spices, tea and fruit. Rembrandt is on his way to the unwelcoming city weigh house, and he doesn't know that the man in the hat who has just passed by him is Spinoza.

15. Heirs

of the Persian Empire. Maybe they don't even come from Persia, these two that so suspiciously glower at the guests. And besides, which Persia is Simon thinking of: the pre-Islamic or the Islamic? Before or after the coming of the Mongols? Baghdad, Isfahan, Nishapur. Everything lay in dust. Somewhere, in some magazine devoted to the paranormal, Simon had read that in 1221, when the Mongols took Nishapur by storm, they cut off more than 1,700,000 heads. Lord-a-mercy, how many people lived in that Nishapur? Did they round them up from near and far? The author of the article obviously needed to spice up his work somehow, or the graphic designer told him: Please, I need three lines more, otherwise the layout won't look good. He calculated that if the Mongols really cut off that many heads in a day, they must have chopped at least 30,000 per minute. What a lot of Mongols there must have been! In those times they were said to have a million-man army. Probably not just Turks but Mongols too had overrun those parts, where some centuries later Anton Blef, father of Simon Blef, was born. And therefore, it cannot be ruled out that in Simon's veins, apart from Turkish–Sephardic blood, a few drops of Mongolian circulate also. Mongols, the story goes, were strong men, because . . . because they lived on raw meat . . . No, no. These curve-nosed pub proprietors do not come from Persia. From Turkey, rather. Granted, that's just a fine distinction. Turkey was Persia too.

Simon once was fascinated by dervishes, but today those times are past. Today, in the pub at the corner of Gravenstraat and Nieuwezijds Voorburgwal. Fascination with dervishes came to Simon in waves, in quantum leaps, so to speak. Mostly when caught up in crisis with a partner. Or some other mania. At such moments, he fell on the couch and gave himself up to reverie. He dreamt of camels, deserts, Lawrence of Arabia, lavishly coloured mosques and mysterious Fatimas. No, not Fatimas, that's not compatible with ascetic resolve. Simon's imagination was as crammed with kitschy expectations as the House of Rembrandt with exotic props.

Ah, what naivety, to head off blindly to somewhere in the steppes of Anatolia! Enviable naivety. Today's Simon catches himself envying that Simon a few years younger, just stepping onto the Turkish Airlines plane . . .

'Mag ik nok eentje . . . ?' Simon waved timidly at Jooske.

'Jenever?'

'Ja, graag!'

You must follow your dreams, as the Brazilian wizard wrote, lolling in his apartment with a view of Copacabana or Corcovado. He wrote that in a story about a poor shepherd who took it into his head that he must see the pyramids. Since nowadays few people read *One Thousand and One Nights*, it could hardly bother anyone that the author had cogged this story, without giving it the slightest added value. Well, no matter. Simon knew this, but he decided that for the moment he would believe the Brazilian charlatan from Compostela and test whether we should really follow our dreams. So then, the poor shepherd lad dreamed of the pyramids, and Simon in broad daylight, on the couch, dreamt of the mosques in the dervish city of Konya. A single grainy black-and-white picture gave him justification for such dreams.

He found it in Eva de Vitray-Meyerovitch's *Rumi and Sufism*. The illustration showed Rumi's mausoleum in Konya. Minarets like someone had whittled them. It put him in mind of the illustrations in a slim volume of fairy tales that included the finest tales from *One Thousand and One Nights*. Even the story of that eternal roamer, the *mariner* Sindbad, was among them. To set one's breast to the sea wind. Then one's face to the desert wind. Stride forth to meet certain nothingness.

A thought occurs to Simon: what would happen if he asked Jooske for a small favour? Whether she would show him what's up there, above this pub. A hotel, obviously, but still: how does it look? First, though, he must somehow formulate his request. He could ask her in English too, but why not practise his Dutch? But how to start? For example, like this: *Het spijt me, mag ik iets vragen?* And Jooske would say: *Ja, 'tuurlijk.* And he thereto: *Ik wil graag de kamers kijken. Kan dat?* And Jooske probably would say: *Ja, dat kan!* But why should she agree? But why should she not agree? She couldn't know, after all, whether Simon mightn't like to stay there. And maybe she would not permit him to spend the night here. Well, what was she, poor creature, supposed to think of him, who spent hours here imbibing one gin after another, all the while scribbling something in a grubby notebook?

No: Simon will not ask. He would rather tilt this gin into him and go. For today, this is sufficient. In this establishment, definitely. He'll pay and he'll go.

16. But even so—

those hotel rooms! Judging by the appearance of this pub: in what state are they likely to be? Something like the dust-coated inns of Anatolia? Here too, in this little hotel on Gravenstraat, is there a doleful, damp cubbyhole awaiting the confused traveller? A bed with a sag and suspicious cracks under the shutters? Just the kind that a rat can commodiously squeeze through? Vile pieces of battered furniture? Dusty lampshades? A night table creaking curses? A yellow-rubber shower curtain with dubious brown and green stains? And what if he were to ask Jooske to show him one of those upper rooms? And suppose he stayed in it just for a single night, would a dreamless delirium transport him once again to Anatolia? To the Hotel Imperial, Royal, Sultan, Saray and Séma? And what would he be doing there, in the Anatolian dreamland?

During the two weeks he spent in Konya, in that sleepy town which no one would know about today if it weren't for Rumi's mausoleum: how many times had he changed his hotel? Five times? And what was he pursuing? With that never-ending dragging of his baggage?

Was he following the followers? Was it his following then, that he was dragging? Or his idea of followers? In one of those hotels, not far from the small mosque consecrated to the masterly master, the saint, the mendicant vagrant from Tabriz, he found a room where he slept for two nights. In the wall by the bed was a gaping hole, such that a full-grown rat might have slithered through it. The groaning of the wooden stairs came insistently from the corridor. And at night, when the lodgers came stamping upon them, heads fuddled with who-knows-what, he never shut an eye: to him, it sounded like a new pogrom had erupted against the Armenians. Another hotel, three streets further on, was a yawning emptiness. The brown and sleepy vacuousness that they simulate in old films set in India or Arabia: pompous facade and wide stairs in the vestibule, a mocked-up colonial style crossed with the copycat pomp of the decadent Ottoman Empire. Simon immediately conceived a trust in this hotel. Though he couldn't explain it, he did feel it. He could not have foreseen that precisely here, in this brown monstrosity, the night would come upon him, such a night as he had seldom known in his life: a night of lonely and causeless weeping; a night of self-pity; a night when he drank the last of the brandy he'd brought from home, intended for disinfection; a night of elongated minutes, during which he sat unthinkingly on the edge of the bed, only afterwards to stand by the wall and start banging his forehead against it. But even the nights in other hotels brought no redemption. The only difference was that he pulled himself together somewhat, acted the adult and no longer had the idea of splintering his head on the wall. But the dull-witted sessions of sitting on his bed continued. Head inclined, gaze scrutinizing the surface of the wooden floor, elbows on thighs. Thus, he sat and brooded, in that town lying on steppes that spring had not wakened. He pondered and vacillated and kept watch for some activating thought, not knowing if he should immediately lie down and attempt, via the cave-like fissures in his fatigued mind, to slide through to a land of fantastic dreams, or put on his boots and head into the night streets, among distrustful merchant countenances into the crowd, amid silhouettes and shadows and movements, so as to end up in the small square once again, before the mausoleum to the dervish master, in the little park with semi-abandoned trees and saplings and a non-functioning fountain, where he found a bench to spend ages sitting on, musing on the incomprehensibility of this entire journey of his. He'd sit there till the bench began to pinch him and the cold of the night made his teeth chatter. Afterwards he'd get up and make his way to a bus stop, to a knot of silent people, he'd attach himself to them, exactly like a few days ago, and he would speak to one of them, hoping that thanks to an unerring intuition he would hit upon the spiritual advisor whom (according to a fortune teller) he was to meet in Konya.

Since Jooske isn't coming round, Simon decides to pay at the bar counter. Rising, for a second he seeks his balance. Picking up the denim jacket he has hanging on a chair, he sweeps his eyes over the table, in case he's forgotten anything. The notebook, pen and mobile are secure already in the two bags, everything is prepared. He may calmly set sail.

Behind the counter he sees something like a noticeboard. Photos on it. He recognizes the Persian faces there. Wait, though! Shining above the photos is a massive white cross, decorated with false pearls. So, neither Muslims nor Zoroastrians. Not Persians, but most probably Aramaeans, running restaurants with Greek specialities. He wouldn't come back here again, as he knew something about this nation's ardour: once in Enscheda he'd almost got a box in the teeth for daring to doubt God's benevolence. Dark thunderbolts swept their eyes, snorting mouths spattered spit, jaws opened to reveal grinning teeth. Some odious astral mist must have darkened Simon's mind that night, something that culminated afterwards in one of his scariest experiences. Never again with Aramaeans. Not a glug of ouzo nor a morsel of moussaka. They boast that they still speak Christ's language. What if that language has hidden codes of holy confusion?

Out of doors, the rain whips him, unnerves him, wisely he fumbles in the bag for the black rain hat, precisely the kind worn by Dutch peasants, at least according to Simon. Go this way or that? Along Gravenstraat, then turn right and along Eggertstraat, crossing over to Dam Square and on down Kalverstraat to Spui Square? Or follow his nose straight ahead and cross the tram tracks to the other side of Nieuwezijds Voorburgwal, pass beyond Magna Plaza shopping centre, built in a bizarrely florid pseudo-gothic industrial style, and via Raadhuisstraat, quick march to the Jordaan district? Jordaan! That's the one! Simon pulls the rain hat lower down on his brow, thrusts his hands in pockets, rucks up his overcoat collar and walks forth.

17. Still, he isn't staggering,

though it's a close thing. Still, he is lord of his motion. He could perfectly well simulate an uncertain gait. Whimsically. So as to draw the
attention of passers-by.

Jordaan. Now it won't be like before, he mumbles to himself. This
time, assuredly not: this time nothing will deter me from it, he smil-
ingly growls, but without showing his teeth. They're crooked, quite
plainly they're crooked, dancing out of step. From childhood. And
roughly a year ago a dentist deprived him of two back teeth together.
One above, one below. Their embarrassing absence is not, however,
visible: the cheek doesn't even sag in those places, though it might
have, indeed he'd have preferred it to sag rather than have his head so
swollen. Better get rid of them now, the dentist said, rather than spend
lots of money on examining, maintaining and coddling them, because
the decay is unstoppable; better get rid of them beforehand, after all,
you still have something to chew on. A far-sighted dentist.

He'd be able, then, to simulate staggers. The main thing is that
he still has something to chew on. He'd stagger so as to be like a

bohemian, a disorderly drunk, a bowsie. Lighter by two back teeth. *Mariner* on dry land. A paper sailor, furrowing the seas on the paper decks of Hermann Melville, Joseph Conrad and Malcolm Lowry. A spelling-bee *mariner*, weak swimmer and nervous case, who cannot see a puddle without immediately starting to fantasize about seaweed-festooned tentacles.

Simon, a name for seafarers. No: fishermen; Simon, son of Jonah, do you love me? Aagh: a moment ago still sea, and now just some Palestinian fishpond? And Blef? What kind of name is that? Name of dwarves? The permanent gnome, the lackey Blef from a small stifling country without a sea? Does have a few fishing lakes though. With some braggart pike. Something for Uncle Albert. Once a 'fish' took a bite out of little Simon. Albert was standing on the far bank of a back-water, catching fish. He waved to Simon to come over to him. The water was only ankle-high, supposedly. Seven-year-old Simon com-mitted himself to a big effort. Dipping the sole of his foot in the warm water, he said: Uncle Albert, but what if the fish bites me? He won't bite, Albert said. But he will, Simon said. Just come on, there's no fish here at all, Albert told him, laughing. That's when Simon felt a crippling pain in his heel. The water around his feet turned blood-coloured in an instant. He began roaring for his life. The fish bit me! I said he'd bite me. Albert ran into the water, took Simon in his arms and raced to the car. Gizka, we have to go straight to A & E. Simon stepped on a broken bottle.

He walks softly, the warming liquid sustains him. Down Raadhuisstraat they flow: moulting fifty-year-old punks, sixty-year-old metal girls, grey groupies of Simon Vinkenoog, the King of Amsterdam, or Herman Brood, the Netherlandish Jagger, a cluster of mummified Janis Joplinettes; the first superannuated generation of rockers, those that in other parts of Europe are near-immobilized grannies and grandpas but over here are perpetual adolescents, who before too long will enter the netherworld carnival without ever having stripped off their black leather jackets or been unfaithful to sex, rock and roll and booze.

18. You live like a hermit,

like Saint Simon on his pillar, remarked Jan van Der Vlucht, former teacher of IT, one of Simon's Enscheda friends.

I do what I can, Simon said. Can't do more. I come to this pub, I get to know people, we have a good time, we swap addresses and sometimes even phone numbers, but nothing happens after that. Silence. It's hard to adapt when I have no feedback.

You're impatient, Simon, Jan said. And you take everything too logically. You can't expect people to be constantly behaving logically. But even so. You ought to use every single opportunity to meet people. And not cower on a pillar. The legend says that St Simon spent forty years there.

Jan is a weirdo, Jan's friend Kees Visser once explained to Simon. He's an educated man. And he has such physical condition that at any old time he'll cycle to some neighbouring town. Almelo, for example. And that's 25 kilometres. Just imagine it, Simon. I mean, the man is seventy-five. And that's not all. He's enrolled in a Chikung course. On Thursdays he goes to the choral society. Besides that, he plays in a string quartet. Fridays, there's the Club of Amateur Translators of Poetry. He has the strength of three. Not like myself. I have to have injections. Thrombosis.

Kees? Jan becomes earnest. He used to be like you, Simon. Never crawled out of his house for thirty years. And look at him now. Seventy years old, and head over heels in love. And with all that he's a grouch, believe me. And a bit crazy. Once upon a time he had talent, but the paintings he does now aren't worth much. Though he grouses about all the other painters. He damns them as mafiosi and aliens from space.

I get on perfectly well with Kees, Simon says. He reminds me of a portrait of an old man by Rembrandt that hangs in Mauritshuis, if I'm not mistaken. Oval face, plump cheeks, small eyes, white hair, broom's-end moustache.

Do you know his *meisje*? Jan asks.

I saw her once.

And what do you say?

A bit cold. Clinging. Women like that scare me.

But she looks well, what? Would you ever think she was sixty-eight?

Must be admitted. Slim, lissom. But too active. Do you think she really loves Kees? Flaming love at that age? And for what? A person should already be preparing for the passage to another dimension . . .

What dimension? Simon, I don't believe in such things.

No? And what about the chichi-kung?

That's something else. It's an affair of the body. Good condition matters to me. Look at Kees. A second youth has come to him. He

77

knows he won't live that much longer, but he wants to savour these few years properly. Kees never used to travel, now every spare moment he's in Amsterdam. With Janneke. She comes from a bourgeois family. You know what that means. They owned textile factories in the east, in Twente.

I can imagine it. A fellow in Bolwerk told me his granny used to slave in that kind of textile mill. As a twelve-year-old, nine hours daily. He said that they had to put boards beside the belts, because the kids didn't have enough reach.

Everything has its price, Simon. Yes, people don't talk much today about these things, about child labour, about the fact that someone got rich from child labour.

Children/non-children, does it matter?

I understand you, Simon. You don't have children, so you don't have regrets.

But indeed, I do. I have compassion for those who will have to bear the consequences of overpopulation and the general upheaval stemming from it.

On that I've a different opinion, let's talk about Kees instead. So, that Janneke of his has a snazzy villa in Oldenzaal and an apartment in Jordaan. And she drives Kees there. To the love nest, where they listen to jazz and classical music afterwards, with a bottle of red wine. Her deceased husband was a composer. What does she see in the same Kees? She coquetted with me too, the swine, but I didn't come flying to her. Imagine it, Simon. Kees has been thinking for some time that I have an itch for her. Hasn't talked to me for a month.

I swept her from Jan, Kees had boasted to Simon. He'd been slavering over her, but eventually she decided for me. Intelligent girl.

Tomorrow I'm going to the doctor, I'm considering Viagra, but I have to take advice. Admittedly, Janneke and I can stay together even with platonic love, but if something more was possible, why not have the benefit? She's beautiful, really beautiful. *Een karakter*. An exceptional woman.

It could kill you, Kees.

And what if it does?

19. A stir

on Raadhuisstraat: a Chinese couple with an empty pram, the child is running loose and the parents are pitter-pattering after him and screaming. Behind them, dilly-dallying, are two black nippers with red-abstracted gazes and patches low down on the seats of their trousers. And further: a little group of Muslim women, all swaddled up in beige and giggling, one of them flashes her eyes at Simon and covers her smile with her palm. Behind those: four hulking girls with braying laughs (certainly they've got the loss of virginity far behind them and they've already managed to experiment with all the body's orifices, anal sex is, so to speak, a required test today, openings are there for not just fingers and members to be stuck in but various objects besides, from flagons to model cars with a condom slipped over, it's been demonstrated on television, no milksops these, they don't heed pain), immediately behind those: an electric-powered vehicle, upon which is a little heap of something anthropomorphic: a probably thirty-year-old (by the face) woman without hands and without legs, what else is there to follow? Limbs from Brueghel and wheels from Bosch, genuinely: without hands and without feet, by some mysterious means she controls her little vehicle, because what she has under the torso cannot be called even stumps of legs, and the fingers, the fingers on her upper limbs grow straight out of her narrow shoulders, from the right one three, from the left four, they are long fingers, one like another, one cannot at all determine which is the index, which the middle finger and which the thumb; and before this apparition even the rain seems to draw back; the armless and legless woman overflows with life, in this carnival maelstrom she obviously feels a whole lot better than any of the fully equipped passers-by. And it does not feel cold, this limb-shorn torso, it thrusts between the legs and the arms of the urban mob proudly, almost ruthlessly, a very monolithic, or actually mini-monolithic, piece of picaresque pre history; a piece of a story that may give us a sense of where we've come from, what kind of marshy, limbless, fins-and-gills existence, and towards what marshy and crippled (and perhaps for that reason with limitless chemical inventiveness) and probably once again fins-and-gills being we are heading, on the wheels of auxiliary machines.

20. On the bridge

over Herengracht he stands, gapes for a moment into the light curtain of rain, somehow, he doesn't want to believe that this too is Herengracht: where is all that ostentation, where has the luxury and hauteur of the merchant palaces withdrawn to?

He takes a step, once more he stops.

He leans with his elbows on the railings of the bridge. The mob around him submissively flows onwards, tyres hum. Raindrops vacillate. Plummeting through his mind is a dream sequence from a few days ago. Twice he has dreamt of some South American city. He's been dreaming of South American cities since puberty, from the times when his Catholic piety blazed with the tallest flame. He wanted to become a priest or a missionary. To head off for the South American tropics. But even so: where had they all come from, those shabby Peruvian, Bolivian and Mexican cities with their half-ruined cathedrals in the style of colonial baroque? And that baleful dark-grey sky above them, and before them again those ostentatious broad steps, upon them leprous beggars and destitute Indians? Once he dreamt he was a member of a guerrilla band, wearing a grimy uniform, driving with others in a jeep; they had just dashed to a certain bare peak, up above the jungle, and upon that peak stood a cathedral with two towers, but filthy as a stable, leading up to it were the broad steps occupied by beggars and Indians in hats, their hefty backpacks by their feet, some had little camping tables in front of them and were selling souvenirs to the pilgrims, and shoots of tropical vegetation were bursting through the cracks in the steps. Familiar backstage phenomena and requisites, all of it. But a few days ago, he had dreamt of a specific city. Rio. And a further novelty: his wife Estrella. A South American element in her own right, she's half-Mexican, after all. But they had never talked about Rio, never planned to go there, they wanted rather to go to Mexico, her father's country.

He pulls a crumpled map out of his bag. Placing it on the railings, he toils over it awhile, as motor barges roar under the bridge, then he realizes that he doesn't actually need a map. Enough to keep on walking straight ahead, enough to steer by the slim tower of the Westerkerk, that'll tell him when he should turn off.

21. Suddenly the drizzle stopped

and glaring sunlight poured over the canals. It stopped, but in a moment it would start again. Stop, start, stop, start. Otherwise pure spitefulness: the sun was not suited to Amsterdam, let it shift somewhere further to the east, to the pasturelands, after the cows. Though the Dutch knew how to enjoy the sun: let it heat up even a little, they'd straight away put on their shorts, T-shirts and sandals, as if they longed to live somewhere else, for example the Mediterranean; to all appearances, it would not have bothered them if the rainy Netherlands changed to a tropical country.

Even the tourists feel a bounce in their mood when the sun rays touch them, as if they'd come here to sun themselves. They stroll round the city like it was a beach; as if here they had fast-food stands, changing rooms, deckchairs and sunshades for hire, ready and waiting. It's plain to see that they traverse the museums only from duty; what they'd love to do is clear off out of here and loll about by the sea leafing through tabloids. In reality, this whole junkshop of culture bores them. They twist their necks, pretending to be awe-stricken, they yawn, scratch themselves and sneeze, each one tripping over the next. Inside every urban tourist there is a slumbering beach bum.

Simon obediently waits for the green, then crosses to the Westerkerk, a building incomprehensibly short, as if it had been sliced in half. The Protestant lack of a sense of proportion: the arse of the nave does not in the slightest make an impression of sacredness, no rounding, just wall and window and that's that. But even so, there is something frivolous in this building, something ludicrous. Maybe this bell tower, the highest in Amsterdam, is meant to mock the little godforsaken Catholic church on Kalverstraat, which, probably for its eccentric pseudo-gothic design (reminding one of the backdrops in old Hollywood horrors), has been conferred by the city's inhabitants with the nickname of The Parrot.

The guidebook says that in Westerkerk (where exactly, no one knows) Rembrandt is buried. His second wife, Hendrickje Stoffels and son Titus lie here also. Simon is not ashamed of having a head stuffed with superficial information from guidebooks. Well, so what? For a time, information like this, imparted in this manner, is in fashion, then afterwards some other kind. Guidebooks are the rage for a while, then there's a rage against guidebooks. Currently we are living in the era of *Lonely Planet* and *The Rough Guide*, which do not shrink from sarcasm, cynicism, deterrence. Don't go here, don't go there, but if you nonetheless happen to go there, pay attention to this and to that. This museum is admittedly famous, but in reality, it's not worth a lot. Such-and-such a hotel may have four stars, but you know (as the rule is in Asia), you'd better subtract two to be sure. The tourist is not even left enough space to be able to grumble: the guidebook will do it for him.

22. It speaks

to whoever is ready to listen. This architecture (the books say). Architecture not at all ostentatious or the least bit monumental. The waterlogged ground would not have supported higher buildings. But even so, what is most attractive is the pulsation. Life (the books say). It flows, dynamically flows, the people here are active and industrious. A paradise for non-conformists. Provocative initiatives are tried here (they say in guidebooks). Simultaneously, tension grows. Disparity of wealth increases, social-welfare payments fall, relations between religions are sharper edged. But the city continues to speak. Where Damrak is today, the port at one time functioned. Canals came into being because building land was needed. For *packhuis* building. The city speaks, but Simon only indistinctly makes out its language. If he were writing a novel about this city and the novel had a principal character equipped with interior monologues, that character would grasp, would understand well, the city's language. But Simon would prefer to write a novel without a main character, one where the character with the interior monologue would be the city itself. Sun, rain, sun, rain. That tremendous glittering ball on the Westerkerk's helmet.

.

23. By the church

there are stalls with postcards, handbooks, brochures, depressing can-vases by amateur abstractionists, on occasion portraits of pets. This colourful jumble almost drowns out another of the city's attractions: Homomonument, a memorial to all possible homosexuals; those who at one time were persecuted by the Nazis, and those who today sup-posedly do not bother anyone, and probably also those whom some-body will again begin to bully in the future. The memorial consists of three triangles of polished pink granite on the level of the pave-ment. Each of the triangles represents one of the apices of a still greater equilateral triangle with sides more than 30 metres long. The apex of one of them passes into the steps (like a sort of saggy Camembert), almost as far as Keizersgracht, and points towards Dam Square, specifically to the 22 metre obelisk, a monument to the vic-tims of the Second World War. This triangle symbolizes the present day. A further triangle, a kind of podium about half a metre higher than street level, represents the future. Pointing to the past is a triangular surface at pavement level that is turned in the direction of the nearby house of Anne Frank.

From the canal a motley procession approaches: transsexuals, lesbians embracing and swigging drinks, sun-browned and sports-trained fairies in white trousers and with dyed hair, occasional transvestites with gigantic false eyelashes and timid sympathizers who are still just preparing to swap their unattractive grey clothes for carnival outfits. Some are waving placards with hurriedly scribbled slogans, more distribute leaflets, others just smile or wiggle their bottoms. In merry knots, they banter with passers-by. The 'birds of paradise' dispense smiles, coquette with the tourists and provoke them. Cautiously, at snail's pace, a white pick-up moves along in the midst of the procession, a powerfully crackling loudspeaker fixed up behind. Simon can distinguish notes, instruments, music: the Prince song 'Shy', spilling out in a rhythm of footsteps, as if created for the march of gays heading towards Koninklijk Paleis and Dam Square.

But Simon is moving in exactly the opposite direction. By the Westerkerk belfry he turns right and walks parallel to Prinsengracht for a while. There he runs into a triple row of tourists.

Oh, but of course: Anne Frank's house, the place that irritated Estrella so much last year. She announced that no one would ever get her in there, any more than to St Peter's in Rome. Because who ever saw the like, making a global attraction of the home of a family that had been gassed? At that rate, they could make a museum of the house of a victim of any traffic accident. The crowds of tourists could assuredly quite also go to the home of some driver, from anywhere at all, who died in a blaze on the highway. You're exaggerating, Simon said, but mentally he was hearing this with pleasure. I'm not exaggerating,

Estrella snapped, all of these sweating, bored cretins in shorts who are squeezing in there will gasp, wheeze, sigh, exhale and drool. And when finally they bowl back out, they'll remember damn all. It doesn't occur to them that if somebody once again organized a transport of a group of the population that was unacceptable for something, for example people like the two of us, so if someone organized a transport to extermination camps, these here who are now cramming into that museum, they'd nod cheerfully, they'd keep their heads down and they'd inform. They'd squeal and squeal again, just to save their own shitty skins. They'd lower their eyes and ears, tuck in their tails, and shit themselves, and us with them. Us with them, stop thinking. And they'd say, what were we supposed to do, we have our families, we must take care of them, it's necessary to live. The human being is not a beast, after all, he must protect his family. Yes, family, so that afterwards the kiddies and granddaddies can swagger around the world in fart-filled aeroplanes and visit the shelters and homes of those who died in the camps. You know what, Simon, that all makes me want to puke, just like in Rome, in St Peter's Square. Because, you know, let them keep all that bric-a-brac, and stuff themselves with it till they choke, that most sacred temple of theirs, when you can only get in there through detectors and I don't know how many security controls. I'm not letting myself be groped, they can keep their chunk of stone, I don't want to smile politely as if nothing had happened, I don't want to answer questions, to bow and bend and shrink back, patiently waiting to see the marble hand and the sanctimonious smile of that *Pietà* . . . Oh, if he could see this circus, the old prick that it's all happening on account of, Saint Peter I mean, or if his boss Christ could see it, I'd like to hear what they'd say, probably they'd curse all those people to fuck, because what kind of Christianity is this, tell me? And what's Christianity to me? What concern is it of mine?

24. On that day

when Estrella, in front of Anne Frank's house, swore that she'd never set foot there, it was sunny like now. Estrella's words seemed to put a curse on the remainder of the day: between Hilversum and Amersfoort the railway line was closed, which meant that the train, taking a diversion through Utrecht, was bursting at the seams. It was Saturday, at the start of holidays, children multiplying the crowds. Families returning from an outing. Teenagers charged with energy drinks. Moroccan adolescents and yelling Scouts. Simon and Estrella at last found a small place on the corridor, by the toilet, but quickly the corridor too filled up. Someone trod on Estrella's foot, and panic seized Simon. He was gripped by a fear that he'd vomit, piss himself and faint. A horrifying thought that his body would slip out of control. Everyone was rubbing against him, poking and prodding him, breathing in his face, howling in his ears, baring rows of teeth, sprinkling him with spittle. He wouldn't have imagined undergoing this kind of thing again. More than twenty years previously he'd had similar panic attacks, on Sunday evenings returning to his university hostel on a jam-packed train. He thought that the panic would dissipate over time, but now and again it reappeared. Like in Rome, in the metro, at Termini station, when such a powerful desolation beset him. A repressed disgust at people. Simon's grandmother, the one who used to keep bottles of white wine in her wardrobes, had suffered from the same. No one believed there was anything wrong with her really, everyone thought she was just absurdly over-sensitive. But what if I faint now, Simon was harping on to himself in the train between Amsterdam and Utrecht. What if? What if? What will Estrella do? What can she possibly do in this crush? Simon didn't know if he should breathe quick or slow, but in either case he was sweating like a pig. When he imagined that he was sweating more than others, that he was sweating conspicuously, he began to sweat still more. Everyone was watching him, though pretending not to, but observing him sidelong; they saw his sodden shirt, definitely they hadn't seen the like before, a man dripping like he'd just come from under the shower. He turned to Estrella and whispered: Let's get out of here. Immediately, let's go. Anywhere, just let's go. Let's try the other end of the wagon. I'm going to faint, I'm going to wet myself, let's try there. Estrella didn't ask any questions, instantly she understood what was happening, experiences in the Roman metro were fresh in her memory, she moved and Simon followed her. There was indeed more space at the other end of the wagon. Simon's breathing relaxed, he sat on the stairs leading to the upper floor of the train. He took the packet of paper hankies from his bag and wiped his face. Estrella passed him a bottle of mineral water. He drank, and the panic subsided, but the sweat continued to roll. Soon even this bit of space filled up. An older woman got on with her two daughters, each of them dragging two fair-haired children behind them, who immediately took to crawling among the passengers. One of them, a boy, wanted by hook or by crook to break through to the upper floor; he was not deterred even when Estrella put her leg in his way and glared at him threateningly. The lad glowered at Estrella, crossly stamping his foot, and darted in beside Simon on the steps leading to the upper floor. Little squirt, Estrella snarled. Standing directly behind her was a buxom woman clad all in black, who kept constantly looking out the window. Dandruff and shed hairs gleamed on her shoulders. A flush of mild alcoholism gave some variety to her round face. When the train moved off, she drew a half-litre can of beer from her bag, thus meriting Estrella's and Simon's appreciation. At the next stop a Black couple squeezed on: he was tall, broad-shouldered, with long straight legs, an athletic deity from equatorial Africa; she was small and dumpy. The Black man stood with his back to Simon and his powerful body curtained off the view of the children's lit-up faces. A wave of gratitude came over Simon. Members of family groups kept shouting to one another; the buxom lady consumed beer; children swarmed; somewhere a toddler bawled; elsewhere someone guffawed in a coarse peasant voice; two teenagers sat on the steps with Simon, incessantly busying themselves with their iPod settings. It occurred to him that the difference between travelling like this and a transport to a concentration camp was rather small. Lack of air, jolting of torsos, screeching, claustrophobia, panic, suppressed disgust. Retention of pressing body waste (numbers one and two), fainting spells, swoons, hysteria, epilepsy, hebephrenia, bragging, paranoia, hyperactivity. Tourists, willingly undergoing the duress of travel: standing in queues, waiting for the plane, the bus, the security check, the baggage, the toilet dish, or for service in the bar, cafe, buffet, restaurant, souvenir shop; adapting to the regime in the airport, regime in the hotel, regime of local mass transport and long-distance transport, regime of the sly taxi men, outlaw manners of the local political regime, exotic customs; the impossibility of escaping from unforeseeable hardship and complications, which at first seem like negligible trivialities but afterwards grow into life-threatening peripeteias; communication lapses; sophisticated and not always evident stealing, unforeseen illnesses, insects, lizards, rodents, impudent monkeys, cats and begging children, rotten foodstuffs, careless doctors and the avaricious mob and refrains and seriality and uniformity: a modified continuation of the holocaust, only in pink.

25. The queue

in front of Anne Frank's house brings him back in memory to Rome, to the expanse before the church of Santa Maria in Cosmedin which has the *Bocca della Verità*, the stone face in the vestibule. Even before this plate-like piece of flattened stone with a surprised, indeed somewhat Christ-like peering gaze in the middle, there were tramping tourists with their cameras, each wanting to be Gregory Peck or Audrey Hepburn for a moment, all of them, the fatties and the weaklings, the suits and the Bermudas. Simon suggested to Estrella that they too should take their place among the tourists. Are you serious? Estrella gave him a look and Simon immediately knew that he hadn't been serious, not very. She grabbed the camera from him, rushed from the entrance hall, leant against the metal bars outside and began snapping the fatigued faces of the tourists. This is much more interesting! she shouted at Simon. Yes, this, their stupid, unwitting snouts! D'you see? They're much more interesting than all those ancient curiosities they come scrambling to see!

In Jordaan, Simon has the peace and quiet he depends on, all around him: some streets are entirely empty, literally desolate, no shops or pubs there, only studios and small, bizarre, seemingly abandoned and vegetating galleries. Estrella would like it here, he thinks. He'll tell her he's found a peaceful quarter, and he'll bring her here, he'll conduct her through these parts. Now just to find a cosy pub. Where Estrella too, the arcanum of Simon's life, would feel relaxed and safe; where she'd enjoy herself sitting and philosophizing, listening to Simon's chatter and straight away undermining and ridiculing his words, and then immediately admiring and reinforcing them. To find a bar, gloomy and chilly, walls panelled with wood and a dust-grimed painting of *Our Lady of Guadalupe* hanging in the window: her small pale-brown face with prominent eyebrows, often seen here in shops with South American merchandise, made Simon think of Estrella's countenance. And besides, the plan for a great journey.

26. Mexican Virgin Marys

surfaced on the streets in the vicinity, unexpectedly in shop windows, in every conceivable size and presentation, from quite small pictures (the kind that people insert in prayerbooks) to plaster statues nearly a metre high, dappled with bright colours all over and dusty all over too; if painted on metal plate, then rusting, covered in layers of a dubious patina, like something deposited by cooking fumes. There is no knowing why the Virgin Marys enjoy such popularity here, even more, they say, than Buddha, Guanyin or the little god of contentment Hotei: whether it is that more South American emigrants live here, or whether it's yet another Dutch caprice, hobby-time fascination with Latin America, naive esoteric superstition, or one of the spiritual excesses of the still-living hippies. But it isn't only from the windows of ethno-shops and pubs and stores with occult 'requirements' that Nuestra Señora looks out on the pavements; she is there too in shops with exotic spices, on tobacconists' doors, on the come hither signs to fortune tellers' dens, even on the lintels of dark, scruffy cobblers' repair shops.

The Marian cult had never fascinated Simon. In vain his Granny (mother of old Blef) had dragged him to distant places of pilgrimages, huddled in depressing valleys or set amid fertile plains. The cult of the Virgin Mary was something he simply did not understand: the Virgin could perfectly well float on a cloudlet and tread upon snakes, all the while emitting sinusoids of golden rays. She could quite well suffer her seventy-seven sorrows and parade her seven daggers, yet giving an impression of irony or even complete indifference. He did not understand how in such a prudish religion they could so openly discuss the delicate matters of virginity, pregnancy, birth, hymen, pregnant women, blood, placenta, sweat, umbilical cords, breasts, milk, stinks and sounds and all that related paraphernalia, because the father was somebody else, far-off and manipulative. That whole ensemble of the Marian legend comes across as the last sleight of hand of the Middle Ages: immaculate pregnant virgin, grizzled husband and a son that crawls out of the synagogue, looks at his mother, and sovereignly declares: I do not know this woman.

But a fellow who has a few chalicefuls of jenever circulating inside him, supported by the robust and consoling taste of Amsterdammer, will eventually come to love even Nuestra Señora, those gilded flames that flare out from behind her and which an alchemist understands as the lightning-bolts of the senses, gushing from the spirit of fire. She is an agreeable and cultivated lady, floating in an oval glow as if garlanded in flowers. And her face, a joy to look on: not at all pale, but pale brown like milky coffee. Virgin Mary of Guadalupe: mysterious queen of the Amsterdam curiosity shops, radiant amid plaster and porcelain statues, antique bathtubs, pre-war radios, personal mirrors; between brushes of various sizes and shapes, minutely detailed model railways, cats sleeping in display windows, and white T-shirts, towels and loud carpets. *Nuestra Señora de Guadalupe* with the eyebrows of Lily Downs or a young Chavela Vargas; with the eyebrows of Estrella. The eyebrows of the Guadalupean thaumaturge are a call, a summons to Mexico, more piercing perhaps than the colours of Casa Azul, more irresistible than the uproarious din of *El Día de los Muertos*.

27. Six years ago (or just five?)

he had still not known Estrella. He lived some life, he was in some relationship and more often than ever he had the feeling he was changing into a mummy. He kept up a kind of hibernating state, giving the world a bared-teeth grin. Then one May or April he went into a travel agency, deliberately choosing the one that had given him his ticket to Konya some years before, smiled at the clerk and asked if he could buy a ticket to Mexico City. Just one moment, the woman said and tapped something into her computer. You say you'd like to fly at the beginning of July, right? That's possible, there are still empty seats. But coming back . . . hold on. Could it be in the middle of August? Yes? There's still one place. So shall we reserve those? And you have a visa already? I need one? Simon stiffened. I honestly never knew that. For the present yes, for the present visas are still necessary. And how long would it take to sort one? Probably a month. I can't wait that long. And how much would a ticket cost, for example, to Cairo?

28. On one of the little streets

in Jordaan he finds the cat-requisites shop. A bizarre construction can be seen in the window: a precarious multistorey den, upholstered with coarse fabric of some kind. A ruddy-haired cat sleeps on the lowest floor, compact as a pastry curl, head averted, whiskers pressed to the face. Another creature sleeps on the second floor of the 'hut'. Black. Simon looks through the glass. In the room, plunged in semi-darkness, he makes out sculptures of cats of varying sizes and colours, unidentifiable toys, artificial bones, artificial mice, portable dens and baskets. These representations of the feline cult make him tranquil; he'd have liked to go in, just that he doesn't know what he could do there, what to take in his hand, which attitude to assume.

In front of another shop entrance a hippie woman is sitting, her clothes brightly coloured, her person somewhat worn. Actually, she gives the impression of a parrot that has crashed into a tree. From her brown face, dried up like parchment, dreamy emerald-green eyes are shining. Simon turns his head away and ups his tempo.

At the corner of the street, for an instant. he's enclosed in a cloud: stink of freshly grilled chips and raw herrings, scent of vanilla joss sticks and marihuana. Looking up, he sees bare feet about two metres above, him placed on the railings of a little cramped balcony. Does Janneke too thrust her limbs out over the street on scorching days? Or would you believe, even Kees?

Simon found himself in a rectangular square. Actually, it's a street. He doesn't need to look for the cafe, it's directly to his right, on the corner of the street that he's just emerged from.

He glances through the glass doors, to see if there's a free space inside. Then upwards, looking for the street name. Elandsgracht. And the cafe, which by noise and smell is more like a pub, could not be more banally named: Cafe de Jordaan! Massive dark-brown tables with spotted waxed tablecloths. Each table has some red-faced loner sitting there. Simon heads for the bar.

He hoists himself onto one of the round stools (red fake-leather cover), places his bag on the beer counter and looks at the sturdy back of the stout barmaid, unhurriedly counting coins by the till. *Intermezzo*, the Saturday supplement of the daily *Volkskrant*, is flapping on the counter's edge.

He reaches for the magazine. Transferring his bag from the counter to the stool beside him, he begins browsing the supplement. On page 21 he finds a large colour photo of the seventy-one-year-old Romanian Adriana Iliescu and her four-year-old daughter Eliza. The mother is clasping her offspring like one of Raphael's Madonnas. The eyes of the girl emit an unthinking, domineering coldness. Her wrinkled, small mother has strikingly rouged lips. Mockery of ageing, hatred of the body. And blood-red nail varnish. Eyes, predictably, big and dark. Something like ardour is smouldering in her. One of the forms of Balkan witchcraft. No less witchlike and cynical is the article's title: *Een extraatje van God.* How then *extraatje*? Unexpected gift? From God? From the God of gaming doctors, who *gamefully* 'managed' the artificial insemination of sixty-six-year-old Adriana? Eliza will soon, perhaps, go through the experience of her mother dying, and she will be able to grow humanly. Because the suffering of our nearest ones helps us, we are told, to *grow humanly*. But Adriana Iliescu is no longer the oldest mother in the world. She has been outdone by the Spaniard Maria del Carmen Bousada de Lara. Competition is possible in anything.

The squat barmaid slowly turns round and Simon says:

'Een oude jenever, graag!'

The female behind the beer-pulls makes some rejoinder, unclear what, it sounded like: *even kijken*. Can't see it, he thinks. A bad sign. If she can't see it, definitely she doesn't have oude, only jonge jenever. That foul-tasting slop.

And indeed: the barmaid confirmed Simon's baleful prognostication.

'Goed dan,' Simon said, preparing himself for the slimy taste of jonge jenever.

Just as the woman placed the tipple before him, the phone wailed in his bag.

29. Oldie

Simon? Hallo? Can you hear me? Hi. It's me. Your mother. Listen. Do you have time? There's something I want to say to you. Don't worry, it won't take long. Listen to what I've just read. Incredible. You must hear this. But wait a second, till I run into the kitchen. I have it there, on the table . . . Here I'm back. Now, my glasses . . . Ah, here they are. Just imagine, the things they write today. The advice they give young girls. Where you are it's certainly the same, in your magazines. It's probably a worldwide trend, right? I marked that down as important. It must be a worldwide trend, because our local news rags don't invent things of their own. We'll never have anything original. They snoop, those amateur journalists and dilettantes, snooping is what they do well, and they steal and bastardize whatever they can. Simpletons. So that any shepherd and media poltroon can understand. Listen, they write that . . . *You have to treat men as animals.* D'you understand? It's what they write. They fling that in your face, just incidentally. Quite upfront. And they're not ashamed. How did we come to be like this? They write such things openly. As animals.

If you want to keep a man as long as possible, behave towards him like he's a household pet . . . What do you mean, am I alluding to something? Which dots are you joining now in that noddle of yours? I see there's no use talking to you at all. You're morbidly sensitive. And what are those sounds? Where are you? In a pub again? Always the same one? Days on end you get sozzled, then you become paranoid about any triviality! I'm not alluding to anything. I only wanted you to know. They're setting out point by point how to proceed. Understand? Step by step, getting a man to the stage where he's . . . *Eating out of the woman's hand.* They give directions how to behave towards a man, meaning a husband, how to train him, teach him obedience. Do you want me to send you this? You don't want it? Well, you ought to read it. Maybe, so that you'll see what you . . . OK, OK, you needn't flare up. But even so, it'll do you no harm to stay alert. If you stop being careful for a brief while, that's enough, they've got you . . . I'm not alluding to anything. I'm your mother, I may be stupid and uneducated but I do have experience. Does any mother want anything bad for her son? Does she, well? I only want to take care . . . Yes, yes, I know, you're not ten years old. But believe me, women can be tremendously subtle. I know what I'm talking about. This field I'm familiar with. Women will always obtain what their hearts yearn for right now. And when they achieve one thing, right away they want something else. For them, a man is just an instrument. An object. An animal, you understand, an animal! Doesn't matter what kind. Draught, decorative, for exhibition, for use, a domestic or couch pet. Simon, you're worth more than that, than letting yourself rot on a couch . . . OK, OK, I'm not going to annoy you. Should I send you that magazine? Maybe you should read that article to Estrella. I only wish you the best. Both of you. Have you noticed that over time Estrella is beginning to take after her mother? That's the iron law. Nothing you can do about it. She'll become a robust Dutchwoman. I've taken the measure of that mother of hers. A major-general, a domestic tyrant. No wonder her husband so quickly drank himself to death. And her new one? He too has a face worth looking at! How long has he lived with her? Eighteen years? For eighteen years he's been impotently loafing on a couch. A regular Birdbrain Bill. A ninny. Otherwise, a likeable fellow. It's she that makes such a wreck of him. Don't deny it! I have a nose for this. She suppresses him, she doesn't let him breathe. I know how that happens, don't you worry! How women stifle fellows. So take good care that they don't turn you too into such a . . . What? What are you babbling? What plural form? Did I use the plural form? I'm not alluding to anything by that. Can't I even ring you now? You ought to give up drinking, for good and all. You're becoming a paranoid narcissist. Oversensitive. That's the alcohol. If someone has to watch every single word . . . Still on about the plural form? I didn't mean anything by that! I made a mistake, and so what! I'm not perfect. Estrella? Yes, I know, she's different. Different from all your other ones up to now. We know. All your new ones were different from those preceding. And where are they today? Always, eventually, I turned out to be right. But OK, fine. We don't have to talk. No need for you to listen to me. When you're the world's wisest. And you want to rot on a couch. Whatever you like. I'm a dunce, yes, I'm uneducated, I chatter to the winds. Forget what I told you. So I won't send you the magazine . . . What?! You're not trying to tell me that all of your failed relationships were destroyed by me? You're sick, really and truly! Have yourself examined. So that you'll know. A while ago I was watching this TV programme and a psychi-atrist, a coarse little fellow, overbearing, roughly your age, he was saying that sons, when they seek partners, should be prepared to take advice from their mothers . . . I swear, he said that . . . I didn't invent it . . . And do you know what? I noticed that Estrella has an exceptionally good relationship with her mother. Exceptionally, you get me? That's not natural. When I visited you, I saw how she used to dance attendance on her mother. How they'd whisper things after supper. I heard some of it too, but I'd rather keep silent, I'm not going to irritate you. I'll be mute, because I know what a brooder you are. And you can't keep anything to yourself. You'll spill this to Estrella, and that's all I need, when I visit again, she'll give me the evil eye. So, take it that I haven't said anything. Just be on the watch. That relationship of theirs is not kosher. Daughters and mothers shouldn't get on that well together. I mean, you know what kind of relationship I have with mine. That mother of hers is certainly passing on ideas—to do with men. I'd stake my life on it . . . OK, I'm not saying Estrella is identical with her mother. Certainly, she also has something from her father, some of those Mexican genes. But she's a woman. Simon, you're naive and you don't have any grasp of female thinking. I know you, I'm your mother. Any one of them can make a booby of you. I don't want you to suffer, do you hear me? I don't want *my* son to suffer. You don't understand because you don't have children. You don't know what it is to be a parent. But there's nothing anyone can tell you any more. Nothing. OK. From now on I'll be silent. From now on, when you need something, you'll ring, but otherwise . . . Otherwise, do what you like. Let everyone screw up his own life as best he can. There's no sense in us talking any longer now. I'm not going to concern myself with your relationship. Calm down. I don't know what's got you so indignant . . . OK, I understand, calm down now, because you'll have a stroke. Why are you so aggravated? Have I hit the nail on the head?

What? That's how it is? Maybe I'm simple, but my intuition's never yet let me down. Ciao.

Ech! For years he'd supposed that the fetters had long ago been severed, the leading strings cut and that he could fly about the world freely. But geographical parameters meant nothing to his mother, would not budge her: she would not let her property be taken away. Physically Simon might be free, yet his psyche remained in his mother's house, in a corner of some mental–emotional dungeon. Simon's body may go wherever it likes, but natural laws are not operative in his mother's reality, the flow of time is not operative, the chemistry of free thinking, gravitation, electromagnetic laws, none of those things are operative. *Behave towards him like he's a household pet . . .*

He pushes away the *Volksrant* supplement and calls:

'Een Amsterdammer, graag!'

30. On the couch,

anything, really anything, only not to die on the couch, on its hollowing, sweat-stained sag, in the bluish light of the screen. Better to suffer, lose everything, break off relationships, drink bad beer, drag oneself from one Amsterdam drinking den to another, just so as not to die on the couch. Not to turn out like Estrella's stepfather Jaap, actually not stepfather but uncle, Estrella calls him uncle, and after all, Estrella's mother had not married him, merely given him shelter, and now allows him to vegetate in quiet semi-darkness, on the couch, in the bluish light of the screen.

Jaap has no plans, no ambitions: already he has found his 'Mexico', he has it in the garage, in the middle of which his old white Volvo is rusting, and otherwise every available inch is crammed with incredible objects, his trophies from bazaars, Saturday flea markets and scrapyards. Jaap has his experience and he also has connections: he therefore gets to go to places that the ordinary mortal doesn't even know the names of. If Simon wanted, Jaap would certainly have procured for him any quantity of skeletons, paper, plastic, rubber and tin, or probably even the genuine articles.

Jaap's garage: a monument to lifelong labour, patient searching and amassing, an assemblage abounding in minute detail and with the motley variety of a Spanish cathedral, composed of thousands of cans of varying sizes full of nails, nuts and bolts, rubber bands, washers, springs, syringes, hoses and screws that don't fit anything. Packed in back of the cans arranged on metal shelves, there are hundreds of sweeping brushes, brooms, paintbrushes, garden shears, spanners, coat hangers, broken office lamps, non-functional transistor radios, orthopaedic insoles, protective masks, potholer's goggles, old calendars, filthy diaries and components of decommissioned hoovers. What if they're just right for something, what if one day someone is looking for that kind of thing, what if somewhere a scarcity breaks out?

While Estrella's father Ernesto collected dreams and books about forgotten civilizations, Jaap by contrast has been building a private place of pilgrimage, a hall of initiation, a shrine to his lifelong collector's patience.

31. The heavens cover

the dead. When he was on the plane heading for Cairo, he didn't yet know those words of Lucan's. But he did sense that he too was among the crowds of those who for centuries had been striding to meet— what? Dissipation in boundlessly wide space? A fusion with the desert, which is spreading out everywhere, without regard to what corner of the world we find ourselves in? Amid the night over the Mediterranean Sea, suddenly it was all the one. It didn't matter whether he died or didn't die, or how he died. Whether the plane disintegrated right now, or whether it crashed and burned up on the ground. He didn't care if he landed in Cairo or not, or was swept away by unexpected death in some feebly lighted lane. Suddenly he felt light and free. What will be will be. Without long speeches, the heavens would embrace, accept, include him in themselves.

No: he was not able then in the half-empty plane to think about this, *the heavens* which would accept him, the heavens *which would cover him*. Simon didn't yet feel this like Port and Kit in the *The Sheltering Sky*. It was only after his return from Cairo that he discovered that he too was like them. Crackbrained and pathetic. Watch this film, Simon's mother said. I recorded it for you from the television so that you'll see all that can happen to you. Simon watched it once, twice. A few months later he was watching it with Estrella.

We're like them, she said. We don't know either what the desert is preparing for us.

But to go back: Simon in torrid Cairo didn't know what *the heavens* had to do with *covering*. There he was heedless of the heavens. He didn't know Lucan's name and was unaware of his unfinished work *Pharsalia*, which he wrote about the crossing of the Rubicon and the murder of Pompey in Egypt. In the Black Land. *The heavens will cover.* The warriors scattered on the Pharsalian plain. In the desert of reality. Where meanings collapse. Only that one true cover exists: *caelo.* For those who have no grave. We can sleep peacefully. *Caelo tegitur qui non habet urnam.*

And meanings may well collapse further. The meanings of everything that Simon had hitherto lived, experienced, performed, neglected, dreamt, squandered, recollected, written. Those alternations of employments, all the disputes, conflicts, alliances, analyses of friendships, partings, conquests and seductions. A while on this side of the barricades, and again a while on the far side. OK on both sides, but by no means so essentially. A while protected, a while protecting. No permanence. Insomnia and the quest—for what? For anything. In any desert at all.

In any desert the heavens will cover him, for whom it is too late to start saving up for a grave.

What you don't sort out in your twenties will stay with you all your life, Estrella said once. *You should have sorted out your mother at age fifteen. Do you understand? At fifteen.* Well, OK. So at fifteen. But this isn't a film, you can't rewind, that reproach in the eyes is vain, and futile too is the assurance that it isn't a reproach but only a question mark, a decorative component that does not ask for an answer.

32. There was a time

when he flew from job to job, from one editorial office to the next, slamming doors and telephones—he, the notorious recorder and pub seat-keeper. Driven by an unrest that he'd inherited and a curiosity that he'd cultivated. What if beyond this corner, behind these doors, on one of the floors in the building yonder, some surprise awaited him? Or better: some solution. He still believed that at any time he'd be able to launch himself into anything. That he'd always be brimming over with subversive ideas. That opportunities would always be at hand (the finest, needless to say). And even if not, *the heavens* would certainly not forget him. He was, after all, the possessor of a conjuror's talent, and the heavens never forget the conjurors. If he were ever at a loss in life, he could always get some guidance from Blef the elder, an exemplary charlatan. *Simon, I don't know if you'd feel in your own skin as a healer; you're not a lover of mankind. You don't have patience.* Ah, the old Blef. He was mistaken in countless things, but maybe not in this. *You're not a lover of mankind.*

When old Blef betook himself to pension, he did not forget to acquaint his kindred with his plans. Spectacular plans, of course. How else: he had sailed spectacularly through life, always before witnesses, never in solitude. Now, he was aware, a time had come for tightening up, but even so he required spectators. As in his youth, now also he had plans in abundance. No one else would have managed to invent them, but old Blef contrived to: here he strummed a guitar, there he lifted a barbell, browsed some esoteric handbook, bought himself a battered computer in a bazaar, set up a telescope, jogged to keep in condition, continued his career as a recreational marksman and above all did not forget to move from the hated capital city to somewhere amid the evergreen slopes, to a mouldy and semi-derelict shack, which he was helped to purchase by his second son Felix, Simon's half-brother, a financial advisor and an admirable zealot.

Zealot. Simon truly wouldn't want to label anyone, but in this case he cannot help himself: for Felix there's no help. What can be done, when he came into the world such an enthusiast? Felix arrives, understands, takes action. Simon once almost succeeded in an attempt to make friends with him at the festivity after the funeral of old Blef's Blef. They drank toasts, and Simon thought they were well on each other's wavelength:

And do you have a girlfriend?

Well. We've two rounds gone in the group phase. That means one point for a draw in the opening game.

Aha. We could meet now and then. Maybe I'd be able to help you in all kinds of ways.

We have to beat the reigning champions and get at least a point in a match played in parallel.

I'm sure that'll be possible.

At the end we lost our playmaker. After his second yellow card for an elbow dig, he had to go prematurely under the shower.

For years afterwards they never saw each other. The next occasion that brought them together was old Blef's sixtieth. When old Blef revealed his plan to move to rural parts and withdraw forever from the revelry of big city life, it caused a rupture between the brothers. According to Simon, old Blef would never cope with seclusion, accustomed as he was to the bustle of social and cultural circles.

Felix said, however: This is the very best thing that Dad can do.

When Simon tried to make some objection, Felix smiled indulgently and began to tell some instructive story from Tibet.

Simon turned red.

Old Blef put a hand on his shoulder and said: Leave him be, Felix knows best what I need. He has lived with me for more years than you.

33. I'm taking up

photography again, old Blef said, puffing himself up. I'll have time
galore. Once I used to take splendid photos. I still have hundreds of
slides from those times. I don't have anywhere to project them or
anyone to do it for, but I don't want to throw them out.

Old Blef from time immemorial had been overspilling with
hyperactivity. Even before that word came into fashion. When young,
he had played accordion and guitar, set up a telescope, modelled plaster sculptures, went to play football and handball, even judo seduced
him for a while. Later, when thanks to his political functions he'd
become more solvent, he bought expensive cameras, lenses, stands,
and he equipped a dark room. And snapped everything: family members, atmospheric phenomena, the Algerian desert, the Mongolian taiga
and rainclouds which he suspected were actually the masked airships
of extraterrestrials. He photographed the forests, glades and gorges of
his native land, and coves on his beloved Mediterranean coast.
Though he was already over sixty, he still felt flushes of creativity: to
set up a pensioners' football team in the village, a chess club, a debating

circle (he would discuss philosophical questions with the locals, and paranormal phenomena), a homeland study society, a choral group. From the zealot he received a mountain bike for his birthday; here at the end of the garden, beyond the little gate, a forest path began, adventure waited. *Felix knows best what I need.* We understand that you've never been interested in football. *He has lived with me for more years than you.* Old Blef, his will unbroken, wants to utilize the time he has still remaining to the full. Although present-day society does not favour the all-round development of the harmonic personality, nonetheless he, Anton Blef, wants to depart this world *harmonized*. He must therefore grant to the body what belongs to the body, and to the spirit what pertains to the spirit.

Simon orders another jenever.

The brawny body of a probably thirty-year-old Black woman, out of breath, sails into the cafe. She makes for the beer counter, places her sunglasses on it and fishes a sheet of paper from her handbag.

'Is Eddie here?' she asks the barmaid in English.

The barmaid stops wiping a glass and sets it on the edge of the sink. Sizing up the newcomer, she leans both arms on the counter:

'No, he's not here.'

She takes the glass, holds it against the light, examines. Another fat woman has come into the bar, strikingly like the barmaid in facial features, probably her mother.

The Black woman fishes a pen from her handbag.

'And where would I find h . . . '

The barmaid turns wearily, takes the pen from the Black woman's hand and scribbles something on the sheet.

'Here,' she says, and hands her mother an apron.

The radio plays a song by the BLØF group, 'Eén en alleen'.

The Black woman affixes her sunglasses, puts pen and paper in handbag, and with languorous movements sashays out in the street.

Misschien dat ik weer verder ga, misschien dat jig nog naar me zwaait, misschien dat ik nog even blijf, sings BLØF.

Psychotronic abilities, old Blef said, when acquainting Simon with his plans. I must not forget those. We all have them, you too, Simon. Just that you don't have patience. You're no lover of mankind. Thus far, you still don't know why you ought to help people. But me, I do know, that only this has meaning. To go and to help.

Did you know it back then, when you were climbing the asses' ladder?

Sure. Then too, I was helping.

Including those you got rid of, who were in your way?

Simon, you can't understand that. I'm curious what *you'd* have done if you'd been in my place? Judging is easy, but measuring up is harder. I have a clear conscience. For me, the interest of my native land was always in the first place. If a few heads rolled, it was not my doing. Such is life. Such is the fate of man. I'm not saying that I'm totally innocent. No indeed. But I'm not worse than the others. And now, at the latter end of life, providence has vouchsafed me a little time to cleanse myself of the last impurities. And so, I will help people, but now it won't be from the position of my function. Spiritually, I will purge myself and I will transmit my energy to people, *healing* energy, energy of love and *forgiveness*.

What do you want to forgive them for?

Not just their actions, but even wrong intentions.

And what if there were more of those who would need to forgive you?

I did not consciously injure anyone. If someone feels that I did,
it's his affair. The world is full of primitives. But now I'm in a different
place, now I must devote myself to other, *more sublime* matters, cul-
tivation of spiritual energy. I'm accomplishing in myself what many
philosophers only dreamed of. I have everything here: solitude, a roof
over my head, Nature, stalwart people around me. I've a few important books; I'll find whatever I need in them. And here, look, two
strong hands, my mind still serves me, I have adequate will, so why
shouldn't I be able to become someone different?

You were always someone *different*, Dad.

Now listen, Simon. I always wanted to serve. To serve the good.
Whatever I thought important for the prosperity of this country. We
made mistakes, yes, sometimes we erred, but don't forget, we were
starting with only the green grass.

The red grass.

Simon, please, don't be malicious.

I'm not malicious. But you people managed to start on red grass,
on bloody grass, and not on the green grass. Everything was moving
nicely then, the country would have pulled itself together despite its
war wounds, only that you arrived and instituted terror.

Simon, you simply don't know what you're talking about.

We haven't talked for a long time.

True. But is that my fault? Well . . . irrelevant. In short, when I
was young, twenty years after the war, there was more dedication and
solidarity in people. No one questioned the interests of the homeland,
do you understand? Now I'd be interested to know, what interests

you, Simon? What is your highest interest? But d'you know what? Better not say, I don't want to hear. Your generation no longer interests me. The revolutionary slogans, the purges, they were yours. But what's to become of us, who are entering old age, that doesn't interest any of you. I really would be interested to know what care those who come after you will take of *you*. Because you take no care at all of us. You flung us out on the streets, the sick and the feeble, and bye-bye.

You're exaggerating, Dad. Look, you've a mountain bike.

Everything is a circus, and for some people there's even enough bread. Do you think the world cares about anything other than a full belly? We gave people bread and places to live; what are you giving them? In one part of the world they've got the circus, in another the bread; one lot is shivering, the other lot is bored, but the result will be the same for all. You can choose, so as to have the feeling that you're free. But from what I hear, you've made your choice already, Simon. You're throwing away your country like a dirty old rag.

Well, it is rather dirty, don't you think?

One day you'll regret, you will bitterly regret such words. Do you think something different is waiting for you somewhere else? Rivers of gold, roast pigeons, milk and honey? Political arrangements don't matter. All that counts is what you feel towards your country. Changes of regime? Stage-managed masquerades. So people won't get bored. But nonetheless I love my native land. And what do you love, Simon?

What native land? Do you mean the country whose borders were determined by more powerful people whenever they liked? Dad, the only reason this homeland of yours could come into existence was that it was never sufficiently interesting for anyone. They invented its borders, they invented its history, so that they could straight away forget about it. Don't tell me you're not aware of that.

But at least there's peace here. Look at those peaks. Those costumes. And those girls. Look at that sunset, at those proud ruins high on a rock. Listen to those folk songs. Take a look around you, and weep.

At this last dialogue with old Blef Simon did not look around him and did not weep. He'd drunk his fill, so he wasn't far from bursting into laughter. Ah, but once again he had ended up in his father's empire! This, after all, is Amsterdam, the Jordaan district, the wide world, where no one owes anyone explanations and apologies. When he finally launches into his big-city novel, fathers and their empires will on no account appear there.

He turned to the sturdy barmaid and called:

'Betalen, graag!'

34. That dandy,

that brimful-of-health, sun-bronzed race driver from Algeria, in his slim novel genuinely captured this. Simon has noted the words, though imprecisely, not literally, from time to time he rereads them, they terrify him, make him incapable of writing his big-city novel. Simply, he must acknowledge that the race driver from the African continent made do with a few images which Simon . . . it wasn't that they'd escaped him, he'd just never thought them worth recording:

Holland is a dream . . . a dream of gold and smoke . . . heads plunged in a mist of neon green and red, jenever and peppermint . . . jenever, the solitary light in darkness . . . dreamily riding their black bicycles with high handlebars, funereal swans drifting along the canals . . . grimacing gods of Indonesia with which they have decorated their shop windows . . .

No depressiveness, just an unengaged observation of life, a full-blooded indifference, so essential for those who love speed, the wind that rises up from the sea, the wind that raises women's skirts. Who else but this gladiator of hedonistic philosophy, who lets death leap from a window in the body of his wife, could describe Amsterdam exactly? Need one seek further inspiration in the guidebooks?

35. In Jordaan,

fancy that, in Jordaan she has an apartment. Now isn't that tremendous? She comes from a very rich family, and right to this day she is very, very rich. How many times have we walked through Enscheda and she'd point to houses: this house belonged to us, and that one, that over there too. It all belonged to my family. Váu.

Kees Visser paused briefly, and continued:

The apartment isn't large, but it's cosy there. Just exactly like I'd imagined. A beautiful woman by my side, best-quality music, wine. Now it's clear that we're lovers. I hope Jan too grasped that. Lovers, váu. Some time back all three of us stayed overnight there. Janneke and I stayed up, Jan went to sleep. After a while I went to see if he was sleeping, and guess what I saw. Tears were rolling down his face. Well, I'm not altogether sure, but I think they were tears. He was crying. Don't ask me what for. Probably he was jealous. Probably he wanted Janneke, except that Janneke made it clear she wanted me. Váu. Tremendous woman. Sharp. And that sense of humour. And educated. Once upon a time she used to organize concerts. In

Amsterdam too. She's got a son in Britain, first violin, world-famous quartet. But you know Janneke, right? Some time you and Estrella could come to her villa in Oldenzaal. Magnificent city, váu. I have photos here, look.

Kees pulled a digital camera out of a cloth bag with inscription *Free Tibet*.

Hm, so that *meisje* of his has a little flat in Jordaan. Maybe I've strolled right beside it. Maybe it was the one with those bare foot soles sticking out from the balcony. An old Spanish superstition, related by Cervantes, says that whoever bathes in the river Jordan becomes young again.

Simon imagines a dusky apartment crammed with books and vinyl records. He imagines Janneke in it, that fidgety woman with the sharply carven profile. So Jan van Der Flucht wept. Kees is exaggerating. The likelihood is that his eyes were watery from sleeplessness, from weariness. Undoubtedly, they'd done a tour of some of the surrounding establishments, and for all that Jan was in good condition, a pair of seventy-five-year-old eyes cannot take too much of that. And maybe it really was weeping. With these goofy carcasses one never knows: instead of preparing for a stoic transition to *non-being*, with their last reserves of strength they are fanning *romantic* ambitions. Elderly weeping has its place in the line afterwards. They don't need skeletons of paper, or a draught.

36. What brings Peter

here? For indeed, that's Peter. To all appearances! How did he get here? And does he know I'm in Amsterdam too?

Simon stops and gazes, quite stunned, at the rather short stocky man with the carefully trimmed red beard. No, that's not him. But those clothes . . . Those spick-and-span ironed jeans, dark-green spring jacket with hood, chamois-leather shoes. That's Peter. No one else dresses like that. It's him. Set in stone.

The red-haired man registers Simon's gaze. He sizes him up for a while, then turns away. Simon's face, by all the signs, did not strike him as familiar. So then no, that's not Peter, quite conclusively. And what if it were him? Would he converse with him? What would they talk about? After such a long silence? For Peter undoubtedly it would be a delicate situation; and Peter, if he found himself in a precarious situation, would simply cease to reply to questions. He would only smile craftily, avoiding eye contact.

After so many years! Virgin Mary of Guadalupe, how many? Ten, twelve . . . thirteen? After thirteen years? Or fourteen? When had he last seen Sandra? Seven years ago? She was pushing a child in a pram ahead of her, and Simon, waiting for tram number 8 on the concrete island, was pretending he didn't see her. Sandra though had no embarrassment, headed straight towards him. They ended up having coffee, though they didn't have much to say: how's Peter? Peter's fine, he's teaching at a tech, how are you, I'm fine too, I'm not complaining, things are OK, I'm working in the editorial office of a women's magazine. Afterwards Simon gave Sandra some tram tickets and she gratefully accepted the gift, from which Simon deduced that financially her and Peter were not exactly thriving. It must be longer again since he saw Peter. Although yes, once he did, once he picked him out from the tram, walking sedately, briefcase in hand. He'd got out of the same tram that was carrying Simon; evidently, he'd spotted Simon before Simon managed to spot him, and he took to his heels at the next stop. And maybe even that man with the briefcase wasn't Peter.

Chances are that Peter today would scarcely look as he did in those days, when they used to skive off from morning lectures and spend whole days in buffets and bars. They'd begin with potato salad and bread rolls, continue with coffee and cola and end in a wine cellar with a few bottles of white. Even then, Peter was developing a beer belly. His leisured, as if meditative, gait, his incipient bald spot and his statements given with an air of infallibility, made him older (and hence more trustworthy) than he was in reality.

Peter must be long settled down by now, and definitely he'd taken on the task of building the family home. He, the teacher from the tech. Courageous. Simon would have portrayed him as courageous, if he'd allowed him to figure in his novel. So that even supposing in reality he had not yet embarked upon building the family home, in Simon's novel he would have the house already. Simon would wish that for Peter. And not only on paper. But again, not from any spirit of benevolence. On the issue of courage, Peter had never been courageous, though he'd never been a coward either. Only a pedant. This is a problem Simon has, that he confuses pedants with cowards. Justin, for his part, confuses thoughtfulness with snobbery. There's some nuance that escapes everyone. But not the pedants. They think that they think of everything. And who else could embark upon building a house, if not pedants?

Are you not getting ready to procreate with Sandra? Peter asked him once on the way from the wine cellar to the hostel.

Simon instantly sobered up. He had a whole day's drinking behind him, a whole evening vilifying professors and almost a whole night discussing Dostoevsky. He was scarcely able to stay on his feet. Simon suddenly didn't know what to say to that, eventually he stammered something to the effect that time was *like fir-tree branches*, and they'd see each other in school. Peter just walked on silently, his gaze skewered in the asphalt, then out of the blue he gave Simon a nudge and roared: Go and get yourself in line, you mortal! Just go, if you please! What are you waiting for? Get into line *with them*, that's where your place is!

With them? Who was Peter thinking of? Presumably those whom philosophizing and boozing students regarded as meriting only scorn? Those *common and simple* ones? Peter had once, indeed, despised the order of everyday life, that is to say, he despised especially those who sleep at night and wake up early in the morning to be fresh and industrious.

To procreate. Simon does not know a more disgusting word. As if someone had deposited a dead eel in his hand. *Go and get in line!*

Eventually Peter himself had got into line. He who had despised all lined-up people. He scorned the in-line communists, and he himself had become an in-line Catholic. Now he was building a house for his wife and two kids. The life of those in line. Or could it be that he'd wanted, by that gesture, by that nudging years ago, to put Simon in another line, to thrust him away somewhere else? Among the godless and the damned? Because he had not obeyed the law of ages, God's law, and had not gone forth and *not increased* and *not multiplied*? And *not filled the earth*? Peter had said *get in line* and Simon had fallen silent, not asking him what he meant. Though he should have done, he ought to have asked immediately. Peter, whom he'd regarded almost as his father, a spiritual authority, an infallible guide to life. Obviously Peter had seen deep into Simon and knew well what his soul yearned for, and he had decided to let his friend go on simmering in the cauldron of his doubts. Peter did not need Simon, he had no need of any friends; his best friends were his siblings, his parents, Russian classics, Catholic theologians and Italian cinematography of the 1960s and 70s.

Simon had found the nicotine smell of Peter's room somehow calming. In Peter's room he had fancied that his great-grandfather (the one who smelt so much of tobacco and after First World War spent seven years returning from Siberian captivity, judging by how judicious he remained lifelong, he'd brought back with him a bit of the Asian wisdom, broad and coarse as the steppe) came to life again, in thick blue smoke in a subterranean room illumined by a single lightbulb. Then and there, in Peter's room, the great-grandfather's moustachioed, parchment-coloured face appeared again, the face of a poor gardener from Salzburg, a face that immediately dissolved over the opened book that Peter handed Simon, that he might read the lines underscored in pencil. While Simon was reading, Peter narrowed his eyes and slowly, enjoyably blew out smoke. When he'd finished his butt-end, he stretched out on the couch, propping his head with his hand like some old Roman after a feast; he seemed to be drifting off to sleep but in fact he wasn't, he did not succumb to slumber. Simon felt he ought to say something, that he should comment on the passage he had just read, but finally he too smiled and reached for his plastic cup of Moravian Riesling. He was thankful for every minute he could spend in Peter's presence. He wouldn't have minded changing to being Peter. Certainly that did not hold vice versa, Peter felt just fine in his own skin, he wouldn't have changed, and he definitely never would have wanted to be Simon and absolutely not be a Blef, a son of the discredited Anton Blef.

37. Piety,

that incomprehensible dense Catholic piety. It was trembling in both of them: in Simon and in Peter, though in each differently. Peter was not very interested in the induced reveries that Pasolini's and Fellini's films evoked in Simon; he thus had no means of comprehending Simon's childish daydreams about the *Eternal* City, which his granny had once infused in him. Even Simon did not understand his own affinity with Rome. Years later, however, he found in an exemplary tale by Cervantes, *Doctor Glass-Case*, a passage that gave him absolution and definitively confirmed the claim he had to such fantasies:

> *He visited its churches, reverenced its holy relics and admired its sublimity; and just as one knows the greatness and ferocity of the lion by its claws, so he too came to know the greatness of Rome by the fragments of marble, by the preserved and broken sculptures, by the cracked arches and ruined chapels, by the spectacular columns and enormous amphitheatres, by the famed and sacred river that constantly replenishes its banks with water and consecrates them with many relics from the bodies of the martyrs*

*who found a burial place there, by the bridges gazing one upon
the other, and by the streets whose very names surpass the streets
of all other cities on Earth: Via Appia, Via Flaminia, Via Julia,
and others of that kind.*

Today there's some kind of clamour by the canals. Today? This
city never stops celebrating. Rain, sleet, mist, sun, wind—nothing
matters, the merriment never ceases. By some miracle, the rumbling
motor barges with little groups of beer-crazed youths never collide:
somehow at the last moment one always manages to avoid the other.

In all the world there is only one real city, the city of cities, an
indestructible city, and that city is Rome, Simon's granny, mother of
old Blef, used to say. So then, what was he up to in Amsterdam, when
in every city he was only seeking Rome? He had even dragged Sandra
there, poor wretch, as if she could have grasped something he didn't
grasp himself. Half-light of temples, columns, rippling cornices, bro-
ken-off noses of saints. Cracked orange-coloured plaster, fragrance of
pine woods, Tiber marsh, stink of soutanes and smoke-blacked fres-
cos. And he had dragged Estrella there too, to St Peter's Square, so
that she might swear she would not set foot in that church ever.
Sandra had gone in there, she'd still been able for that; it was two
years after she had become Peter's lover, behind Simon's back. Simon
took almost half a year to be able to come to terms with that, more
or less. It didn't occur to him that he needn't make any strenuous
effort, he could walk out of Sandra's life and thus pre-empt later,
much more devastating events. Except, it appeared then that Sandra,
thinking things over, felt she would rather be with him than with
Peter. He had accordingly forced himself to *forgive* her, and he had
forced her to go to Rome. But he didn't have to force her all that

much. They had not regretted the trip, of which a few grainy photos survived: Simon on the steps of the fountain in Navona Square; Simon on the pavement before the Angelic Castle; Sandra in front of Bernini's colonnade shading her face with the guidebook, where nothing was said of the fact that St Peter's Church contained the last remains of Simon the Zealot.

Simon Blef too had sometimes been a zealot, a kind that Peter never could have been. That was why, in the films of Fellini and Pasolini, Simon had first and foremost seen Rome, the indestructible city, whereas Peter had found there his own favourite themes: guilt and punishment, pride and humility, sloth and penitence. Slowly, smoke blown out with relish. Although Simon did not fall to his knees in the churches, each time something within him flung its entire (astral) body on the cold floor and crawled to the altar, in a childish hope of experiencing an ecstasy like that which contorts Bernini's Saint Teresa.

What would he say to Peter, if he unexpectedly met him here? In Amsterdam, the city that knows no distinction between sin and forgiveness? He would say: Hello, this is me, Simon, do you remember me? Shall we go for a beer? Let's turn the page, let's forget everything, what has been has been, there's no undoing it. So, are you in favour? And Peter wouldn't say anything, he never replies to questions, after all: he'd lower his eyes and a patronizing smile would appear on his face. *Let's turn the page*, but we won't go for beer.

38. Best not to go that way,

best not to think of casting anchor in Spui Square. To pass close by it, at most. Some might like to be there, the guidebook praises it, but it's never been to Simon's taste. The bars, the beer halls, the cafes: alluring on the outside, but jam-packed inside in wintertime, empty and unfriendly in summer. Abandoned gyms. They say that here (here too?) smoulders the authentic (nicotine-poisoned) heart of Amsterdam. Nevertheless, he'll go to Spui. He'll give it one more chance. What if something has fundamentally changed there? It's a good distance away, first one must go back, cross bridges, Prinsengracht, Keizersgracht, Herengracht, Singel. After that, it wouldn't be a bad idea to arrange for a short pause, take a break and fortify himself; one needs to come reinforced to Spui, so as not to be overwhelmed by all that racket, rumbling trams, swishing cyclists, gnashing jaws, spits, smiles, plen-itude of limbs, shawls and shorts, colour prints and old books. From there it's just a little way to Rembrandtplein, not that one may look forward to relief in that quarter, only the identical din that prevails in Spui. So why is he thrusting himself into all that, why is he rolling in that direction, when he's disgusted even now? Why not go to the De Pijp quarter and take refuge in one of the dusky restaurants on Frans Halsstraat? He has no answer. His legs hurt. Yes, probably they're hurting, that tension in the thighs and calves might possibly be pain. And then: above all else, he must think of the flight arrival. Walking from De Pijp, he wouldn't make it so quickly to Central Station, assuming that, come what may, he wants to go back to the station on foot. The flight . . . when does the flight arrive? At quarter to nine. And what's the time now?

He thus forsakes Jordaan, over the Prinsengracht bridge. Today was not the proper day for this quarter; no newborn prophet appeared from it today. Jordaan evidently hasn't had its proper days for a long time. For example, the day when he was here with Justin: what kind of a day was that?

It was no small achievement, persuading Justin to drag himself hither. From that stinking birthplace of his (Simon's stinking birthplace also, in fact). But eventually he gave in and actually dragged his person. And what awaited him here? Stinking Jordaan. On the positive side, he made no remark on the stink. Not here. Later, at home, safe in a native pub, in the circle of his own, he would certainly have glossed the experience in his distinctively pungent manner. Once again instructing those sitting round him that it's futile and ridiculous to travel, because a stink is a stink, every stink is the same and the native stink is always best, safer than the foreign. But it's not so, but it isn't, Simon mentally objected. However, this is a thought that someone like Justin has no way of arriving at when once he has concluded that the world can only be such and such, the same thing, and on no account something else. *No-o-o-o way.* The world is always identical, to a hair and all over, and whoever maintains something different, whatever that difference may be, is a liar and a deceiver. But the fact is Jordaan nonetheless stinks differently if only for this simple reason: that whatever is spat out, sweated and puked out here comes from entirely different, maybe worse and maybe even better beers, from worse and better breads, condiments, broths, chops, ribs, fish and greenery, relative to those that are dished out in Justin's true-blue pub in his and Simon's native town. In short, man in every corner of the earth farts differently. But Justin is right, why write novels about that? What's the point of convincing anyone that a change of place means also a change in the pong of the fart, the consistency of the stools? Needless to say, most people are happy even without that knowledge. Stink, however, is the foundation. If the stink changes from town to town, then all kinds of other things may be *different*. Feelings, customs, reactions, thoughts, words.

One way or another, Justin finally succumbed to persuasion and arrived. A year ago, roughly at this time. Simon had one objective only: that Justin should have a few days' change of air. That he should arrive at different thoughts. But why did it matter so much to him? He doesn't know. Probably he loves poking his nose in other people's business. If he wrote a novel, he'd unpack all that. The character in the novel representing Simon would presumably know why he needed to drag the character representing Justin away from home and show him a different corner of the world. But Simon did not want to show Justin anything, parade anything before him, harass him in any way. He just wanted to spend a few days with him, and to once again go through stories they had raked over a thousand times before—banal experiences from student life, the political situation, manias to do with women. Stupidity: he had never talked over any experiences from his student life with Justin and he never would, even if they should chance to meet again. Because in their schooldays they had scarcely ever had an adventure in common, they had belonged to different *parties*, they were different *sorts* of boys. Hence Simon did not wish to demonstrate anything or show off in his friend's company. Justin cannot stand hyperbole, of which he himself is an ever-gushing spring. Justin cannot stand travelling, he loathes famous places, tourist attractions, tourists, miscellaneousness, chaos, lack of the unambiguous. And all the time, paradoxically, he lives in the permanent *baroque* delirium of his exaggerations. Simon decided he would be considerate and behave as though they were going for beer in their native town. Let Justin in Amsterdam discover whatever he wanted to, even if it meant him sitting the whole time in one solitary pub. Ultimately, it turned out almost like that. All of the pubs in Jordaan were full to bursting, they barely managed to find a free table, right by the canal, under the pruned maples. The beer had a bitter taste, and their spirits fell.

If only this stuff doesn't give us the runs, Justin remarked then.

Look, you can scutter straight into the canal.

Afterwards they moved to Spui Square and sat for a number of hours on the rickety chairs in front of Cafe de Zwart. Daylight faded, Simon drank toasts and, forgetting his resolution not to force anything on Justin, proposed that for fun they should go to the red-light district.

No way, said Justin, and withdrew into silence.

So let's go to Rembrandtplein, Simon suggested.

Is it far?

A bit from here, the way the tram is going, see?

OK. Rembrandtplein, but nowhere else.

So let's have one more beer.

Justin is a pragmatist, at least he claims to be, and for the most part he really does behave pragmatically, though it sometimes seems that by stubbornness he robs himself of the joys of life. *Pragmatically* attainable joys. But one can understand that, truly one can: how can one have joy in something that the majority enjoys? Justin must have *his own* joys. Secret, exceptional. Secret pleasures, but when afterwards we come back out on the street, we see that others who discovered them long previously have eroded and degraded them. And we, two small-town laddies, in arrested development, from a land full of brag-garts, yet again we've arrived too late. Justin needs his exceptional pleasures, but they shouldn't be revolting. He's actually a careful fellow: in his opinion, so many injustices have been visited on him in life that by now he is entitled to caution. But caution itself is probably the worst *injustice* that a person may visit upon himself.

Justin had never had it in mind to visit Simon. Justin actually didn't know how to sustain relations with someone who had emigrated, he had no experience of that. Most of us don't, in fact. Simon's problem was that he had abandoned his country, his place, his pub, where he could meet with Justin. Naturally, according to a harmonogram designed by Justin. Because Justin, if he didn't have his own iron in the fire, would not adapt himself to anyone. That's something one gets used to. Justin *does not invest* in the maintenance of relationships. If anyone's interested, go ahead, let him be the first to ring, because Justin will not ring first. Simon had often pondered this manner of Justin's, and it took him a long time to discover, actually only here, in the Netherlands, did it dawn on him, that Justin is right, that one can only concur with his communicative *habits*, they do not merit reproach; the individual who pushes himself about too much in maintaining diverse relationships will sooner or later founder. Simon himself had foundered. And when that happened, all of a sudden he had begun to admire Justin. He admired his clear-sightedness, the unerring, implacable logic that protected him from *foundering*. When a person founders in youth, all very well. But with the advancing years one finds it ever more difficult to recover from such crashes. With advancing years, one must don the appropriate armour and be heedless of backbiters and sneerers. Justin therefore has the gospel truth (and incidentally he always wanted truth, even when it promised to be frightful; there was nothing he could do about being born with a knowledge of truth—being born *unto truth*): if Simon feels lonely in the Netherlands, let him not complain; it was his choice, after all, no one forced it upon him; his grumbles aren't worth a straw. *Not a straw*. Let him not go crawling to anyone. Let him not keep writing to anyone, or ringing.

Listen, where are we going? Justin asked. His speech was slurred now.

We're gradually making our way to the station.

But through this district?

Shortest way, Simon said enigmatically.

But we're not stopping here, OK? I'm not curious about these farm fowl in the windows.

Simon knew that Justin would not regret this trip. When he returned to his loved and loathed backwater, among *his own*, with whom one could stubbornly, pathetically grow old, the very next day he would announce enthusiastically that he'd seen things. A copper-skinned drunk on a bicycle. He was wobbling, all but tumbled into the canal. A guitarist in a green coat, an authentic water sprite. A brown tart, old and fat like this pub lady here, imagine, there's some-one who still wants such a creature. She was there in the window bowing to customers, she gave me a mocking leer. A two-metre-tall transvestite, who had half her arse sticking out of her shorts. Tattooed on that half was the smiling head of the Pope. Sixty-year-old punk women with pea-green hair, kilos of chains on their leather jackets and beer cans in their hands. Junkies dressed up as Easter Bunnies. Goths, head to foot in black, and with such wide trousers that they couldn't walk. Pink bicycles with turquoise spots. Buddhist monks with laptops under their armpits. One-hundred-and-ten-year-old hip-pies with white hair down to their shoulders, in top hats and with hundreds of badges fixed to their pink jackets. A Black man who had bionic protheses in place of legs. A blind poet who was giving out autographs. Drunken female students dancing on a motor barge, while their male companions uninhibitedly pissed in the canal. Women in black chadors. Indian women in fiery-red and saffron saris. A houseboat that served as a refuge for dozens of cats.

39. It'll be sufficient if he gets underway

sometime before eight. From Centraal Station to Schiphol is a quarter of an hour's journey. The flight gets in at half eight. Or even later. There's time then for a session at Rembrandtplein, so put nerves aside. Before that one could have something at Spui as well, maybe a beer for sobering up, but now just a coffee and glass of water would go down well. Right there, for example. Seems they've an empty space, they've only recently opened. *Harry's*. Sterile name. So. In we go.

The barman, with his back turned, is occupied with the coffee machine. Face brown, haircut impeccable, ebony hair oiled. Probably Moroccan. The walls are adorned with various bits of wooden, paper and copper junk. Ethnoshop merchandise. The space fills with the aroma of a vanilla joss stick. Electronic world music slithers from speakers, sounds of a Spanish guitar interweaving with the ethereal notes of a Turkish bamboo flute. Subdued lighting.

'Dag,' Simon says.

'Hello,' the barman says, sizing up the intruder in a flash and turning back to the coffee machine.

Simon hesitates a moment, whether to stay on the ground floor or go upstairs. He opts for the upstairs. In a nook by the window, under a massive beam, he finds a small table. Enough for the brief while he plans to stay here.

Minutes go by, the Spanish guitar is replaced by strumming on a sitar, instead of the bamboo flute Indian violins wail. A tram comes clattering down the street. Then another. Someone yells. Something bursts. Night is coming in, the mood on the street heightens.

Simon pulls a jotter and pen out of his bag.

At the ground level the stairs begin creaking, and Simon sees the bald crown of the barman nearing. Obviously, he's in no rush.

'What do you want to drink?'

'Ik . . . ik spreek een beetje . . . Nederlands,' Simon stammers.

'Sure,' the barman continues in English, and waits.

'Ik will graag een coffie en een glas water,' Simon says.

The barman nods and leaves without a word.

From the street, the insistent wail of an ambulance.

Maybe he doesn't come from Morocco, Simon speculates. But straight—from Egypt. From the 'Black country'. Not from the desert, where *the heavens cover the dead*. Damn it, straight from five-million-strong Alexandria! Where, in a cafe on the seashore, they had put a bottle of vodka on the table in front of Simon, he could pour for himself. In a decilitre glass, as much as he liked. And there he found refuge from the importunate street hawkers selling socks, watches and paper hankies. Only to find himself in the snares of two insatiable waiters. You're White, you're not in rags, so cough up! The waiters propped their arses against the bar counter, crossed their arms, transfixed Simon with their eyes and waited to see what he would do with the bottle of vodka and the decilitre glass. Simon had no liking for vodka and especially not the kind that they offered in Egypt, but he had to take a swig or two of this prophylactic to ensure that the intestinal plague of travellers (Tutankhamen's curse) would not compromise him somewhere on the street. That was all he needed. Especially since, that morning, he had swallowed an unknown insect. And yet normally he didn't walk the streets with his mouth wide open. Alexandria offered nothing to leave one rapt with admiration. Whether that insect was poisonous would be revealed in due course. Or not. In any event, he did not need to diversify the phobias that ever and anew possessed him in dusty Egypt with an attack of diarrhoea on the street. Which is why he had resorted to vodka (though it was scarcely stronger than tea).

The barman places a cup of coffee, a glass and a bottle of mineral water, on the table. Then, without the least inhibition, he asks:

'Where are you from?'

The question surprises Simon, but not so much as to leave him incapable of lying. He cannot, after all, say where he comes from, because this fellow would not believe that such a country actually exists.

The barman says: 'Oukey.' But he makes no move to leave.

Simon is stricken by fear that the Arab will want to make him company. That he'll want to be amused. To divulge confidences. Or to gather intelligence. Maybe he's working for some secret service. In the museum in Cairo, crammed with mummies and sarcophaguses, a guard had called him over. Simply to confide in him, an unknown tourist, what a potent male he was: apart from his wife, he also had a girlfriend who cried out in rapture when they did it together. Simon listened to the guard's tale, nodded affirmingly, but didn't believe that this was all he wanted. Who knows what feints and coded approaches may be used by the Egyptian secret police?

'And long time you live in the Netherlands?' the Moroccan asks.

Simon thinks of a number and reaches for the sugar bowl.

The Moroccan stands over him silently for another moment, observes Simon's trembling hand, then takes himself back to the ground floor.

What does this Mustapha or Achmed want from him? What's pestering him? Doesn't he see *the fact that*? What doesn't he see? He doesn't see that I, Simon, that *in short*. Or does he really see? Is this actually the very thing that he sees? Does he see precisely the *that* in him? That Simon is one of those who scarcely are *here, in this world*? And those, precisely those, have got to be pestered. Their lapels tweaked, so they don't fly away. So that they comprehend the fact that gravitation applies to all persons without exception.

Simon opens his notebook: where did he stop?

He browses.

Scrawl. Beer stains. Notes from the pub on Gravenstraat, almost illegible. Now he can more or less decipher them, but tomorrow, tomorrow at around this time . . . He won't understand a jot from these wavy lines. Tomorrow he'll have to tear out these inscribed pages and throw them away.

He browses.

But it wasn't only the guard in the Cairo Museum, no, he was not the sole pesterer. One day, after a long time, he went to have another look at the Citadel. This time he approached it from the other end. Suddenly some fellow addressed him in English. He explained that today there was no access to the Citadel, because a terrorist attack was anticipated. Simon was astonished, but since he had come to Cairo for a month, he told himself he'd return to the Citadel another time, tomorrow or the day after. But that other fellow would not release him. He proposed to Simon that he could show him somewhere much more interesting than the Citadel, a place tourists know nothing about. And what would that be? Simon asked. The Blue Mosque, the lad said. OK, Simon agreed, even though this situation reminded him of something. Was it this same fellow who had addressed him in Konya a few years ago, and how did that end? Buying a number of carpets in the underground shop of the lad's brother-in-law. They had simply lightened his wallet. This will not happen now, Simon resolved, and he let himself be conducted to the half-ruined mosque, whose courtyard was crammed with scaffolding. Passing through the gate, they met an old man, probably the imam, in a grey gabali. The imam stretched out his palm and the lad told Simon how much he had to give, otherwise he would not be able to see the mosque. Simon blushed scarlet, but he would not retreat. He pressed a banknote into the imam's hands and let himself be led inside. Turkish glazed tiles gleamed in the half-light behind the scaffolding. The Blue Mosque, said the young fellow. These tiles come from Turkey. Have you ever been in a minaret? Simon said he hadn't, and suddenly his depression passed: he was experiencing something that anyone might envy him, access to a minaret. By a narrow spiral staircase they went right up, to the outer passage that the muezzins had called from in times past. Here the lad took a photo of Simon with the silhouette of the distant Citadel in the background. After that, they went to the roof of the mosque. The lad turned to Simon and held out his hand. Fifty pounds, he said. That's too much, Simon objected. The fellow launched into explanations, that Cairo had been hit by an earthquake, let him just look at those cracked walls and flattened minarets, and he'd lost his parents in the earthquake and his granny had gone blind, let him just give him the fifty pounds. They were only Egyptian pounds, needless to say, not a very large sum, but it was that unheard-of gracelessness that offended Simon. He felt dismayed that he'd once again let himself be caught, and that the Orient was incapable of showing him the merest shred of civility. He gave the lad what he demanded, whereupon the other began demanding a further sum. But Simon was already striding to the exit. The lad began to laugh and kept on crying out the amount that he wanted to extract from his client. And even afterwards Simon heard him shouting that if he liked he could come to him that evening: there would be a large family hooley, at least he would see an authentic Egyptian wedding.

He strains his memory: what was he thinking of when he entered this bar? Where was his mind straying when he crossed the road? When he dismissed Jordaan from his thoughts? What was it that he wanted at all costs to write down? If anything? He has to record something, even if nothing just then comes to mind, something must be there or else he will feel useless. To scribble in twilight, in the twilight of any literature. In the twilight of any *good* purpose. What had he wanted to write? Something about Justin. Or something worse. Something about Peter? And that nameless redhead in Jordaan had wound him up just like that? Just like that?

40. Falsehood

lives its independent life, provocatively flaunting, promenading. It clings to the human being even before his birth. And not only the human being. It clings to anything that moves, breathes, that is subordinate to instincts. Everyone develops a greater or lesser effort to uncover falsehood. Some from the very beginning seek it exclusively in others. Some find it also in themselves, and then they decide whether they will reinforce and enlarge it, or whether they will rid themselves of it gradually. But we are never able to rid ourselves of falsehood, completely and forever. The impulse that compels us to strip ourselves of falsehood once again feeds off (what else but?) falsehood. The notorious recorder has some knowledge thereof. That is why he has a notebook incessantly in his hand. To capture falsehood while it is red-hot, blind, powerless. In a state where it hasn't yet been wrapped up in diverse tricks and ploys. Of the ploys there is a great diversity. Janneke, who thanks to Kees had become superficially acquainted (in the crudest outlines) with the fundamental theses of Buddhism and Hinduism, not so long ago offered instruction to

Simon: The world is an illusion. Simon smiled. Janneke: Everything is an illusion, even this table we're sitting at. Simon wanted to say something, clarify, point something out; he was aware, however, that Janneke was not one of those women who would listen attentively to anything, and so he continued to be mute. Let her be wise. Even Kees was smiling. But differently from Simon. A bit roguishly, as if to say: *Let her be, she's beautiful after all.* Which is the same as acknowledging that beauty counterbalances wisdom. *The world is illusion.* Even this is a falsehood. If Janneke were to apply herself more to Buddhism, in time she would discover that the sentence pronouncing the world an illusion is one more trick of pan-cosmic falsehood. Monks, some of them, know that perfectly well; Janneke, however, will never attain to this insight. It would be an illusion to think that this is a fault. That it is *her* fault. We are all powerless innocents, and the very fact of our powerlessness and being childishly *immaculate* is what constitutes the crime of cosmic falsehood, greatest of all crimes.

The notorious recorder turns the page of his notebook and smoothens it out before him.

What he is relying on is that if he faithfully recalls every trivial thing that surfaces in his surroundings, he will gradually drive falsehood out of himself. He writes the first sentence, but before he has finished it he sees that it is absolutely swarming with adjectives. Need to hold fast to the nouns, says the recorder. Nouns are a guarantee of precision. Adjectives lie when they tout themselves as aids to increased precision. They never make anything more precise: they only befog and enfeeble. How could they enhance precision when they designate qualities and attributes about which no two people can permanently agree? Tomorrow these lines will be indecipherable. Allegedly *indecipherable.* For Simon certainly. But maybe somebody will be found who can puzzle them out with ease, and then Simon's rough copy sentences will be disclosed, the rough copy of Simon's perception of the world will be laid bare.

The notorious recorder ought to remain a notorious recorder. He should never publish a book. A published book, as everyone knows, is tale-telling evidence, the record of a condition of falsehood. It is an immortalization of the author's weak-mindedness, even if a hundred times distilled and stylistically refined. The notorious recorder might plead in his defence: at that time, I didn't yet know that adjectives are a component of falsehood; but now I know it, now I would not deceive, I swear I would no longer befog and enfeeble; today I would not make value judgements or deliver verdicts. Thereby, thinks the notorious recorder, he would become immune to falsehood: he has learnt lessons, he's admitted to the world and to himself that he's learnt lessons; he's admitted that he was silly and conceited. Falsehood, however, constantly grows in strength; it's a viscid puddle, a complex set of which the human being is just one member. All the one if he sinks or swims.

In the publication of books, however, that a book becomes a document of weakness and imperfection is not the worst thing. Most books are forgotten. Authors too are forgotten, but not as many as books; people are more likely to remember a name than a book. The worst thing in the publication of books is communication with the publisher. Because the publisher says: this manuscript is too extensive, or too concise; the publisher says: people today cannot stand this genre, write something else or take it to somebody else; the publisher, if he's dealing with a female writer, may ask: do you wear black or white knickers? lacy? with suspender belts? But also, to be met with is the kind of publisher (Simon had actually met him) who wants to besport himself with the writer for at least one night of sodomy. Simon came to the conclusion that the writer had ceased to be a thinking and writing being, and was more and more changing into some plasticine creature that would gladly accept and do anything, if only his book came out and a pinch of celebrity came his way. And therefore Simon drew back, he became the notorious recorder. But even in this position he no longer felt well. Because what kind of virtue was it to go snooping through the world and write about what you'd seen? And then: there are whole armies of note-takers, no less than writers. At this moment, crowds of note-takers all over the world are recording things as alike as two peas to Simon's things. More than one of them has imagined a novel character and by pure chance has invented the name *Simon* for this character and is whittling out sentences, for example: *If Simon ever happened to write a novel, he would have character B appearing in it, for whom A was the model, but he would imagine certain of B's qualities. Simon, however, is not writing a novel, because his fears that at this very moment someone is working on the same novel as himself and that in said novel, just for fun and by caprice, for light relief, a character appears who is brooding on everything he would write in a novel if he were ever to get down to writing, are simply too strong.* Simon knows there are no tricks by which one can wrench oneself free of unoriginality. And he also knows that any other state besides unoriginality, and any other deed besides the unoriginal, scarcely exists in this world. At the same time he is conscious that not acknowledging originality even in that which at first glance appears as something unoriginal, is an expression of incapacity to stand up to falsehood.

41. For a while he stared

into the empty cup. Then he looked elsewhere. For a while he looked
in front of him. Then he looked out the window. A while this way,
then that way. Trams were pealing, he couldn't hear the cyclists
through the glass, he had to associate them mentally with the murmur
of their tyres. He decided to have one more coffee. Rising, he went to
the stairs. The Moroccan was sitting behind the bar counter, reading
a newspaper. Simon leaned against the stair rail and coughed. The
barman looked at Simon and waited.

'Nog een keer, graag,' Simon said, smiling.

'Koffie?' asked the barman.

'Ja, en ook water,' Simon said, and returned to his table. He drew
his mobile from the bag and checked the time.

His friendship with Peter had ended all of a sudden. Simon could
not have said what day it was and what the weather had been like
that day. He knows only that Peter suddenly slipped away, vanished,
even though he didn't travel anywhere, but it was no longer possible
to meet him on the street. Afterwards Sandra, with whom Simon had

moved to a freshly painted rented apartment, announced that she was pregnant.

She said this at night, before going to sleep. When they lay down, Sandra extinguished the lamp on the bedside table. Silence for a while. Then she put the light on again.

Are you sleeping? she asked Simon.

Not yet, he replied.

I'm pregnant, she said.

Simon, his voice unstressed: That's good, isn't it. What we wanted, after all. I'm delighted.

Sandra retorted: But I don't know who the father is.

Simon, as if he'd been expecting this news, said: OK, tomorrow we'll talk about this, now let's sleep. He leaned over Sandra and quenched the lamp. And then he could not fall asleep.

He imagined men whom Sandra might have liked. Who could it have been? Who had she slept with? Why had she done it? Wasn't everything OK between them? Honest truth: I was cowardly, I postponed *procreation* of a child by every means I knew, but eventually I submitted. She was strange in recent times, yes, somehow cold. But who doesn't have crises in partner relations? I thought she was only tired, fact is, she was going to two jobs . . . So if I'm not the father of the child, who is? Someone she's working with? Her boss? Or has one of her old loves resurfaced? Could it be Peter? Him again? He wouldn't do that, not a second time. He hadn't been able to handle it even when he slept with her behind my back the first time, he couldn't come to terms with it; he ceased to have anything to do with me, although several times I indicated to him that *I forgave him*. Our friendship was more important to me. To him, seemingly not, but one could do nothing about that . . . Could it nevertheless have been him? Not to be excluded, by thunder, not to be ruled out. But how then can Sandra not know who the father is? How can she not know? How?

In the morning he sat at the kitchen table opposite Sandra, as always during those four years when they shared a household, and force-fed on a slice of bread and butter and a cup of tea. At work he mindlessly pecked at a keyboard, producing one typo after another. He had a feeling that all around him were wrapping him in tinfoil. He made phone calls but didn't know what he was saying; he scrawled on a sheet of office paper. His mouth dried up. Something had his chest in a vice-like grip. His limbs were like lead.

What's up with you? his colleague Beata asked him, but each time he replied, nothing. Don't talk nonsense (she would not be fobbed off): I can see that you're not in your skin.

OK, so I'm not, he said finally. Do we still have that cognac in the cupboard?

Sure, come on, let's have a shot, Beata said, livening up and looking for cigarettes. You can tell me what's crushing you.

Simon transferred himself from the swivel chair to the moulting armchair, inclined his head, and told his colleague what had happened in the night, what Sandra had said and what he had said to that, and how then he quenched the lamp, and how soon the working day would be over and he would have to go home, to that apartment, to that room, where the fresh paint was still smelling, he would have to go there, because otherwise he had nowhere in the city to sleep, although he could turn to Peter and ask him for help, but he can't bear to, and he can't bear to go to the apartment, to Sandra, but even so he would have to go there in the end and he would have to say something to Sandra, ask her something, something fundamental, just that he doesn't know what he should ask her.

Bea, honestly I don't know what I should ask her. There's only one single question that comes to mind, always the same question, question, question that I can't stand, and which properly shouldn't be of any importance to me, as a person who doesn't acknowledge conventions. I can't bear to utter that question, actually it's useless, Sandra wouldn't give me an answer. And even so, even so there's nothing else I can do but utter that question, and were it to happen that nevertheless she did answer, I know for certain that I would shut my ears, because actually I don't want to hear any answer.

Simon, stop being silly, Beata said in that hoarse smoker's voice of hers. Stop the craziness right now, calmly go home and talk to her normally, after all you are reasonable, adult, university-educated people, you'll see that it'll work itself out, finally she'll tell you that you're the father of the child, you're the one who procreated it. She's just drawing you out, putting you to the test, understand that.

But I, I don't like children, Simon blurted out. And the word *procreated* disgusts me!

Don't talk gibberish (Beata raised her voice). Now you're desperate, and you're being pitched every which way, but you'll see when the baby is born, then you'll see what a miracle it is, I know what I'm talking about, your whole world will be turned right round, it'll change from the foundations, everything will change, you'll change completely, it'll be a new kind of love, you'll see, everything will work out.

What do you want to do now? Sandra asked, when Simon returned that night.

Simon just shrugged his shoulders and subsided into a chair. After a while he said: I don't know. Should I stay? Will you tell me who the other fellow is?

I won't say, Sandra retorted.

Do I know him? Simon asked.

No, she replied.

Is it Peter? Simon would not give up.

No.

And will you tell me why you did that?

Sandra shrugged her shoulders. She lowered her eyes, played with the lace fringe of the tablecloth. Finally, she said: You know, Simon, you can't deny that for years you avoided us having a child, and by this stage I couldn't wait any longer. I asked the gynaecologist what I should do, and he advised me to find someone and say nothing to you for the moment.

How banal? But just to be certain you slept with me as well, right?

In Sandra's eyes there was a flash of outrage: Simon, I didn't force you to do anything that afternoon, I just submitted to you, and whether you believe me or not, now I really don't know whose child it is, but anyhow that doesn't matter, you know that yourself, that it doesn't matter, it'll be our child, our shared little mystery, if that's what you too want, OK? A shared mystery, we won't say anything to the parents, or to the child, what do you say?

There's a hubbub in my head. I don't know what I should say. Probably I should go, I don't know if I can bear to stay . . . Why don't you want to tell me who the other man is? Why don't you tell me it was Peter?

Sandra vehemently stood up and screamed: It was not him!

42. Fortified by the coffee,

he made bolder strides towards Spui Square. Is he going to ruin the rest of the day? With this never-ending harping upon and winnowing the past? Full of adjectives? All that will remain of any of us finally is the skeletons. And God be praised, skeletons that are at least somewhat *cleansed*. The whole world could change to Mexico, and then El Día de los Muertos would be celebrated everywhere, paper and plastic skeletons would hang everywhere; that would be some show. We would make them dance and they would make us dance in turn, at the spirits' hour, and the soul-healing chattering of paper jaws would be heard from all sides. But all that one hears is wailing and brays of laughter.

One of the most likeable deaths, actually a finished dandy with a talent for cultivated cynicism: Death in Bergman's film *The Seventh Seal*. The characters grope their way and tie themselves in knots, chance and uncertainty toss them about; the only one deserving admiration is Death, patient, cunning, not without humour. Death is a spectator, a connoisseur of good theatre; he knows beforehand what all mankind's drudgery culminates in, but he waits, does not interfere, mostly only looks on in amusement. Simon too would wish to be such, to look on and be entertained, but not let the entertainment smother him. To look on in a long black robe, in the mask of a skeleton. And whose mask does the authentic skeleton wear?

And here we are at Spui, again one must decide whether left or right, whether to Cafe Luxembourg or Cafe de Zwart, whether agoraphobia or claustrophobia. Or to stop still in the midst of indecisive bands of tourists and wait for the attacks of sociophobia. But they're just vagaries, capricious games, all those phobias. As a certain Diderot follower and Cervantes revivalist writes, what they amount to is a fear of dropping out: the human being would very much like to drop out, if possible, in an inhabited area, so he'd have someone to support him and spectators in sufficient numbers; he would gladly drop out, give up his stability, surrender his duty to *measure up* in *his* place, in *this* world. From now on, finally, let other people see to that. Actually, Simon thinks, it's not a fear of dropping out as such (fear of what we wish for most, meaning fear of non-permitted pleasure), but also fear that we will not be able to drop out in an *appropriate* (elegant) manner.

Simon does not suffer from sociophobia, he merely sweats immoderately and begins to choke if he finds himself in a crowd. In a small space. Spui is indeed a small square. Some of the houses give the impression that they're going to collapse any moment now. Under the spreading trees in front of the one-time Lutheran church and along by the Waterstones bookshop's windows, the wind murmurs without ceasing. Irrespective of weather. In the centre of the square and in front of the cafes, there is permanent sunshine. Again, without regard to weathers and seasons. What Simon likes best is the inconspicuous, unmarked gate on the building just next to the American bookshop. One need only press the handle, and the curious stroller enters a dark passageway that issues into a totally different world: the idyllic, medievally strict silence of the Begijnhof. The visitor who approaches Spui from the opposite side, through the courtyard of the Historical Museum, the Begijnhof, and the said passageway with its heavy doors, experiences a still more surprising emergence: into the lively bustle of the square, which seems as if the thought never entered its head that, look, here behind these doors abides a mute, mysterious world. The atmosphere of Spui so far diverges from the mood prevailing on the smooth lawns of the Begijnhof that to Simon the unfathomable, actually quite ordinary short passageway seems to have the inscrutability of Calvino's towns, Cortázar's houses and Borges's gardens, and indeed something of Meyrink's glimmering Amsterdam.

Simon, then, does not suffer from sociophobia. But he certainly does suffer from something, he would not be able to designate it by name, though it occurs to him that he is anguished by uncontrolled pleasure. People disgust him, not only their skin and their breath, but even their glances and their hair; everything about them disgusts him, which makes all the greater the pleasure it would be if he could drop out of their society. Because no one will believe his troubles if he does not drop out, if he does not provide *physical proof* of his nausea. And there's nothing strange about that. All of those *mental disorders*, sometimes alleged to be illnesses, all of those phobias, dyslexias and dysgraphias, are only modern sophisticated excuses for laziness and lack of discipline. Simon is convinced of that. If he were to write a novel, the main character in it would think the same, but Simon would have to present it in such a way that no one could attack him or abuse him as author, and so as to make it clear that the character's thoughts were not the author's thoughts and that the author was not offering the reader any philosophy, neither his own nor a fictional version: he was merely portraying the constrictedness and wretchedness of one character, his contradictory inner world. Simon, although ever more frequently he shunned society and would have fainted in a narrow stuffy space, does not believe anyone who has designated himself as sociophobic. He no longer wants to believe that, and no one will believe anything from him. Time was when he found that troubling. His mother used to say to him: you can tell them what you like and they won't believe you, you've inherited that from me. When you tell people you're feeling fine, they'll say you're only pretending. When you tell them you're sick, they'll mark you down as a hypochondriac. You can live as you like, with any degree of frugality, having breakfast of ordinary bread and butter and disgusting milk from a carton, even so they won't believe you, and they'll spread the story that you're a snob who is stuffing himself with caviar every day. And even if they do believe that you only eat bread rolls, they'll construe it as a pose. Believe me, I know what I'm talking about. I can well remember what poverty we lived in when your father abandoned us. I didn't have another piano to get us out of the hole. We were living from hand to mouth, but everyone in the town (may the lousy dump be accursed!), everyone thought we were rolling in gold, that I was buying the most expensive clothes and cosmetics, and all just because I used to take regular showers and I didn't eat red meat. When finally, we got out of the worst, for a change they began to think I was poor. Simon, there's no help for you, because you have a face that irritates people.

And so, don't torment yourself about whether you're lying or telling the truth.

To Simon, Spui is reminiscent of a small square in Madrid immediately behind Plaza Mayor, a little place nestling in the shadows of crooked buildings, from which one can see the massive tower of St Isidore's Church. Madrid. This Amsterdam afternoon is like that day in Madrid, when Simon was similarly waiting for a plane that would bring Estrella from Amsterdam. Interchangeable cities, substitutable events. In every city there are nooks that make us feel we're in a totally different city, at the opposite end of Europe. *Events.* Then in Madrid he was able to wait for Estrella innocently, cleanly; their shared past was not burdened by even a single smashed plate. Estrella, given copious quantities of courage by red wine, in a good-tempered caprice took it into her head that in pure curiosity she would dash a plate against the pavement: she wanted to *feel* what it was like. Indeed, her temperamental father had once flung an entire pot of noodles out the window. How did he feel at that moment? She too wanted to know. But today the cohabitation of Simon and Estrella has been darkened by something greater, something more menacing than one broken plate; today he cannot wait for her as *innocently* as then. And therefore, maybe now in Madrid she has not actually boarded the plane for Amsterdam, maybe she's decided differently, maybe she's resolved on a new life. A new one, although she knows, she read it in some novel by Diderot's last follower, that one cannot begin a new life, one can only live a variant of the life one has lived hitherto. But once again: only characters in novels believe that, the doctrine about variants of the same life, and novel characters may not be trustworthy, as even that same follower of Diderot says, so their philosophic musings do not have to be taken seriously. Estrella, then, has perhaps boarded a plane heading somewhere altogether different, for example Buenos Aires, where she will start not a further variant of her life but an entirely *lovely, new* life.

43. And therefore he should not have let her

go alone. Not that he wouldn't wish her a new life, not that he would insist on her living just *variant*. Simon doesn't insist on anything, at least that's what he thinks. He is simply afraid for Estrella. A broad-minded novelist would probably write that he fears for her, irrespective of how she might decide in Madrid. Simon, however, would not write that, but not because he does not know with certainty whether he would be afraid for Estrella even if she were to decide that she would not return to Amsterdam. He is afraid for inexplicable reasons, and so provisionally he will leave his fear, which thus far is intangible, unexplained. He is afraid for her, because what if she falls? Stars fall. At least it seems so from Earth. In reality, perhaps they are rising. Carlos Fuentes writes that gravitation is not a fall but a convergence. *Every man and every woman is a star*, writes the masterly Therion. Life makes game with strange *attractions*, he shouldn't have let her go to Madrid. With their gravitation, Jupiter and Saturn protect the Earth from the cosmic *scree*. What protects Estrella? Simon puts no trust in his *gravitation*. What if she stumbled somewhere on the street and fell, what if someone cannoned into her, say somewhere on Paseo de la Castellana, that epitome of cheerlessness and soullessness? Anything may happen, *we live under the volcano*, we live there uninterruptedly and the volcano may erupt at any time, Lowry warns us. That volcano is on Earth and Earth is the volcano, *and the Earth itself still turning on its axis and revolving around that sun, the sun revolving around the luminous wheel of this galaxy, the countless unmeasured jewelled wheels of countless unmeasured galaxies, turning* . . . A trickster from the eighteenth century (which has taught us, as Diderot's follower points out, not to fall in love for any old reason—I swear to God), Tristram Shandy, would not have minded if he had been born somewhere else, on some other heavenly body, but not on Jupiter or Saturn, because rough weather is not for him, he finds it somehow harder to bear. Give me another planet, Simon used to say to Estrella. A planet that turns more placidly than this one, the volcano-sown.

What if she had a fit of vertigo? On the pavement at Paseo de la Castellana. What would she do there, where there's actually nothing, just endless asphalt and endless concrete, glass and steel, glass and steel? Trees and stairs to the metro. How would she manage there? She is not, after all, as crazy as Simon Blef, who on the day that Estrella was to fly from Amsterdam to Madrid took it into his head that he had time, so why shouldn't he go all the way to Barajas Airport on foot? That day too he feared that the plane with Estrella would fall, and so he whiled away the *empty* time without her in senseless activities: on his way to the Prado, where he was planning to spend most of the day, he happened upon the church of Parroquía de Nuestra Señora del Carmen y San Luis; unable to resist, he went into the cold, sinister half-light with the still-lingering stench of inquisition, determined to make peace for a while with God, whom so many times he had sought to kill within him, simply so that the plane with Estrella might safely land. And here, in the dimness of a Spanish church, he remembered Simon Westdijk, the spectral atmosphere of his novel, those grating words: *sanbenitos . . . knotted ropes . . . bellows . . . coffins with the bones of heretics . . . darkening faces . . . blisters and soot . . . stink of a carbonized body . . .* Reading Lundquist's *Fantasy of Goya*, Simon was seized by a similar disgust: the dungeons, the putrefaction, damp, mould, excrement, groans, clinking of chains, metal cutting into festering wounds, rustling sounds of rats . . . Now, where else would someone fantasize about Goya and his century, if not in some hidden-away church in Madrid, in that city whose Manet-beige facades seem never to have been touched by the human race's thirst for blood?

Afterwards he made his way to Museo del Prado. All the time molested by anguish, he wandered through the halls like a soulless thing. Upstairs he found Goya's cycle *Pinturas negras*, a dog inconsolably howling to the yellowish sky. Back on the ground floor, he returned once more to Breughel's *Triumph of Death*, on which one could almost hear the knocking of bones, the gnashing of jaws, the distant wail of those who are sorry they've remained alive. From the Prado he took himself to the Jardines del Buen Retiro, in one of whose corners he indulged in a tasteless and mouth-parching cerveza, but he wasn't able to finish it in peace, because some street musicians, probably from the Balkans, began performing at full blast, and the racket they made compelled him to get out of there quickly. He emerged from the park on Calle de Alcalá, headed left, passed by Puerta de Alcalá, then crossed to Paseo de Recoletos and thence to Paseo de la Castellana in the hazy, unconfirmed intuition that this way he would get to Barajas.

And so, he walked and walked and hoped that eventually he would be overcome by fatigue so great as to make his anguish evaporate. But the anguish didn't abate; in his bowels he felt an ominous shivering, the first indications of panic, panic from panic, where can he run to in this concrete desert if the sudden need comes upon him? And what if Estrella should fall, what if the aircraft skids during landing, what if some kind of rubbish gets into a turbine and the machine goes ablaze? What if he can't run to the bushes in time and here, in the sight of all, he shits himself? How will life continue? If the aircraft with Estrella falls—how will life, Simon's life, continue? How will he manage all the bends and twists that await him still in this variant of existence? Bends and byways like in the Buen Retiro Park: with foul beer and Romanian harmonicas.

There was the baking sun then in Madrid, like at any time in Spui Square, and it now dawned upon Simon, a few steps from Spui, that it was still early, Estrella certainly hadn't yet gone to the airport. Nor had she gone out walking on Paseo de la Castellana. Madrid, perhaps, no longer takes her fancy; she is sitting in some cafe, let's say on Plaza de Santa Ana, and reading Simone de Beauvoir, who attracts and repels her at the same time. But what if she isn't sitting in a cafe but rather lying in a hospital, because when she was going down the hotel stairs she tripped on the carpet and broke her leg? Is she lying in a hospital bed and cannot ring me? Because that could easily happen. She's lying in hospital, her phone was broken, on the little table is Simone de Beauvoir in an English translation which she bought a few months ago right here, in one of the bookshops on Spui Square . . . What sort of city is it, that Madrid: a city where one cannot sleep, because hanging in its halls are *Pinturas negras* and *The Triumph of Death*?

44. He'd have done better

to go with her, not let her go alone to Madrid; what if she fell somewhere, and what if she *fell* also in another, deeper sense? What if she tripped and fell like that time a year ago in Enscheda, on that demonic night? No, she didn't trip then, her legs simply gave way and Simon couldn't manage to catch her. She fell, *sank* like that time in Utrecht, although there she sank only by a step, in her own sphere. But on the Enscheda street, the earth opened and showed its gullet going down to Hell.

In a fuggy Utrecht pub with the pompous name of Café de Postillon she fell merely within her own self, with a smile so to speak, entertained by her own weakness. Her father Ernesto also used to go there, whenever he came to Utrecht to scout the second-hand bookstores. It was there that Ernesto had found Jose Guadalupe Posada's book of prints (*Posada's Popular Mexican Prints*), a collection of mad scenes where one can almost hear *the knocking of the bones and gnashing of the jaws*. Estrella thought of the empty black eye sockets as passageways to Mexico. He shouldn't have left her, Simon shouldn't have left her alone even for a moment in Café de Postillon. Yes, he needed to hop out to the second-hand bookshop on the other side of the canal. Café de Postillon and antiquarian bookshops: a sad repetition of the orbit which had also been Ernesto's. Simon had never had a chance to make his acquaintance, because when he appeared in Estrella's life, Ernesto was already dead. One bibliomaniac replaced another. Simon hopped out then, because he had to, at all costs he had to buy a book that he'd spotted: *The Thirteenth Tribe* by Arthur Koestler. Because the desert. The desert calls, in the desert one observes the stars better, their falling, extinction, ignition. When a little while later he returned to Café de Postillon, in the dusky pub that was governed by a robust publican with the features of a sea wolf and a hare-brained Arles painter, a new star had kindled: in front of Estrella's face something red was glowing—a lighted cigarette. Simon thought he was dreaming. Estrella, while he was away, had bought a packet of cigarettes and lit up. After five years not smoking. Simon felt blackouts circling around him, but he smiled. Clown show. The day he slipped right out of gear. The desert was calling to Simon from Koestler's book and the camel on the packet was calling Estrella. To stride daringly to the desert, not turn round, only mock (but purely to oneself) one's own anxieties, to smile and remain indifferent. In the end the desert blows and scatters all decorations, covers them in drifts, desiccates and burns. All the spiritual decorations. Look, they're only Camels, she said and smiled. Aha, camel, and tapped a finger on the box. And a pyramid behind it. But especially the desert. We're all the time walking through it, aren't we, Simon? We walk through the desert like Lawrence of Arabia, the desert is waiting, we must go on. *The heavens cover him who has no grave.* And let the dogs bark all they like. *This voyage never ends.*

45. Should he sit

at one of the wobbly tables in front of Cafe de Zwart, where he'd sat with Justin a few months before? Or rather retire to the dusky bowels of the Luxembourg Cafe, where he and Estrella had once gone to survive a sudden onset of fatigue? It was an uncommonly scorching summer, and the moroseness, the secessio-fascistoid angularity of that interior, permanently smelling of cinnamon and ground coffee, was convenient. They each had a glass of white wine and their tongues could not stop. Simon was daydreaming, his eyes misted, once again for the umpteenth time he was wandering through the halls of El Prado and stopping before Breughel's *Triumph of Death*; newly he immersed himself in the crowd of skeletons, rampaging in a seared landscape, that he imagined in Ligeti's opera *Le Grand Macabre*.

The action takes place in a country called Breughelland, he explained to Estrella. In a desolate cemetery Amando and Amanda look for a place where they may hide and devote themselves to lovemaking. But then Nekrotzar makes an appearance: a supercilious, demagogic and pretentious creature without a scrap of humour.

Nekrotzar announces the imminent end of the world, but when a comet explodes, he succumbs to panic. Or not: actually, I'm not sure how it goes. But there is some panic, that's for sure. It seems unlikely to me that somebody like Nekrotzar could succumb to panic. Certainly, towards the end of the opera, he shrivels up. In fact, I hadn't yet seen the opera, I'd only read the libretto and seen a few shots. In a 1997 performance, Willard White played Nekrotzar. No better casting! Nekrotzar, *the Black ruler*, and he is played by a Black man with the surname White! Best of all, I like the name of the astrologer: Astrodamors. How many possibilities are latent in that name: *astra d'amor* or *astra da mors*, star of love or star of death? The comet, then, destroys the world, Nekrotzar shrivels, and Amando and Amanda, beautiful as two figures by Botticelli, crawl out of their hiding place pleasantly fatigued, drained by their lovemaking, with no inkling that the world has meanwhile ended. Romantic, too romantic, Rob would say, but for him it was even romantic when I read *Under the Volcano* in his pub.

How concerned you are with volcanoes, here in Holland, Estrella observed.

In Mexico we couldn't ignore volcanoes.

You're exaggerating.

They nattered a while like that in the Luxembourg Cafe, and she recalled the graphic sheets of Jose Guadalupe Posada: his football-playing skeletons, cycling skeletons, skeletons transporting themselves on trams, skeletons dancing in graveyards and finally skeletons with bristling cat's fur and tail. He was still waxing lyrical about Breughel, *The Triumph of Death*, how for years he had wrongly thought this painting was the work of Bosch. He said that exactly as the landscape was painted in *The Triumph of Death*, he also imagined Ligeti's Breughelland, and actually, how banal, because how else could that country be imagined?

Banal/non-banal, Estrella interjected. Does it matter? My father, for example, comes from the same city as Diego Rivera, Guanajuato. Just suppose: if one day you managed to write a novel about us two and you brought in the fact that Estrella's father Ernesto came from Guanajuato just like Diego Rivera, wouldn't the critics think that banal?

Romantic, Simon said. Rob Schutte would remark that it's *so* romantic. *Of that very sort.* From the props room of romantic junk.

Another recollection of Spui. Probably summer. In front of the Athenaeum bookshop's display window Remco Campert, chronicler of Pussycats' days, author of the whimsical book *Het Leven is vurrukkulluk*, was handing out autographs on the occasion of his eightieth. Simon didn't know what to do in this sudden moment: sitting in front of him, by pure coincidence, was a classic of Dutch literature celebrating his jubilee, who might not be in the land of the living the year after. What he wanted was somehow to preserve, retain that moment, but to use the camera he had with him seemed graceless.

Do you want to snap him? Estrella asked. Without waiting for an answer, she took Simon's camera and began forcing her way through the mob towards the writer.

Eighty years, that's some going. This jovial gentleman, his old-world spectacles set on a purple face with cheeks blooming from the years-long consumption of wine, not to mention jenever . . . who can say how long more he will last? In this country the most vital wave of puberty sweeps over men between sixty and seventy. Suffice it to mention the vigorous Jan van Der Vlucht. Whizzing 25 kilometres on his bike and thinking nothing of it. Then in the evening he'll hit the disco, where he'll hop and skip like a savage and be one of the last to leave. So then, perhaps it is only now that Remco Campert, in the eightieth year of his life, arrives at the age of adolescence.

Spui: a cry for emptiness. For greater emptiness, for spaciousness and silence that Amsterdam nonetheless would not endure, because Amsterdam wants to whoop, wants to cycle and skate, get drunk and fall down, in short, it wants to subside differently into the water, less aristocratically, more burgherishly, than Venice.

46. What if he had another tot

somewhere else? Out of order? Is he serious? Not really. He will do just this much, go to Cafe Luxembourg and sit in a corner. So as to not be too visible. What may happen after that, whether or not he will be discovered by some waiter, does not concern him greatly. He will wait for twenty minutes at most. Time enough to jot something in his notebook.

A few months ago, he was sitting in this square with Justin. On the teetering chairs of Cafe de Zwart. Precisely at the corner where a short and narrow laneway named after the Netherlandish Jagger, Herman Brood, begins. Symptomatic. To sit on a chair that's almost capsizing and have a view of the blue plaque, upon which is written in white letters: *Herman Broodsteeg 5. 11. 1946–11. 7. 2001.* (Death by suicide.)

Not alone is it not possible to begin to live a new life, as the Moravian admirer of Diderot says, but one cannot even find *new* friends, only variations on the old ones. The similarity between Justin and Kees Visser was pointed out to Simon by Estrella.

Have you ever noticed his fingers? Take a good look at them next time you meet. They're the same as Justin's. And overall, Kees is like Justin. Body posture, walk, the same impulsiveness and obstinacy. You left Justin in the old country and here you found Kees. No fundamental difference. Or if so, only that Kees is thirty years older than Justin and speaks a different language. But that's all. They're as like as two eggs otherwise. That walk, those little thin legs, beer belly, chubby red face that radiates self-assurance and pigheadedness. On the shoulders of such people civilization rests.

In Enscheda they regard Kees Visser as crazy. That doesn't bother Simon much, but when Kees invited him home to show him his collection of Oriental and African statuettes, he felt a surge of warmth for him. The collection took Simon's breath away. A private ethnographic museum. Statuettes ordered according to their country of origin and size took up almost the entire space along the walls. The largest, about as big as a child in pre-school age, came from Africa; the smallest, elaborated in minute detail, were likenesses of tantric divinities from Nepal and Tibet. In the hallway the visitor was welcomed by maliciously grinning wooden dolls from Indonesia, known as wayang golek. Apart from the living room and bedroom, there was one more room, which served no other function than the storage of further statuettes, Shivaist cult objects, Tibetan dishes. Here one found further wayangs (wayang kulit), dolls used in the Indonesian shadow theatre. The atmosphere of Kees' apartment, imbued with the sanctity and quiet of old objects, seemed to transport Simon to other regions, and especially to other, more peaceful and more *stable* times. The aroma of rare wood and lacquer moved him; for a moment he was overpowered by the feeling that his *real* home was to be found somewhere deep in Asia.

When I think about it, Simon told Estrella after she'd alerted him to the similarities between Kees and Justin, then yes, absolutely: Kees is the very same stay-at-home as Justin. Despises travelling, he despises masses and tourists; he isn't even envious of the great solitary explorers. You'd scarcely get him as far as the next town. He says he has everything he needs in Enscheda. He considers himself a shaman: the essence of shamanism, he says, is everywhere identical and independent of human will, so that you don't need to travel anywhere, to any jungles or steppes, and equally it is a waste of time to study anthropology or to trawl the various courses on transcendental perception. And once a person becomes fully aware of this, he may stay in his town, Enscheda in Kees' case, and spend his time in a relaxed frame of mind drinking red wine in some peaceful pub, for example Cafe Het Bolwerk.

None of the waiters had noticed Simon so far. He wrote the word *Kees* in his notebook. Beside it he drew a horizontal arrow with two heads, and opposite the word *Kees* wrote *Justin*. After that, suddenly he didn't know what else to write. He therefore shut his notebook, leaned comfortably against his chair and gazed at the couple sitting in front of him, on the terrace.

47. Kees and Justin have something else

in common: both have experienced the death of a close person. An experience that Simon Blef has not yet had to bear and to comprehend, which he has nothing to add to, an experience that he dreads and which incessantly, in something like waves, fills him with fears and inspires him to barren philosophizing. But apart from the fears and the prattle, mixed in with his lifelong waiting for this experience of rupture, there is envy. Envy of those who've already *taken the leap*, and yet they'd never prepared themselves to say: HOP! Because Simon, he's the one who's whetting his throat, hacking away at his cough, practising correct pronunciation. He's not, indeed, such an idiot as not to know that in reality all he fears is that on the day of the death of one of the closest persons (his mother is beginning to seem ever more distant and Estrella seems ever closer) he might go missing. Because all of those who retain full awareness will see, in the person who goes missing, an ill-concealed leer of pleasure and triumph.

For almost twenty years Kees hadn't been seen in the streets of Enscheda. He left home only in the most unavoidable cases. His wife was confined to bed by a severe illness, and Kees conscientiously cared for her. Precisely the same as Justin, though he was caring for his mother. A wife dying or a mother dying: the two deaths that Simon did not want to deal with, and yet he thought about them unceasingly; his entire life went by in dread, in a suppressed panic, fearing that at the decisive moment he would not be able to *hold up* and would collapse, or in other words lose control of himself, of how he behaved and looked. He didn't know whether at such a moment he would weep or laugh, or simply fall in a faint.

Simon dear, one day I won't be there. Words that nested deep in Simon's unconscious, words of his Granny, the mother of Old Blef. *I won't be there.* In the unconscious? Maybe people ordinarily had some sort of *unconscious*, but Simon personally wasn't aware of having any such thing; perhaps, though, he'd carve one out for his novel character . . . I won't be there. One day after that, the Granny died unexpectedly, and Simon with amazement discovered that he did not feel any sorrow and was not at all threatened by collapse. Granted, he was then no child, but a university student, whose only concern was sex. Hmm, the trivial couple, sex and death. Once his predominant fear was that there would not be enough opportunities for coitus, then another time it was the anxiety that all of the people close to him would die and he would be consigned helplessly to an unpredictable and unfamiliar world. When involuntary sexual abstinence gnawed at him, thoughts of death receded; when he had sated his passion and, panting, rolled on his hip beside another of the just-*conquered* female bodies, into a pleasant void that lasted only some minutes, the thought of death made its entrance right away. Yes, in his case too, the hackneyed phrase seemed to find confirmation: *omne animal post coitum triste est.* He'd first heard this maxim (axiom) from Sandra. But she said it like this: *post coitum anima triste est.* With a mocking expression on her face. Simon, however, felt no sadness after the act; thoughts of death never filled him with sadness, only with fears. And besides: more than once the thought occurred to him in moments of fresh erotic fatigue—what if he were to pick up some heavy object and crush the head of the woman he'd just made love to?

Simon had never asked Kees what it was like to care for his dying wife. On the one hand, he did not want to spoil Kees' joy of being in love, his joy in the happiness that had fallen into his lap in the form of this intelligent and vital *meisje*; on the other hand, he did not know how to ask, because he still didn't know Dutch well enough and Kees had not sufficiently mastered English, to be able to discuss these matters. So they communicated in stark sentences and washed them down with Argentinian red. But always, hanging somewhere in the background to Simon's thoughts, was the incomprehensible feeling that here he was sitting with a person (a cheerful and carefree person, it must be said) who for years had been watching his wife progressively wasting away.

Justin's mother, fortunately, if one can put it like that, *had wasted* away from this world rather quickly: in less than a month. Simon to this day has not ceased to reproach himself that he didn't stand by Justin then. To assuage his guilt feelings, he remembers instances when Justin didn't stand by him. And what does it actually mean, stand by someone? When Granny, mother of Old Blef, died, her beloved son Anton Blef, dearest of all her three children, did not stand by the catafalque. None of those attending the funeral ceremony knew where he was. And yet he took part in the funeral. He was standing not far away, outdoors, behind a tree. Behind him was the secret service's black car. Simon didn't see his father during the funeral. A few days later he wrote him a letter full of reproaches, accusing him of joining up with the *communist swine*. Old Blef, for his part, tried to explain in a letter that he could not be present when they dropped the coffin with the body of his mother into a hole, because the ceremony was religious and he as a party member was forbidden to participate in such things. And let Simon understand that he must protect his family. His *new family*. His *new children*. And let him understand what he cannot understand, because he doesn't have children; he doesn't know what responsibility is; he does not appreciate that in a similar situation the majority of people would act similarly.

Simon, again, could not be there when they lowered the coffin with the remains of Justin's mother into the grave. He could not shake off the feeling that this was something Justin would never forget. Although Justin himself had never come across as a warmhearted and devoted friend, yet he had regular impulses of yearning for someone to behave devotedly towards him. And perhaps for the very reason that Justin was not overflowing with ardour, he did not have any claims upon Simon, so that he didn't even have anything to forget.

The death of Justin's mother, however undramatic and distant, shook Simon more than he had expected. Nevertheless, he did not attend the funeral. He could not. Afterwards he repeatedly explained to Justin why he really couldn't come that day: the editorial office was closing the latest number, nerves, stress, materials not submitted, computers freezing; his superiors would scarcely have shown understanding of his attending the last farewell to the mother of his closest friend. Simon repeatedly explained his non-attendance to Justin, adding on more and more details. Every reason, every argument, compared with the death of his friend's mother, seemed ridiculous to him. Ever more ridiculous and ever more squalid. Something told him that Justin was in no way resentful. And yet, from that time on, something changed between them forever. More than once the absurd feeling took hold of Simon that the flash he caught in Justin's eyes was a light of triumph. Yes, his friend had triumphed *over him*. Justin had held up in one of the hardest moments of human life, he had honourably passed muster, not crumpled, not fallen, shown his strength. Simon had this test still before him. Justin had triumphed; he no longer needed to cultivate towards his friend the suspicion, the mental *setting*, that had bound them since their student times. Simon suspected Justin of sucking his energy, *consuming* his life. For his part, it seemed to Justin that Simon despised him. Except that it also seemed to Simon that the one who despised the other in this relationship was not himself, but Justin. The reproaches and accusations, unspoken and uttered, never had any end, they endured in the friends for whole decades. But when Justin's mother died, that was decisive: Justin had undergone something for which he deserved respect, and he himself was probably conscious of that.

48. Nothing else occurred

to him, he didn't have anything to jot down, he didn't even know why he ought to write anything, actually he didn't understand why he so obstinately kept dragging assorted notebooks around with him. Later it occurred to him again that after all, he knew precisely why he was dragging around those notebooks, he knew, only that now he could not formulate it; typically, he has these transitory mists in his mind when he knows something, simply that he cannot empathize with it, cannot give it credence, and so now a moment had arrived when once again he didn't trust his notebooks. Each person fixes on something, which is of course no explanation or, heaven forbid, apology; he too was fixing upon something, on notebooks, on scribbling, on the notorious recording, so that he might feel like somebody else, like Lowry's hero that had just returned from the seas, and thus live a different variant of this life. The waiters did not notice him. They were standing somewhere to the rear, behind the bar counter, having an entertaining time chatting. They were doing fine: they did not need notebooks, did not need to pretend they were somebody else; everyone could see clearly what they were and how honestly or dishonestly they were doing their work.

On the glass-fronted terrace of Cafe Luxembourg a man was sitting, grey haired, maybe fifty, in good physical condition, with his, hmm, woman, wife or concubine, not even thirty, ebony-black hair, Asian, probably from Indonesia or Malaysia. They sat silently, both with their backs to Simon, observing the bustle in the square. He did not have the impression that this splendid, fragile Indonesian, truly and sincerely loved the ageing European. And since it mattered to this European (that much might be gathered from his sporty body) that he should attract women's attention, there could be no question here of love. Dutchwomen by now are obviously too emancipated and self-confident, and he required: 1. a young woman; 2. a woman who looked like a girl; 3. a sexual servant; 4. a submissive and quiet woman. Experience as a sex tourist had entitled him to certain expectations. During his most recent trip he'd only needed to enter certain quarters of Bangkok or some Indonesian city and seek out those *right* people, who for a certain portion paraded before him an entire assortment of hopeful *wives*. Satisfaction on both sides: he had found his slave who does not scold, because, for one thing it isn't her custom, and for another she doesn't have a good grasp of Dutch yet; she had made provision for her entire family, and it was now only a matter of time until she moved the whole lot of them to Holland. She was patient. What she desired, she would attain by slow degrees. She was not in a hurry to be anywhere, and in the meantime her big White, stupid husband was getting older and older. She was prepared to nurse him, for her it was worth doing. A cliche, certainly, but what other story could one imagine for these? If there was something that Simon truly didn't like about himself, it was just this imagining of histories for unknown faces. Granted, his intolerance, directed towards himself, against one of his *qualities*, was not permanent. There were days when Simon enjoyed his bent for fabulation. Here and there he wrote down something of those fabricated life stories, but he wouldn't use much of that in his novel. Should it ever happen that he embarked on writing one.

Looking at the crown of the dark-haired woman's head, he ruminated thus: the little inhabitants of Asia are unobtrusively seeping into Europe and patiently changing the customs that obtain there. They are conquering more space for their oriental complacency, corruption, indifference, inconsistency, unpunctuality. Europe will fight that for a while, but the battle is lost beforehand. The *European* youth also are adopting complacency, indifference and unpunctuality from their Asian schoolmates, and precision, reliability and considerateness are becoming like the flies on the old folks, things that need not be noticed. A few years more and Europe will keel over into the gullet of chaos, as Hermann Hesse called Asia. Return to Mother Asia! Migrants arrive here because they are fleeing from that Asia which is turning more and more into a monstrous, though counterfeit, fusion of Europe and America. They come here as dishwashers, as chauffeurs, greengrocers and fruit sellers, chefs and medicine men; as monks, artists and trollops, and most frequently as wives and wives' relations. Nothing of what is European is precious to them, it has no meaning for them. They consume and use everything that they find, and eventually they throw it away on the rubbish heap, among the other plastic bags. For them, Europe has long ceased to exist. There is something stupid and unprincipled in this, and yet also something far-sighted and even prophetic. Europe, after all, cannot be Europe eternally. No continent, no civilization, can forever remain itself. It cannot survive in its *identity*, because no identity is fixed and unchanging. And besides, hardly anyone has a notion of what precisely identity means, how it should express itself and what aspects of it are beneficial, or worthless. These migrants do not think in terms of races, continents and identities: they feel at home everywhere, and so they do not adapt to anyone or anything. But perhaps, thinks Simon Blef, himself an immigrant, precisely because Europe will cease to be Europe as we know it today, perhaps it will return to its original state, will again become itself, such as it had been from the ages. Again it will become a marketplace where diverse races and social strata are yelling uninhibitedly, where they haggle and swindle and yell some more. Now that the ghastly nineteenth and twentieth century is past, Europe will again become a *variant* of Moorish Andalusia, a Medina and a bazaar where Black Africans, Palestinians, Turks, Moroccans and Persians lazily move and stroll about, precisely as if they had never left Isfahan or Marrakesh. They will migrate to Europe, they will halt time and wait until Europe adapts itself to them. Europe? What Europe? Europe swarming with anorexic bimbos, obese binge drinkers, hysterical abstinence, fragile cyber chaps, junkies with the shakes, corroded Catholics and hate-filled Calvinists? Europe of sloth and resignation and insatiable greed? Indeed, it will be better if no one adapts to such a Europe as that. The sort of Europe that mistakes a level of comfort for progress will grind down, mangle and crush its own self.

These two here, the ageing Dutchman, healthy today but mortally ill tomorrow, and his fragile slant-eyed wife, sincerely love each other. Maybe the differences between the European and Asian understanding of love (not only *corporal* love, but also celestial love?) are not that enormous. Love that has overcome time, mountains, valleys, oceans and cultural divides. Universal love: another cliche to replace the cliche about the insurmountability of the abysses of civilization.

49. Some though are

fortunate: they will not become either *cared-for* or *caring*. Estrella too, like Justin or Kees, underwent, lived through one fundamental death, close-contact death so to speak, the death of a person whom she hadn't even had time to get to know thoroughly, the death of a father. Of that inscrutable and opinionated Mexican, who had died suddenly, which is to say, *evaded* the fate of being *cared-for*, and thus spared his kinfolk the cost of the caring *services* (however, Estella's story remains still open, at least while her husband Simon Blef is alive).

When Ernesto divorced Estrella's mother, he spent almost every evening in the Enscheda cafe Het Bolwerk, refuge of the local bohemians and their noisy, affected female admirers. When his imagination ignited after a few glasses of oude jenever, to everyone who happened to be near his table he began to expatiate on his *grand plan*, his long-prepared journey to Mexico. When, after all, if not *now*, on the threshold of pension age and relieved of the burden of matrimony, should he set out for his native Guanajuato? Empire of parakeets!

Empire of lugubrious hard-drinking singers, who would never become as famous as Chavela Vargas! Empire of the dimly-lit, dangerous pubs that Malcolm Lowry wrote about! The journey to Mexico, to the empire of Ernesto's father (and the empire of Estrella's father), should be his reward for the chilly decades he had spent under this dreary northern sky.

Ernesto expounded on Mexico as a kind of enticing marketplace, and at the same time thought of his native land as a coarse, pitiless country, which would nonetheless receive him kindly, as someone who understood. He was fascinated by the ghostliness (which perhaps had long since oozed away out of those parts): mountain scenery, malevolent and unintelligible as Comala (*Yes, señor, Comala. Are you sure you want to go to Comala?*), a city in Juan Rulfo's novel *Pedro Páramo*, of which no one here in Enscheda, or maybe in all of Holland, had ever heard mention. Well, actually, one man: Rob Schutte, owner of the Bolwerk, lover of literature, writers, artists and prattlers.

Rob, that jovial and well-meaning sixty-year-old, conceived an idea about Ernesto that he too, like William Wilmink, the local but nationally known literary celebrity, must surely be a poet who would one day write some important work, and he, Rob, could then take pride in the fact that daily he used to watch the solitary Ernesto bending over his crumpled and smudgy notebook. But Ernesto had no literary ambitions. He pulled the pad from his bag only when he was already well-hammered, and it seemed to him that something had come into being in his mind that he should not let drift off to oblivion. But at the moment when the tip of his felt pen neared the unwritten page, those thoughts changed to isolated words, Spanish words written one under the other in tidy columns, so that Rob, when he placed another beer in front of Ernesto, thought that *gedichten*, poems, were emerging. *Ááá, gedichten*, he cried, so that the others in the room would hear.

Ernesto migrated to the Netherlands at some time in the mid-1970s. Like the majority of immigrants, he wanted to escape from everything in his country that he considered unbearable. Although he had no idea why Holland should be any better, like most of his countrymen he believed that life was easier in Europe. He had come with a clear purpose, and he was prepared to marry out of interest, but something happened to him that he had not expected, even though somewhere deep down he had reckoned with this eventuality: he fell in love. With a Dutchwoman. Yet he himself had declared, while still living in Mexico, but having seen Dutch female tourists, that a Dutchwoman was *something* that falling in love with was impossible. They moo like cows, he laughed. And yet it happened. They say that being in love is something different from love, and love again is something else besides marriage. In a short time, it turned out that he had become a victim of his own illusion. Victim? No one, after all, could say with certainty whether Ernesto had fallen in love with a woman or rather with a country. And whether he had fallen in love at all: whether the drive that was working in him was not in fact the instinct of an ambitious castaway? To simulate being in love, after all, pertains to courage, to adventurousness. Rainy normality, however, washed away all the fairy tale colours of adventure, and Ernesto, with more of the philosopher in his make-up than most of his fellow countrymen, had to acknowledge that the effort was vain: life would not be as rosy as he originally imagined, either with this woman or with Holland. Even so, it was still more comfortable than life in Mexico. It could even be very cosy: here, in this Calvinist vegetable garden, in reality nothing dramatic ever happened, and even if it did, then the drama was quickly stifled, covered up, resolved. Ernesto caught himself beginning to yawn ever more frequently, compared to in his native Guanajuato.

50. Returning to Mexico

was unthinkable. Return would mean admitting failure. He had left that land as a nobody and an outlaw, who had received a chance that the majority of Mexicans could not even dream of. And now he was to return there as what? As a *double* nobody? As a greying vagabond who had fulfilled expectations? *Expectations*! And does a man's life become fuller only when he manages to fulfil the expectations of others? The community expects of the individual that he will have expectations of his own, that he will expect something of himself and others. Specifically: the others expect that the individual will expect from the others only this, that they too will have expectations of him. Demands. Demands of him who decides to leave his country: if you left because you were not contented, in your new homeland you are obliged to achieve greater success. What had Ernesto achieved?

He who leaves becomes a refugee. And he that is a refugee is also a coward. The coward is he, says Kundera (or, more precisely, Kundera's heroine Agnes), who fights tooth and nail against death. Ernesto had not read Kundera, but it was if he were guided by that sage maxim: he never fought against anything. He fought neither love nor marriage, nor divorce, nor even death. Presumably, then, he was no coward. Out of passivity, he endured living in a country in which every Mexican would have gone mad. It is likewise true that Mexicans go mad even from their own country, as Carlos Fuentes says. Ernesto had evidently read Fuentes, or at least one novel, *Los Años con Laura Díaz,* where it is hinted what one can go mad from in Mexico. As is well known, lunatics are not (need not be) cowards.

When the refugee (namely, he who *at home* was not strong enough to battle with his native country, so as to stand on his own feet), achieves success abroad, however inconspicuous, the community (that community which remained at home), the kibitzing and sage community will be able to declare: yes, we knew he would be successful, but, let's say it straight out—is he happy now? Happier than when he was here, among us? And can someone be happy outside of his homeland? All those perpetual tramps, refugees, displaced and resettled, expatriates and immigrants, not one of them is happy; tears roll relentlessly down their cheeks, secret tears, the *inner* tears of darkness, inexhaustible underground rivulets. So that what the community in reality expects is the colossal failure of every refugee undertaking (whether successful or unsuccessful, that does not matter): the adventurer deserves a proper lesson, he is asking to have his mutiny put down and to be sunk.

Ernesto, then, must willy-nilly hang on to Europe, must achieve something there. During the first years he tenaciously strove to get Mexico out of himself. It never occurred to him that one day his inner world would rebel and sadness would overpower him, a long-drawn-out and nagging dejection, a luxurious sorrow, the pastime of the idle, a lordly killing of time. Years fled by, and more and more often his sadness brought up visions of sentimental scenes like on sloppy post-cards, scenes naive and rudimentary as the youth that he'd spent in Mexico.

Rob had pity for all these deracinated people, who struck him as too *romantic* to know their way round in this world. In a corner of his soul, he was glad that he, Rob Schutte, was not rootless, that he was at home, here, among the dark and the hard cheeses, *Herzog Jan* beer and herring salad and that here, in the security of his city, in the fug and dimness of his cafe, he could hear the tales of wandering non-Dutchmen, stories of horrendous conditions prevailing in far-flung, almost fabulous ends of Earth. Rob loved the southern lands; flamenco, fado, samba, bossa nova, sounded unceasingly from the speakers. Equally he was enthusiastic about the learning, or rather the melancholy, of East European intellectuals: he seemed to imagine that in every second Central or East European grumbler there was a bashful Kafka, Musil or Kundera. He even regarded Estrella's father, until he discovered that he came from Mexico, as an East European cultural refugee. The fact is, Ernesto didn't have such a dark skin as a Dutchman would expect in a Mexican; from his pale face, black hair and thick moustache Rob judged that this fellow must come from somewhere in Hungary, or from the ravines of Transylvania.

51. So then, she too,

Estrella, the girl from beyond the river Ijssel, from a region where the foxes say good night and local farmers at the markets speak to the well-nourished fellow countrymen of Goethe and Dürer in their native tongue, she too had undergone that decisive experience for which Simon envied Justin, though he'd never ventured to tell him so. Because he didn't want to insult or delight him. But he did not envy Estrella the death of her father, definitely not; it merely worried him somewhat that if he was going to remain with Estrella, he would also have to cohabit with the death of her father. With the shade of Ernesto, fabled eccentric. With Estrella's perpetual self-reproach that she had never found enough time for her father, whom she now, *post mortem*, felt much closer to than her mother. But what was the basis of this affinity? With a man whom she scarcely knew, and who had battered her mother? Granted, one cannot batter a Dutchwoman just like that. Especially not if she is as self-assured and robust as Estrella's mother. What it amounted to was grotesque squabbles, during which slaps were thrown. Dramatic, but basically harmless.

Simon had felt the desire to stay with Estrella years before, that evening when he was sitting in the Het Bolwerk cafe with a chum that he'd walked through Holland with, and he invited that strange girl with the thick eyebrows to the table. Simon knew that the moment had come to step down from his merry-go-round; he knew that he couldn't let go of the interesting woman with the Spanish name and adventurous origin; he must take hold of her: a further attempt at escape, another Cairo, that would lead nowhere. Simon saw a portent in this. Always he was guided by portents and their weak-witted interpretations. If he wanted to leave behind his life as hitherto, he must also give up the maniacal interpretations. His way of giving them up was to let himself by influenced by them one last time. Since, however, it is not possible to begin a new life, only to vary the old one, as Diderot's admirer says, Simon's interpretations continued, only from now on in a different variant degree.

52. He died here,

in this pub, she said, shortly after they'd got acquainted. I was at uni
then. I'm not ashamed of my father, of how he lived, and not at all of
his death, the place where he died, this spit-coated, stinking pub.
Because it is a pub, let's not delude ourselves, it's in vain that the windows say it is *Café Het Bolwerk* and under that: *Sinds 1904*.
Sometimes I feel that I'm glad he died in these exact circumstances,
not in any other. He deserved a relaxed death, where a humorous
dimension was not lacking. Death in the pub. So then, he died here,
because it was only in a pub he could die, useless for him to put on
airs as a coffeehouse thinker, he was just a pub fantasist with all those
illustrated books he had about the great engineering feats and sacred
buildings of mankind. On the last day of his life he was sitting, aha,
at the table there, right by the bar counter. So that he'd have the beer
closest to hand. He drank *borrels* of oude jenever with it. Actually,
mostly he used to sit on those high stools by the counter, leaning
across the sink and the empty beer glasses to debate with Rob. About
the Mexican pyramids, and how he was going off to Amsterdam over

the weekend, to burrow through the antiquarian bookshops. Ambitions, yes, the summit of his ambitions was to rake over dusty books with low-quality illustrations and dubious details. You'd have understood each other, Simon. He had a similar gleam in his eye, similar energy, similar gestures to you. He'd return late at night from those expeditions to the Amsterdam second-hand bookshops, reeking of beer, jenever and foul cigarettes. Besides Amsterdam, he used to go to Utrecht. Especially to one inconspicuous bookshop by the canal. Though I'm not sure if that too wasn't a make-believe, that Utrecht antiquariat. Even there he spent most of the time in a pub, which also called itself a cafe, Cafe de Postillon, and it looks even worse than this one. Over there he used to sit by the table, take out his notebook and start writing Spanish words. Usually the cat would come up behind him, seeing him as part of the bar furniture, leap up on his table and follow the movements of his felt pen with slitted eyes. That ceaseless recollection of Spanish words was part of his preparation for *the grand journey*. If you ask me, he didn't want to return anymore from Mexico. He wanted to die there. He no longer got on with my mother, I was already an adult, independent too, he didn't need to worry about me now. All he wanted was the one thing: to die at the feet of the Virgin Mary of Guadalupe. Or somewhere else, in his native town, in Guanajuato. Or in some foul dark boozer in Cuernavaca. I don't know. It doesn't matter. In the end he died here, in this pub. There, at that table. He took a bad turn, he felt pressure in his chest. But he still managed to rise and stagger out to the street. And then he collapsed. His face was not distorted, he died with a smile. As if he was smiling at someone. Or as if he wanted to say that *the grand journey* had finally worked out. And do you know what, Simon? I think finally he did make his way there. Rob refused to pour one last tot for him, he said: You've had enough. He said it at the moment when my father clutched his heart. No one took him seriously, because my father was a clown, when he'd been drinking he took to foolery, he simulated heart attacks and strokes. So that evening when he clutched his heart, Rob crossed his arms and looked on with a grin as my father tottered out of the pub. He thought it was just another act. He expected him to come back in and start singing 'Paloma Negra'. Do you know that song? I know it from Chavela Vargas' version. I reckon that my father met some merciful being from beyond the grave out there on the street, who said to him: *Don't be afraid, Ernesto*. That's why he was smiling, you understand? His legs buckled, he fell on the ground and his heart stopped forever. Then that merciful being from the afterlife took him by the hand, the hand of his astral body, if any astral substance or dimension exists, and led him off to Mexico. To eternal Mexico. To the ghostly Mexico of Juan Rulfo. I imagine that after death every person reaches the place that he dreamed of during life. I reckon that even a criminal ought to get to paradise, if he dreamed of paradise. Mind you, for a given person paradise may be hell. But what's the point of some paradise where there's nobody else? Simon, do you think we too will meet after death? And if we meet, will it perhaps mean only this, that neither of us ever dreamed anything for our self? Do I really believe what I'm saying to you here? I don't know. I'm not a believer, I mean, not a person who *has the capacity* to believe in something. Faith's not enough for me. I need facts and data, otherwise I couldn't do what I do. But I find the idea diverting that the believers will get to the paradise of believers, the doubters to the paradise of doubters, which means, in a certain sense, to hell, and those who do not believe and do not even doubt will get to their own paradise, meaning someplace where there isn't the paradise of believers or the hell of doubters. So, to nothingness. Or to some variant of nothingness. I'm weary already of this endless ring-a-rosy. I imagine it something like this, that just as in paradise, so also in hell there's a never-ending chain dance, like the one on Earth here, and so I would rather go to nothingness. And father? He is definitely in Mexico, in his Mexico, behind the table of some eternal pub, with a bottle of mescal that never runs dry.

53. Ah, but he would scarcely commit

such a base act! To traduce the service in this posh cafe! No waiters standing behind the bar counter. That would be a lie. He'd invented everything. Not only the lounging waiters: he'd even invented the couple (the sporty Dutchman and fragile Indonesian) sitting on the terrace of the Café Luxembourg. Originally, he had not intended to stop in Spui at all. And yet in the end he had stopped. Only so as to convince himself that originally he had made the correct decision when he hadn't wanted to spend time here. Because how else to persuade oneself of the correctness of a decision if not by acting at odds with one's purpose? But supposing he had indeed stopped in Spui, then why had he finally chosen Café de Zwart instead of Café Luxembourg? Because if ever he decides to use his *notorious records* in writing a novel and mentions there that he stopped in Spui (in itself as trivial as can be), should that not suffice, then precisely in Café de Zwart, a coffeehouse known for being a meeting place of writers. If Estrella were here with him now, she would say: if ever you should embark on writing a novel that would contain a chapter about how you stopped in Café de Zwart, readers would think either you did it from naivety (because it still hasn't dawned on you that anyone today can get any information, you don't have to spread *enlightenment*, you needn't lecture, put on airs, show off), or from ineptitude, because you can't spot a cliche. In principle I'm not against you putting Café de Zwart in the novel, which you'll probably never write (or if you do, then certainly it won't be about Amsterdam and its pubs). Such a move could be interpreted like this: you're deliberately writing about easily accessible and fashionable places; you're mocking those authors who, whenever they write about cities, try to introduce their readers to the most out-of-the-way recesses and reveal some secret things. That could be *read* on the second level of your design. But you know what the first level would consist of.

He stopped, then, in Café de Zwart, a boozer that seemed to lean out from the square, as if it were veering away from it and wanted to resort to flight. While Café Luxembourg haughtily thrust out its chest and opened welcoming arms to perfumed snobs who were not ashamed of their snobbery, by contrast Café de Zwart had the attitude of a shooed-away dog, a scorned and timorous animal. Of course, this also was only a trick: the two cafes seemed to support, encourage, blandish each other. Simply, Café de Zwart was the refuge of those who carried their snobbery under the local bohemian's nonchalantly crumpled coat. This grog shop pretended that it was authentic, a great deal less touristy than its puffed-up neighbour.

Simon chose a place right behind the window, wanting to see what was happening on the terrace and in the square. Not far from him, an odd couple was sitting on the wicker armchairs on the terrace: a young Malay in knee-length trousers and his friend, a sinewy older man with supple movements. Instantly it was clear to Simon that they were gay; simply, he couldn't figure out what their relationship was, what stage it was at: the beginning or the peak of *romance*. The young Malay was behaving like someone who knew he was the focus of attention; he didn't sit still for a single minute, circled round the wicker chairs, squinted at Simon to see if he was watching. Then he took out a digital camera and began to take photos of his partner. In the meantime, the partner had entered into conversation with a charming gentleman with long grey hair, probably a hard-core habitué of the cafe. Doubtless a writer, Simon thought. The Malay left them to it, let *the old folks* talk, moved to the edge of the terrace, where the legs of the sitting customers poked out into the adjacent cycle lane, grabbed one of the armchairs and spilled into it, pretending he was going to take the sun.

But you know what the first level would consist of. A jiffy ago he still had it, a moment ago he still knew what. What the *first level* would consist of. Now, however, he couldn't remember, so he imagined: *on the first level* of such a novel, which drags the reader through the most heavily trodden localities in Amsterdam, there would be a parody of a guidebook. Would Simon, novelist and zealot, hermit down from his column, really find pleasure in such a parody?

Mindlessly he browsed in his notebook.

The young Malay and his friend had made themselves scarce. At a more distant table, precisely where the Malay had just been sunning himself, a three-member family had ensconced itself. Father, mother and son. The son could have been sixteen, with thick black hair and thick eyebrows; he was so beautiful and ephemeral that Simon could not tear his eyes away. He imagined him naked, making love to an equally beautiful girl somewhere on straw under a wide Provencal sky.

Because he guessed that the family was French. Another family entered the cafe, with two children: two fragile dark-haired daughters, one probably aged sixteen, the other could be thirteen. Simon caught fragments of their speech: Spaniards. He lowered his gaze, afraid he was going to blush. Just occasionally he looked in their direction, to see if those two girls were peeping at the youth on the terrace. They were looking at the square, but pretending that what was happening out there didn't interest them in the least. But Simon knew well that they had noticed the boy and wouldn't mind if they engaged his attention. The boy's father rose and went into the cafe to pay his bill. When Simon heard English, he understood that he'd guessed wrong, because this was not a French family and so the Provencal sky wouldn't do. Although maybe, if the thirteen-year-old Spanish girl were to meet that dark-haired English cherub, it could only be there in Provence, in the countryside, in a summer heatwave charged with eros and the trills of the cicadas.

In the corner by the bar counter sat a loud-voiced, roughly sixty-year-old hulk, in check flannel shirt and jeans. Unquestionably a barfly. His robust drunken babble, just the kind Simon imagined for ruined sailors, drowned out all other sounds; the peals of laughter wafting in from the street and mingling with trams' rumbling and bicycle bells, the snorting of tour buses and droning of street-cleaning and garbage vehicles, none of that could compete. Only now did Simon become aware that in Café de Zwart they did not play music. Presumably they realized it was quite pointless, given that all day they had a door and window open. They had enough in the *music* of the square.

The hulk, whose face bronzed more and more with each further beer, roughly every five minutes slithered off the barstool, pulled a cigarette from his pocket and shuffled off to the door to light up. But he never lit up immediately; he came back in a bit, stopped, almost in the centre of the room and hollered something at the waiter. The latter plainly did not hear him, evidently he'd spent years not hearing him, but considering him an indispensable decoration of the cafe.

Simon looked again at the terrace and noticed a woman in black. Her clothes came from another century: long sleeves, white collar. Her grey hair was coiled behind in a chignon. She gave the impression of a Victorian governess. Authority and sternness oozed from her. Simon had a feeling of admiration. But that did not last long, because when she turned towards the window to call the waiter, he saw her salmon-pink spotty face and the empty gaze of the dried-out (or rather burnt-out) alcoholic, who had drunk herself into the other world years ago, only death somehow forgot to come for her, and so she must haunt these parts a while longer.

Governess, veteran sailor, Spanish girls, ethereal young man. Simon's world, the carnival, or rather, all that was left of the carnival. A world that never accepts people like Simon, but this does not bother him. On each occasion the company of such maskers fills him with faith that he will have something to put in his notebook.

But now here comes something else that presses on his attention, and thence to the notebook: a knot of drunken men in white T-shirts. Tanked-to-death louts; their gestures and lisps give Simon to understand that he's dealing with ossified Spaniards. Two of them in particular are extraordinarily amusing: one is attempting to mount a bicycle, while another smaller fellow (his companions address him as Carlos) wants to be a passenger, but they can't keep the balance. The taller one dismounts and tries to lean the bike against a tree, but he misses it by a few centimetres and the bike falls on the pavement with a crash, causing the knot of lads to roar laughing. Carlos, whose problems with equilibrium are obvious, jostles his friend who is trying to lift the bike from the ground. Both of them roll over on the ground, and Carlos guffaws.

54. Although it seems otherwise, he did not stay there

long. He tossed down a tot, maybe a second with it, but definitely not a third. Rising, he went down to the counter, stood beside the bronzed barfly and paid. He exited the cafe, shoved through the little group of staggering Spaniards, stared at the mind-boggling sculpture of a boy whom Amsterdam, as the plaque on the plinth proclaims, regards as its *lieverdje,* and made his way to the former Lutheran church. But who could that *amsterdamse lieverdje* be, he mused. Is it some kind of metaphor expressing the naughty, immature character of this city? Not that he cared: by now he was where the bicycles are propped any old way against the railings, and behind them the motor barges cheerfully honking down the canal. He headed for Bloemenmarkt. It wasn't easy to force his way through the mob that awaited him there, but he didn't feel like devising an alternative route leading to Rembrandtplein.

Roaring of the barges, drunken cries of celebrants, water and water. Breath of water, air of water, memory of water. At the bottom of the canal, in the mud, bicycles repose in tens of thousands. Water conducts, abducts everything. Water fondles everything, touches all sorts and leaves them so, it will eradicate what's useless. And it remembers everything. In 1421 or in 1530: first a hundred thousand, then three hundred thousand dead. There were scarcely that many people, perhaps, who remained alive in the country then. Water, water, washed up, washed away, and washed-up, abandoned bodies. Waves, ripples, who was counting them then, all those torsos? If someone in those times had imagined Nekrotzar, he would surely have been a merry Nekrotzar. Except then they had other macabre entertainments. Ship of fools, dance of death.

> *Those whose feet move in the dance*
> *with their sergeant must advance.*
> *Minds and bodies, youthful now,*
> *all will freeze and go below,*
> *off to join the dancing moles*

Anthonis de Roovere wrote then. Today his descendants' descendants wave from motor barges, beer can in hand, and death just flows wherever it likes, drifts, *the voyage that never ends*, flows, runs round itself, circles and gushes like in Gorostiza's lines in *Muerte sin fin*.

Simon passes through Koningsplein and already is absorbed in the human river, no less turbid than the canal down yonder; he plunges into the crowd in Bloemenmarkt, where there's a crush like in some oriental city.

55. What to call, how to grasp

Simon's flight to Cairo? If only he had at least died there, if only he had expired on one of those greasy and foul-smelling pavements, among the dusty cats, hunching child beggars and pestering taxi men; if only he'd kicked the bucket and rid himself of himself, his impotence and constant self-pity, his snivelling and his practice of giving pride of place to the past. At least in the hotel (whose name he no longer remembered, but it was a short distance from Tahrir Square), there at least death might have struck him down during the stifling June nights on a sweat-soaked and sagging bed. Or, to make it sufficiently kitschy, he might have croaked right in front of the pyramids, in a mob of stupefied tourists, among the camel drivers and the security men who incessantly walloped the harassing beggars and souvenir sellers with sections of rubber hose.

And he could have suffocated in a crush like he'd just plunged into in Bloemenmarkt; he could have choked among the hawkers and loud-mouthed females in the Cairo bazaar, on rambling al-Mouski Street (anyone who's timid shouldn't go to al-Mouski, wrote Zikmund and Hanzelka). Al-Mouski: crackling of battered cassette recorders and hoarse speakers from minarets, whirling dust, crowds of veiled women raking through the heaps of dubious-quality goods laid out on quilts, mats and bath towels, or tables constructed of cardboard boxes. And he could have been struck down by the strong coffee with cardamon in the air-conditioned Naguib Mahfouz Cafe close to the Khan el-Khalili bazaar. One of the millions of cars might have hit him while he was trying to cross to the al-Azhar Mosque, where the courtyard gave him refuge during the afternoon heatwaves. He was indifferent to what would happen to him, whether he would breathe his last on Talaat Harb boulevard or in Tahrir Square, or somewhere else, in the torrent of sellers of paper hankies, socks, cheap Egyptian perfumes imitating luxury Western brands, video cassettes, children's toys, clinking trinketry.

With the passage of time, he must admit that he had actually gone to Cairo to learn indifference. Not only towards the noise and the perpetual pressing crowd, which after sunset took on such dimensions on the paved sidewalks of the European part of Cairo that he constantly had to step out into the lanes of the cars wrestling with a hopeless traffic jam; more especially, indifference towards himself. After the first week spent in that metropolis scorched by a cruel June sun, he no longer resisted. He let himself be dragged by the mob, by the silent men and the rapaciously gesticulating stocky women, who looked like white grubs in their chadors. He no longer felt like a hunted beast, pursued by a band of bloodthirsty nomads, when the taxi men began screeching at him the moment he emerged from the gloomy hotel. Eventually he became cynically accustomed to looking at poverty the like of which he had never seen before: grubby skin-and-bone children in rags, trudging along with two-wheeled carts piled high; a girl beggar who approached him through the pell-mell of the bazaar, looked pleadingly at him, then caught his hand and fondled it, at which Simon bent down to her and the girl, not even ten-years-old, kissed him on the neck while behind her elongated eye-lashes tears glistened. And then the City of the Dead, where among the tombs, mausoleums, abandoned mosques and minarets the out-laws of Cairo live, a city within the city with its own post office, police station, hairdressers and shops; a city of those who do not belong to any social stratum and of whom no one takes any care except the heavens.

56. Spreading out from the stalls

is the smell of clay. It permeates everything. It cuts through all layers of the aromas of Bloenmarkt: through the scent of tulips, gerberas, asters, onions, seed bags, seedlings, flower pots. The smell of clay in these places even steals into the tourists' perfumes and the random whiffs of marijuana. The smell of clay conquers, inconspicuous, as if it existed only in memory.

Simon remembers this scent from his grandparents' garden. Someone else who grew up in that garden was Simon's father Anton Blef. Simon remembers the flowerbeds, remembers the vegetables, even the knife, the garden knife, originally a kitchen knife, later it rusted and was then used only in the garden, for outdoor purposes; yes, he remembers that knife, a number of such knives, stabbed into the damp spring clay. Maybe it was one of them that was meant to end up between the ribs of the unfaithful locomotive driver. Write also how the blade gleamed, Estrella would have said, if Simon were to set out to write a novel in which he would incorporate the episode with the jealous wife of the engine driver.

Blade. Broad blade. It gleams in the ill-lit evening street. From nearby fields comes a smell of autumn. Where the gardens end, they are burning weeds, leaves, old newspapers, filthy rags. But the blade is not all that gleams. Leucoma too, malign, wakeful leucoma. In one of the buildings belonging to the national railways, the railway choral group is rehearsing. That evening, however, no blood flows: the hand with the knife dropped down, the blade disappeared in the folds of an undulant black shawl. What would a family be without a dark secret? A secret that ultimately does not remain concealed; by meandering paths it does nonetheless break through to the light of day. Maybe the actor herself will tell the story of the kitchen knife and lurking under the choral group's windows to her children, by then adult. She'll tell it, which is to say, invent it. Nothing ever happened. She never stole away with a kitchen knife in her hand after her husband. But she would have done it, no one doubts that. Which is why I've told you this story: so that you, Gizka, will know how you should behave towards Albert when he turns into a slob.

What if she'd really skewered her husband that evening, Simon fantasized: probably his father's empire would not have emerged and he, Simon, would never have come to be. Even though Old Blef at that time (the time of the alleged episode with the kitchen knife) was already in the world, his empire certainly was not. Only some bits, unassembled, weak, sickly germs. Anton Blef then could not have been more than ten years old. So, if his mother had managed to eliminate her husband, he'd presumably have ended up in an orphanage, probably in a different town, another corner of the republic. He'd never have met the girl—the lass with the concert grand—who later gave birth to Simon. Nor would those germs of the father's empire have afterwards come together in a ghastly whole. But, Simon reflects, to whom are we born *more*: father or mother? In which is there *more* of me? Old Blef could have fertilized a completely different woman, some beauty of the hills (blood and milk, milk and cream, potato and fried leftovers). And not some hysteric from the lowlands. Simon could have been born in the shadow of the peaks, somewhere in green spaces, under woods and in mountain hamlets, by the light of an oil lamp, and he would not be called Simon but, let's say, Jacob, and it would never have occurred to him to go off to another country, to rainy and hill-less Holland, a country of potatoes and thick soups, and he'd never have met Estrella and now would not be squeezing through the crowd in Bloemenmarkt. Even so: who has the greater contribution to the fact that Simon is Simon and that he feels that he is he and not someone else? Whose *consciousness* is in him more? If Simon's mother were to find another suitor—in whose child would there be more of Simon's present-day *essence*: the one born to Anton Blef and an unknown bride from the mountains, or the one that the butcher's daughter bore to some dashing lowlands lad? If the engine driver's wife that evening really had packed him off to the other world, presumably her funeral, which took place roughly thirty years later, would have looked differently. Simon would have had no need to write a letter to his father accusing him of banding together with swine. If Old Blef had ended up in an orphanage, most likely he wouldn't have made a career in the party that prevented him, as he stated, from taking part in the church funeral of his own mother.

Initiating mantra: *Simon dear, one day I won't be there . . .*

From the stalls at Bloemenmarkt came the spreading smell of clay. Even here, so far from his own country, earth has that same smell, more intensively in fact, able to transport a person across the decades to the past. And mixing in with that smell, the stinks rising out of the canal: the race driver from Algeria wrote something about a specific Amsterdam stink, a vapour of stagnant water and a stench of withered foliage percolating in the canal. Infernal arcs that distributed this mortal and yet irresistible stink beneath the windows of palaces and one-time merchant storehouses . . . Simon does not think, never has thought and never would write in a prose piece or even in his notebook, that Amsterdam is the Venice of the north. Besides, how many such northern Venices still exist? Stockholm? Petersburg? And not one of them has water splashing in the squares—what kind of Venice, then? Let Cervantes speak:

> *And he went off to Venice, which if it hadn't been for Christopher Columbus, would not have had an equal in the world: let thanks be given to the heavens and to the renowned Hernán Cortés that he conquered the renowned city of Mexico, which can equal renowned Venice at least in something. These two far-famed cities resemble each other in their streets, which are entirely flooded with water; the European city is famous in the Old World, the American city is a wonder of the New World.*

Ah, where, oh where! Where else but in the flower market can the Amsterdam pedestrian feel (one last time) that there is something Venetian here, in this city of flowers withering, city of merry death? Smell of clay ascending from barges loaded with flowers. Smell that rises from the graveyard where they used to bring little Simon on All Souls, and he knew that the moisture bursting out of the ground was the breath of the dead, breath interchanging with candle smoke and the smell of rotting flowers . . . He perceived the smell of old black coats, shawls, dresses and handbags with scrunched-up rosaries, handkerchiefs, decomposing hymnbooks and prayerbooks. Which they handed down from generation to generation like some feminine mace, like collections of wise saws and charms. Somewhere under those black handbags, which his grandmother brought exclusively to church or to funerals, lay the new catechism that smelt like a spelling book: Set out on your journey, Christian soul, from this world . . . Smell of the garden where, as in some time loop, bound to endless repetitions, the shades of Simon's grandparents slaved away. One of those shades, the granny, would rise at dawn and set off for the market to sell flowers. He would never be able to pass through Bloemenmarkt without his senses dragging him into a funnel of time.

57. He stretches his neck

to see past the stalls to the helmet of Munttoren. Whoever sees it will not go astray. But even someone who finds himself in Bloemenmarkt will not go astray, so it is pointless stretching one's neck. Even so: he stands on tiptoe and stretches his neck. As if he were paddling in air and calling for a lifebelt, to save him from this sea of flowers and flower pots, onions, seed bags, postcards and compass apparatuses with swelling pink busts or the sloping shoulders of windmills.

By now he is almost at the end. Just cross over to Munttoren, wait for green at the crossing and head off down Reguliersbreestraat. He looks at the ludicrously big clock dial on Munttoren. *Has my watch stopped?* Simone de Beauvoir asks right at the beginning of *L'âge de discrétion*, and immediately answers: *No.* He is amazed that he's remembered the first sentence of a book that he never read. Is it possible to write a more impressive first sentence? *Has my watch stopped?* Simon has never worn a watch. His wrist is too narrow, he's afraid it will slide off. And the hand under the watchstrap is sweaty. And the shrinking expressed by numbers causes tension in his stomach.

In town, on the street, he therefore relies on towers. He could look at his mobile display, but why make superfluous motions when there are clocktowers available? Once again he looks at Munttoren.

58. And he plunges into the crowd

on noisy Reguliersbreestraat. Particles, bacteria, viruses. Cell structures and molecules. Well, there are no such things as molecules, academician Ernst Mach once declared. Thereby causing the suicide of Ludwig Boltzmann—who has heard of him today? Hanged himself from a window sash. Torsos, limbs, torsos. Galloping and gesticulating, smacking and slurping jaws. How many of them are rushing home at this time so as to engage in more and more alteration of their dwellings? To go drilling, hammering, nailing, sawing, cutting, grinding, chafing. Unto stupefaction. Unto improvement. The world passes through endless reconstruction so that it may be better tomorrow. When, however, tomorrow comes, there will again be devised some improvement, plan, strategy of betterment. So it is never good, it is never better. Now and then it's more beautiful and in some measure less practical, another time hideous but cosy.

They're hurrying. The one that hurries, Simon muses, also has regular employment. He doesn't hurry without reason. Has a secure job, a secure office table, unshakeable regime, regular pay. Desk diary.

Doesn't loaf around pubs like some people. Like this here, this Simon Blef. Who has migrated hither from who-knows-where, who-knows-what burrow, from some trap hole on the periphery of Europe. Here, in this damp green country full of striving, industrious people, he has dragged up his body, half of his personal junk, almost a hundred per cent of his woes and his infantile daydreams, and settled here; he thinks he has settled here, that finally he has dropped anchor, he thinks he belongs, and here and now he just parasites, day after day, loiterer, good-for-nothing. Hauling around his crumpled notebook. So that he seems to be working. But is it work, to spend whole days scribbling about torsos, bones, bowels, limbs, pub castaways and ambitious American girls? It's work when it leaves a person weary, when the sitting and scratchy writing exhausts you, sends you to sleep and flips you over to an everyday somnambulism.

They hurry, they roll along, bump into one another, these torsos, these intoxicated volumes, they give way before nothing and no one. Maybe Simon too, though he has neither regular employment nor desk diary, will in a moment begin hurrying: if he forgets himself in the next pub and gets into time pressure. But no, he will not. He has no fear of that. Certainly he will get to the airport in time. That much self-control remains. Where else besides this country could he better refine his self-control?

A motorbike with silencers removed thunders by. Rage rips through Simon. Often he has imagined buying a gun and simply shooting the noisy bikers. Who did they want to impress with that racket? What did they want to convey? He thought that in this land he had escaped from the din. That discipline reigns, that they penalize rowdies. And actually: not so, not since the distant past. The police have an air of timidity, and noisy behaviour seems natural around here. Who do they fear? Who do all these monstrous, well-fed descendants of sailors, peasants, millers, shopkeepers, hydraulic engineers and harridans fear, when they yell like that? Are they afraid of anyone? Yes, the motorcyclists, those noisy ones, he'd shoot them without a thought: they could never again be reduced to order. The noisy ones need to be shot in time, in their tender years, otherwise they'll proliferate. And you'll never get anything through to a noisy person at an advanced age. The racket-makers aren't even bothered by the racket that others make; they are unteachable, really, they will never amount to anything, they will not be transformed, they will not change into aware, considerate, ethereally gentle beings, they simply have to be shot.

Mouth, eyes, incompatibility of cells. Cells condemned to constant changes and divisibility. And along with these torsos, torsos with all their mitochondria, rhizopus, cytoplasmic membranes. Torsos that daily manufacture syllables and smiles and stares. Prostheses grate, tongues slurp. On this street there's nothing special, this short nasty Reguliersbreestraat. No *callejón de los milagros*. But after all, the Cairene Mahfouz's *Alley of Miracles*, which the filmmakers set in Mexico City, also was not distinguished by anything remarkable. Aagh, that couple again: Cairo and Mexico City! So then, if Simon were to write a novel occurring one afternoon in Amsterdam, he would leave out this street.

59. And what if she doesn't come?

Because she decided otherwise? Decided she will not return to Simon? Because Madrid bewitched her and she understood where her place was? Understood that, if Mexico, then minus Simon. He wouldn't have thought it strange of her. Minus Simon. Maybe just a few hours ago this happened: she left the hotel and somewhere on Plaza de Santa Ana, actually by Lorca's statue, she ran into Peter Bilý, a poet and attractive lad, whom Simon had introduced to Estrella during one of their infrequent trips to Simon's homeland. Peter is strikingly good-looking, women tend to feast their eyes on him, though again there's something in him that leaves them unsure what they can hope for. And now Estrella had run into him, both of them smiled at such a coincidence and promptly made their way to a cafe. They ordered churros with the coffee and Estrella, maybe for pure fun, uttered one of the few Spanish sentences she knew, which she'd learnt from a poem of Lorca's: *Por qué duermes solo, pastor?* Then she shifted to English, helping herself out now and then with Spanish words, and without inhibition began to expound her plans to Peter, about how she was preparing to go to Mexico, because, as the ship's doctor Jan Jacob Slauerhoff writes in his poem, 'In Nederland will ik net blijven'. Peter, who has still not found work in Madrid, suggests to Estrella that she stay a while longer in Madrid and then they can go off together to Mexico or Argentina, and the devil take Simon: foolish to go back to that rain-sodden country, to the still more sodden Simon.

Would Estrella really be capable of something like that? No, probably not. Ah, how often had Simon woken in the middle of the night and with bated breath watched to see if Estrella's chest was still rising! Estrella sleeps so quietly that he thought . . . Hadn't her father Ernesto died of heart failure, and what if she'd inherited that? What if, out of the blue, she was to stop breathing, die unobtrusively, in darkness, without warning? They say that death revives our feelings, says a narrator in a story by the Algerian race driver. Maybe so, maybe death indeed revives feelings, but Simon is not curious about such feelings. He wants Estrella alive and well.

He passes in front of a mournful facade with the inscription *Theatre Tuschinski*. At one time a theatre, today a cinema with six auditoria. In their time they might have shown *El Callejón de los Milagros* with Salma Hayek in one of the lead roles. Marlene Dietrich too had a part, allegedly. Simon imagines that surely, she sang the ditty *Peter, Peter komm zu mir zurück*. Goths, in a little bunch, stand before the entrance. They would be excellently suited to that facade, which evokes an unbridled fusion of crematorium, dragon's den and haunted castle: two disfigured Goths. Among the personages clothed from head to foot in black, Simon recognizes Analis. Anna lies. Anal is.

223

60. The space finally expands.

And this is Rembrandtplein. The twilight lends a certain malevolent expressiveness to the expanse. There are glowing inscriptions COF-FEESHOP * SMOKY POOLTABLES * JUICEBAR * at the opposite end of the square. Merry salutations of eccentrically painted bicycles, gallop of eccentrically dressed and unkempt figures of Amsterdam's bohemia. At a tram stop stands a maestro, in the guise of a water spirit. Long grey hair, red trousers, green tailcoat. Guitar in his hand, which he's ceaselessly preparing to play on, but ultimately he doesn't strum it even once, merely with expansive gestures fixes the attention of bystanders and tourists sitting before the cafe, inviting them to a performance that he will never accomplish. Perhaps these protracted preparations, courteous bows, temporization and assurances actually constitute the core of his act. Unquestionably an elegant concept, a thematization of artistic *depletion*, artistic void, emptiness and helpless incapacity to do any artistic deed. An aesthetics of the void and silence. Aesthetics of the pause. To which also belongs the *aesthetics* of these musings that I attach to this street event, Simon thinks. He daydreams: if I wrote a novel, it would be set in the course of one year, one day or one afternoon, and likewise it wouldn't matter whether the protagonist was able for a deed or for a thought: *Dillinger is* (nevertheless, even so) *dead.* And along with him, everything else is dead that might have been important not just once, but principally today. And Simon dreams of his protagonist further: definitely he would have to be a composer. A hero that would not want to be a hostage to the artistic machinery and publicly manipulated taste: he could have composed and hammered away on the piano, but he would rather go out on the street and invite the swarms of tourists to a fictitious concert. Yes, that's it, that's the one, the street conjuror will settle himself nicely on the vacated throne of the King of Amsterdam, the throne which the sulphureous and bilious provocateur Simon Vinkenoog once sat on, who will never again surface from the canals of the otherworld. Or will he? Well, for sure. In Simon's potential effort at a novel, assuredly.

61. When the plane

lands, certainly they won't immediately go to the train: they'll sit in one of the airport bars and have two tots each. For welcome. Estrella will surely tell him all about her time in Madrid, and even if it was good, she couldn't wait to get back. Among other things, Simon will learn how she went to the Church of San Isidro, to find out if they were holding the procession that the two of them had joined a few years back. But the Estrella he knows is more likely to tell him about what she's read in Simone de Beauvoir's *A Very Easy Death*, which sometimes repels her, at other times fills her with curiosity. According to Estrella, though, the French do not understand death; they may write what they like about it. How do they portray it? Do they let it dance at all? Maybe I'm wrong, but I don't remember any skeletons even vaguely resembling Posada's, dancing in French art. What do they know, these frog eaters, of the graces of the toothy thing that Mexicans can so splendidly bedizen? Those French deaths, what kind are they? Easy, happy, airy, cold, rococo-sadistic. Objects of intellectual reflection. French death does not know the whiplashes of the flagellants, the rattling of inquisitorial chains, the stamping of the carnival crowd, the grinning motley Mexican skulls for El Día de los Muertos; it's lacking *fatum*, the overlap with spectral worlds; El Greco's feverish light doesn't shine there, Goya's night doesn't swallow it up. In French death there is only the gurgling latrines of gormandizing marquises, or more precisely, variations on latrine merriments. Well, all right: a classic extols the century of Diderot, century of variations. Actually, which century wasn't a century of variations? The difference will be only in this, that the eighteenth at least didn't try to hide it. Wig, variation on hair.

62. And they don't move aside and they don't move,

they just yell and yell. They would not move aside even if they had space to. They march, with gaze fixed on the stupefying glimmer. They stride, (one scarcely needs to say) like mechanical toys. They are free, and yet are stretched to the limit. Free, and yet no joy. Only variations. When they block one another's way (as happens often), they fall or they stop still. If they stop, even that does not compel them to look before them or at least under their feet. Gaze fixed forwards, and yet they do not look before them. When their paths are crossed, they halt, look sideways, wait until the other one reacts. Each time the other one must react, not them. Thickening biomass, accumulation. Voices accumulate, eyes accumulate. Granted, not only in this square in the middle of Amsterdam, at evening. Fingers, nails, limbs accumulate, more and more rivers of cells. Skulls, collarbones, bowels, glands accumulate. They accumulate. It doesn't bother anyone. Each one has heard, several times in a life, that it's natural. That accumulation. Each one knows that it's natural to listen to sermons about what is natural. After all, there has to be something too that's natural.

Natural is accumulating. There's ever less space, but accumulation must happen. It is natural to believe that this world is not perfect, but there isn't a better one. Accumulation there must be. A universal merriment thus reigns, a merriment that squashes down every loner. Merriment with a wind-up key. At the end, a bell rings. Before the first cock crows. Worldwide mechanism of confusion. But even the confusion is no longer authentic. It's become a decoration. Something that's considered natural. They fall, they rise, they crumple. And continue not looking in front of them. They gaze, they gaze, but they do not look. They look, but they don't see. They gaze into the stupefying glimmer. And they multiply. Descendants drop off them, to whom they afterwards say: See how beautiful it is here. Bodies pervade the city, and the city pervades them in turn. Bodies circle in space, unanchored, unweighted and unrelieved. They transmit information. Information in turn shifts bodies. More bodies require more information. More information diffuses bodies. They multiply, as if they knew they no longer need fear wars: hurricanes of information, avalanches of details, exchange of pictures and text messages in real time, sensors, cameras, electronic cells and digital eyes make secrecy impossible, and with it discipline and advantage. No one knows where he is. Or where the food that he shoves in his maw is grown, processed and wrapped. Because: let us grow such and such here, in our own land, afterwards let's export it to Asia, there let's refine it and wrap it and then let's bring it back again, to our supermarkets. Because that way it's cheapest. And whatever is cheapest contributes to civilization. Simon must once again tell himself: *Give me another planet.* Because he feels threatened on this one, whenever he looks at what present-day zombies can suppose is logic.

63. If some day, after all,

he decided to exploit his notorious notebooks to compile a novel or at least a novelette, he doesn't know, thus far he does not know, whether he would have Justin and Peter appear there. If Justin nonetheless happened to feature, Simon would put the following words in his mouth:

Well, OK. If that's how you wanted it, OK. To tell the truth, I thought it was only big talk on your part. Somehow, I believed you'd never do it. You'd never have the guts. You wouldn't dare. You wouldn't go off, escape from your mother, your town, you wouldn't leave me alone here to rot. I still think you won't slough off the past. You can go wherever you like, your limitations will go with you. You can only begin to live a further variation on what you've lived till now. I don't know what your past is like. My guess is, it's false. Falsified. Because you're a forger, which, I must admit, impressed me for a while. You're a forger, son of an apparatchik, what can be expected of you? Better not say. You went away and you refused to measure up to your own country's demands; so, endure your further variation on

life by yourself! I always sensed that eventually everyone would aban-
don me. All the lovers, all the friends, all those who get married. They
all move somewhere, even if only to a neighbouring town. All of them
are dead for me, you know that very well. Either you're with me or
you don't exist for me. Whoever is not sitting in this pub with me,
behind this table, for me he is dead.

64. More people and more people

and more people and more bodies and torsos need more foodstuffs and liquids and more foodstuffs and liquids. Vain is this Rembrandtplein, vain is this Amsterdam, vainly a while ago Simon Blef almost cannoned into two lesbians who were going to get married the week after at the Town Hall in medieval costume; vain the eighty-year-old lovebirds with clacking dentures in passage round him, and vain, vain, all those peculiar perfumes and pongs that hover here; vainly the punks have garish hair and vainly the Goths do their blackness and vainly the water spirit in green tailcoat waves his guitar without strings and vainly by the stall over there an amateur artist dressed in Dutch folk costume offers her winter landscapes for sale and vainly the cyclists sit so straightbacked on their machines and vainly they carry their children and vainly the windmills and sunflowers and tulips make richly coloured postcards, vainly we know a thing or two about this Holland and that Holland, that here this is permitted, and not just this but also the other, vainly we know that, always there are people and more people need more information and more people need more

232

foodstuffs and liquids. This whole colourful and sounding circus is only one of the modes of masking what in reality is going on. (*Viva Ensor*! Lucebert understood that Ensor's skeletons, sometimes surfacing in the carnival procession, required the Spanish word *viva*! *Viva*, skeletons, for you every day is El Día de los Muertos!) In one of the variants of reality. In the one that entitles nobody to optimistic prospects. If something is sufficiently dispiriting, it begins to be regarded as reality, as a serious thing. Something more real than other real things. The manufacture of foodstuffs demands ceaseless development of new technology. Thanks to new technology, people can make real foodstuffs even from the most incredible materials. Therefore, human dung also is differently real, to begin with. Synthetic additives in human dung are slowly poisoning the earth on the inside, as plastics, asphalt and steel do on the outside. Tourists lolling on wicker chairs before cafes turn their faces to the last rays of the setting sun and superciliously inspect the passers-by. The earth is inwardly connected by a network of passageways and canals, precisely as shown in the illustrations of Athanasius Kircher. Instead of red-hot magma, rivers of synthetic dung course through those passages. More people, more information, more pictures, more flashes, more noise. Bodies collapse, those political torsos, representations of what is sometime convenient, they collapse and pour down to Amsterdam to seek life, gorge on life, trample down and excrete. To excrete all possible liquids, secretions, emulsions, phlegms. The earth detests those ingredients by now, its entrails are rebelling, crust shaking, volcanoes snorting. *Mundus Subterraneus* is preparing to vomit: preparing to vomit, not just magma but also an amassed freedom, changing to cannibal hunger. Will ruin come from below? And not from the sky? Not in the form of sulphureous rain? Not in the form of the imagined pandemic or a hundred-metre-high wave hurtling in at a thousand-kilo-metre speed? The fat women stumble and fall. Or they buy rubber paddling pools to put in their gardens, turn on the water and settle in them like pyramids of meat.

65. This one will do OK,

it seems to be empty. He knows it vaguely. Café De Monico. So then, here. But it isn't completely empty. Sitting over here are two, what should one call them, girls. For girls, though, they look rather experienced: they smile expertly, expertly they move their fingers, expertly they curl their lips.

'Hoyyy! Komm binnen,' one of them says, waving at Simon.

Simon blushes. Actually, he doesn't know for sure if he's really blushing, even at his age, but he thinks yes and brightly, as he feels the feverish heat. After so many jenevers, too. But with a bit of luck, he will seem to have come with sunburn. He stammers his usual apologetic phrase: 'Sorry, ik ben een buitenlander, ik spreek Nederlands heel slecht.'

The woman who greeted him smiles and changes to English. She explains that the owner has just gone off somewhere, but the cafe is open, he may sit down at his ease. If he likes, he can go to the upper floor, where there's a dance hall, music; he can dance there, the girl says, and smiles again.

Simon thanks her for the information (devil-knows-how intended), moves deeper into the room, into the half-light reeking with disinfectant, air freshener and little pools of spilt alcohol. But underneath all those stinks there is one central unifying stink cutting through: the stink of foul water. He remembers that smell from his youth, from his native place: in the summer, when he and Justin used to walk by the river, it stank precisely so. Once they were wandering there by night and Simon suggested they should strip naked. He doesn't know what got into him then; today he would call it enthusiasm for life. It was only a few months before the country was possessed by a non-violent revolution, a theatrical and more or less lethargic regime change. Simon and Justin were sitting in a suburban so-called workers pub (the workers called it *The Brawlshop*) and debating, neither one being the taciturn type. Darkness fell, it was after closing time, and the two friends took themselves off down the nearest street to the river. Simon spied a junk container on the street, the kind they load onto lorries. He could not resist the dark lure and slid into it. After a while he clambered out of it with a triumphant expression on his face. In one hand he held a fragment of a mirror, in the other a score with the heading Beethoven.

He is weighing whether to sit at the bar or seek a table elsewhere. The chairs strike him as low, angular, chilly. He looks towards the wall: high tables and high barstools without armrests. By no means reliable looking. But if he sits there, at least he'll be able to blend in with the dark brown wooden panelling of the wall. Accordingly, he sits there. He tosses his coat on a second chair, pulls the notebook from his bag, throws the bag under the table.

Nothing is moving, only the street beyond the great glass windows separating the cafe space from the terrace. The girls who spoke to him take no notice of him any longer; they laugh, occasionally whoop disagreeably, first one, then the other, sometimes both together. Simon calms down, as the vertiginous street recedes.

He imagines: what if the upper floor that the girls drew his attention to were not a dance hall but something entirely different, where admittedly one could dance but not very, not much, just by way of show, as an introduction; what if that room served for altogether different purposes? Bed on a podium, mirror along the floor, wash basin, shower, white terry towel thrown over a chair. Hidden cameras in the corners. Here? Such rooms? In Rembrandtplein? On the upper floor of a pub? Like in the red-light district?

A powerfully-built Black man emerges behind the bar counter, something between Forest Whitaker and Lawrence Fishburne. Or better still: a younger edition of Willard White in the role of Nekrotzar. He comes over to Simon's table.

'Kan ik u helpen?'

'Ik wil . . . ' Simon stutters, 'Ik wil graag een oude jenever met een glas water.'

'Geen oude jenever,' the Black man slowly turns his head and sizes up Simon curiously.

'Goed dan, jonge is ook goed,' Simon says, and his stomach rises.

The table he has chosen doesn't have enough space for the drinks menu, the notebook, and the tray with the glass of water and the jenever. He realizes that he cannot write and comfortably slurp jenever at the same time. Closing the notebook, he turns his hip to the table and his back to the wooden panelling, so that his face is towards the bar. His gaze meets the Black man's. The latter has just placed a small glass of beer in his own proximity. Simon raises his spirit glass and drinks the man's health. The other also raises his small beer, then with his free hand unexpectedly points to the table in front of him.

Simon evaluates how much he'll be able to stand in that stink of rotten river and disinfectant fluids. He takes bag and coat in one hand, the spirit glass in the other. He'll have to return for the notebook. Having shuffled to the bar, he threw the bag on the ground, the coat over a chair, and immediately headed back for the notebook. Only then did he notice that hanging, pinned, over the table he had originally selected was a huge reproduction of *The Night Watch*. And this to boot, he thought. All that incredibly nauseating kitsch in the square, the twenty-two bronze unfortunates made according to Rembrandt's painting, could not suffice. But whoever displayed the wretched reproduction here, what was he thinking of? That the poster in the room and the sculpture group in the square set up some magical interaction which no customer could withstand? Be thankful for so much, that this boozer isn't called Rembrandt, Saskia, or even Nachtwacht.

'Ik ben Eddie,' the Black man says.

'Ik ben Simon, aangenaam,' Simon says, taking hold of the spirit glass.

Eddie asks Simon in Dutch how long he's been living here and in which city. Simon again (nothing better occurring to him) asks Eddie in turn if he comes from Africa. No, Eddie replies, he's from the Caribbean. From Haiti. Haiti? Simon raises his eyebrows and says, that must be a very nice country. Well, it is too, Eddie concurs languidly, and unexpectedly asks Simon in English if he's married. Simon answers that he is, and immediately asks Eddie if he too is married.

Eddie replies that fortunately, not yet, he prefers freedom, currently he has three girlfriends. At once.

'Three?' Simon wonders, and feigns an amused laugh. Since now they are using only English, Eddie underlines his announcement with the declaration:

'I fuck everything. Believe me, I'm forty-three and I fuck everything. I don't care.'

They both laugh. Then they look through the great glass panels, across the heads of the two girls sitting in the cafe and the heads of some guests sitting on the terrace, out onto the commotion of the street. Simon recalls, he doesn't know why, the Roman Square of Santa Maria in Trastevere, that day when he and Estrella had Fernet at one of the pavement tables, because Simon's stomach and legs were trembling, impossible to know the cause, maybe the dimensions of Rome and maybe the clamour of demonstrations and chaotic traffic. But calm reigned on Piazza di Santa Maria in Trastevere: not many tourists strayed in there, the cafes and restaurants had a yawning emptiness. Simon observed a pigeon that was stubbornly trying to land on one of the tables: he waved his wings so vehemently that he swept a glass and cup off the table, scaring the other doves that were strolling between the chairs.

After a moment's silence, Simon observes that in Haiti it's certainly very warm, there's pleasant weather, bananas and sea, and if he'd been born and lived there he'd never in his life think of leaving to go to Europe, especially such a country as Holland. Why hadn't Eddie stayed in Haiti? Why did he come here, it's cold and wet here, after all, and even the people have got part of them frozen. Eddie doesn't come up with an answer, Simon hastily says sorry, he doesn't want to be intrusive.

'Eddie, you don't have to answer if you don't want. I mean I know there's poverty in Haiti, no prospects. Understandable if someone over there hankers for life in Western Europe.' Eddie agrees. Haiti is a beautiful country and one day, when he's got enough money saved, he'll return to Haiti, he'll go back there and buy himself a grand hacienda. But till then, till then he's OK in Holland, he doesn't lack anything, got a marvellous boss, actually the boss is his father, this is a family business, and he's also got marvellous brothers and sisters, really he cannot say anything bad about them, even if he isn't his actual father and the siblings aren't actually that, he's a Dad, a White man, the siblings too are White, and the stepmother too is White, the mother of his foster-brothers and sisters.

'That must have been hard,' Simon says. 'Living among whites. So many whites.'

'Yes, it was hard,' Eddie attests. 'At first it really was hard, but by now I'm one of them. They behave towards me as one of their own.'

Other customers enter the bar. Eddie observes where they settle. Once they find a table, immediately he goes shooting off after them.

'Even so, it must have been hard,' Simon says, when Eddie returns.

'It was hard,' Eddie says, and he guffaws. 'And you? What are you doing in Holland?'

'Well . . . all sorts,' Simon says. 'Little bit of this, little bit of that. Actually, I'm a journalist. Actually, I was. Actually, I could be if I had something to write in. I can write, but not in Dutch, I haven't mastered this language yet. Actually, I do have something to write in. This notebook,' he smiles mockingly. 'I'm a journalist who doesn't write, a person who hasn't got a language. Am I at all?'

Eddie gives a loud laugh.

'Probably it won't be that dramatic,' he says.

'Not dramatic,' Simon says. 'Definitely not dramatic. But something else. I don't know what. And my situation is like that—*I don't know what.* I actually can't do anything properly. I can't do most of what most people can do, and the little I can do either is not significant, or I can't do it properly.'

'Interesting,' Eddie says, and gazes out at the bustling street.

'My parents,' Simon continues, 'have a kind of romantic disposition. *Dreamers*, you understand. *Daydreamers.* They equally have no proper command of anything. They never learnt anything properly. No craft. Expert competence. What could they teach me? My mother openly admitted that she gave me nothing. No *tricks or skills.* Nothing for life. The grandparents supposedly yes. Supposedly they did give me something for life. But that too is something you can't make much money with. Decent behaviour and a sense of order. Considerateness. With that, supposedly I'll get far. And indeed, I have got far—here.'

Simon smiles briefly.

'But I don't know if it's thanks to considerateness. Aach, what am I chattering. What they gave me was not a sense of living, not a sense of order, but an intuition. Intuition of some kind of order. Intuition of the order that they lived by. This intuition is pleasing sometimes, when a person recalls it. Otherwise, it's worthless. In these critical times. If they really are critical. Eddie, do you sense a crisis? Does your business sense a crisis?'

'To some extent, yes. Quite a lot of Poles left the country in recent times.'

'Did you have Poles coming in here?' Simon asked with interest.

'No,' Eddie said. 'I just happened to mention that. They were working all over the country, plenty of them, they used to install and repair things. The Polish girls, I won't say, they didn't look bad, mostly in pizzerias. They're fewer today. Maybe there are still some in the red-light district.'

'So, the people you regard as your parents are whites. Did they adopt you?'

Simon knocked on his forehead:

'What a dimwit I am! I didn't even ask you about your mother.'

'She died.'

'That too! It seems I only have friends who have had one or other parent die. And in one or two cases, both parents. Mine are living and I don't know how to deal with them. How to behave with them. How to deal with the past, with their past, which they manage far more easily than I do. And how old were you when your mother died?'

'Nine.'

'That must have been hard,' Simon says.

'Well, it was,' Eddie says, and adds: 'But you know what, I don't remember anything. All I remember is that Haiti is warm. Here it's always raining. So, one day when I'm rich, I'm going to return to Haiti and buy a little house on the seashore.'

'My Mama,' Simon says, 'told me that she hadn't taught me anything properly. And do you know when she told me that? It was when she was old enough not to care what she said to anyone. Even so, I think that she still hasn't made a full confession. She'd never taught me anything: she told me this after I'd thrown it in her face for years that I was lost, because my parents hadn't trained me for any regular life. And for years she defended herself, contradicted me, declared: That's not true, Simon, that's not true! But I kept repeating my story. Until one day she acknowledged: I know that I haven't given you anything precious in life, I know I wasn't a proper mother, I shouldn't have got pregnant so early. And when she said this, I began to esteem her. How many mothers are able to admit such a thing? I began to esteem her and suddenly I discovered that although I'd never learnt anything proper in life, with the possible exception of a certain *considerateness*, nevertheless I am not lost. Now she says that although she taught me nothing, that doesn't mean that I cannot learn something by myself. And that's what I think too. I do not feel lost. I'm a journalist who doesn't write, a newspaperman without newspapers or a newsroom, a newspaperman that never studied journalism, a journalist that became a journalist only from dire need, so to speak by chance, I'm a journalist without a theme and without a language. And yet I do not feel lost, here in Amsterdam, whose language I haven't really grasped and where I know no one, I do not feel lost, and my life's ambition today is to get to the airport and wait there for my wife.'

66. 'And have you got a photo of her?'

Eddie asks.

'I don't. It never occurred to me that I should carry one around with me. Do you think it's a mistake? That I ought to? At least on the mobile?'

'I don't know.' Eddie grins. 'I don't know. I've got three girl-friends. I shouldn't carry their photos round with me. But I carry them, look.'

Eddie opens his wallet and shows the photos. One is White, young. 'This one's twenty, I'm forty-five. I shouldn't carry them round with me. Because here,' (Eddie was pointing to his heart) 'here I feel that one day I will meet a fourth, and she will be such that afterwards all these three will have to . . . '

'And then you'll take number four to Haiti, to your little house.'

Eddie smiles: 'I'll think a while about that.'

'It's not easy,' Simon says, 'to spend so many years among whites. And then to return among your own.'

'Well now, it isn't easy,' conceded Eddie. 'But nor is it difficult.'

'In any event,' Simon says, and takes a sip of the jenever, 'I cannot even imagine, I can't imagine how it is when someone is born as a *Black* and afterwards lives among whites. White people are quite disgusting, no? Sticky, smelly and sneaky.'

'Not all,' Eddie says. 'Not all. I've been lucky, my parents are wonderful, they allow me to work here, to save, to get rich. My father gives me money. Apart from giving me regular pay for this work. When I've had enough of it all and I'm feeling pretty weary, I'll go off to Haiti and buy my little house.'

'Was it you who pinned up the reproduction?' Simon adds and nods in the direction of the poster with *The Night Watch*. Eddie wrinkles his forehead and says after a brief pause:

'No, not my doing. My brother must have put it there. I've no idea when. My foster-brother. Or Jouke, the waiter who works here. Why do you ask?'

'Something silly,' Simon says. 'A song came to mind. King Crimson, d'you know it?'

'The name rings a bell,' Eddie says. 'But I can't place it immediately. Boxer? Basketballer? What song?'

'It's a rock group,' Simon explains. 'One of their songs is called "The Night Watch".'

'OK, so . . . ?'

'The song goes, I don't remember all the lyrics, just a few lines, it goes, *Three hundred years have passed, the worthy captain and his squad of troopers standing fast.*'

'Nice one,' Eddie says. 'Three hundred years? I'd never have thought it. That's about the painting, right? And the painting is that old? Man! So those there are standing for three hundred years and these here,' waving in the direction of the square, 'didn't last even for three years.'

'And where did they put them? I read somewhere that they shipped them to New York. The entire sculpture group, all twenty-two figures. Presumably forever.'

'I won't miss them,' Eddie says, pulling himself another small draught beer.

'Crazy. What will they want those sculptures for in New York? They could have manufactured the very same. Even so, to my mind they're valueless. A crazy idea in the first place. Isn't Rembrandt's statue sufficient? Did they have to display that kitsch in front of it? A three-dimensional copy of a two-dimensional painting?'

'Those statues didn't bother me,' Eddie says. 'Like it doesn't bother me when they're not here.'

67. He imagines

Eddie's childhood. He has no points of support, no facts, no emotional stimuli, so his ideas will be vague. Carefree Black boys skipping in the dusty streets of Port-au-Prince or some other Haitian city. A ruddy or ochre clay covers the streets, no sewage, just rivulets of dirty water or urine. A boy skips, a sea breeze stirs the crowns of the trees, the sky is blue to satiety. The boy skips over to a wooden veranda attached to one of the tin buildings. On the carelessly sunken wooden veranda stands a broad-smiling Black woman, stretching out her arms to him. Simon imagined an erupting volcano. But are there any volcanoes in Haiti? A volcano erupts, smoke rolls from it, ash rains, stones, gravel. Then he remembers the news stories and it amuses him how volcanologists feed on erupting volcanoes and outdo one another in frightening people: it's dozing now, but no one knows when it will erupt, and if once it erupts, it'll be quite another party. Mobs in gas masks and rubber cloaks; maybe he ought to buy a protective mask. Actually two, one for Estrella. Again he imagines Eddie as a small boy. Suddenly he concentrates on Eddie's mother. A slim woman, simple white garment, skirt. Something like a turban on her head. Does she attend magic rites? Does she take her son along?

Simon squints at Eddie's watch.

'Will you have one more?' Eddie asks.

Simon nods and again catches the other man's interest. Eddie pours, places the tot in front of Simon and says:

'And what if you don't find any work?'

'Me? Actually yes, you're right. Why don't I find? Good question. I'm waiting for an idea, you get me.'

Simon takes the glass and lifts it to his lips. But he doesn't drink, and places it back in front of him.

'Why don't I find any work, hm. Actually, I'm looking for it, I'm thinking about it, opportunities, steps that might be undertaken, really, just that . . . '

'Just that what?' Eddie asks.

68. If he were to write a novel

and if a character resembling Peter were to appear in it, he would
make him say . . . What words would he put in that character's
mouth? What would Peter-in-the-novel say? Nothing. He'd be silent.
He'd smile cunningly. Like the real Peter. But Peter-in-the-novel
would not be entirely like the real Peter; Peter-in-the-novel should
have something to say. In the novel he can speak, in novels there are
just mute letters; the real Peter can therefore within Peter-in-the-
novel, no matter what a chatterbox Peter-in-the-novel may be, cheerfully remain still silent, cunningly smile.

Peter in Simon's novel would probably say this:

Go and take your place! Blend in with the superficial ones, run
to it. Humility never meant anything to you. And don't show your
face in this country again. Don't return, don't try to find me. And
don't try to find Sandra. Sandra's a saint. A solid, straightforward
human being. Don't come near our children. Don't look for us. Don't
try to find our house. You're lost. You've understood nothing, our
conversations were pointless, you'll burn in Hell. Don't even try to

reform yourself. You don't have to repent, not that you understand what penitence is.

You'll burn in Hell! What else, my friends, what else? What other destiny pertains to someone who is called Simon, and not only that but Blef? Ble-ble-ble: Beelzeblef. We'd have the Hell already: the race driver from Algeria wrote that the Amsterdam canals made him think of Dante's *Inferno*. He wrote that in *The Fall*, so fall and Amsterdam seem to belong together; when someone wants to fall, Amsterdam is available.

But afterwards Peter too ought to come here. After all, he's a kind of rescuer of fallen women, women whose *fall* Simon had induced. Isn't he? Should he not come here to rescue all those who fall? Or were those falls, those few falls of women, not actually induced by Simon? Induced / not induced—even so, Peter is a rescuer of fallen women. When Sandra's legs (figuratively speaking) buckled, he came and raised her up. Rescued her from Simon's insecurities. And megalomania. Previously, however, he had rescued Anita. Granted, not to the same degree as Sandra (by espousal), but at least symbolically— with an offer of marriage. When Simon had left her. Because he returned to Sandra. Thereby causing Anita to attempt suicide. A hysterical, theatrical act, Simon thinks even now. But that doesn't matter: the main thing is that Peter came after Anita, travelled to the country to see her, rang at the gate of their house and offered her marriage. Certainly, he did not offer that immediately. If Simon knows Peter, assuredly a few hours of conversations followed. They smoked dozens of cigarettes, drank quantities of coffee. Or they went to the pub and drank till they gibbered. And then Peter came up with his What if. What if she and he. For Peter, fixing Simon's (purported or real) blunders seemed to have become his life's role. His mission. Peter the repairman.

All this transpired while a particular political regime was in its twilight. Does Simon now regret that, pursuing his private peripeteia, he suppressed his direct experience of the social upheaval? When we take into account all that has happened in the intervening twenty years, then no, he does not regret that he wasn't more immersed in the *revolution*. By now he knows that it was only another servitude replacing the preceding servitude: the mob or the individual may choose the regime that they suffer in most pleasantly. But this is not about regime changes, but about Anita and Peter. Here is how it occurred.

During the summer Simon and Sandra agreed they'd had enough, full stop, they were going to end their relationship. And the quarrels, misunderstandings, reproaches, had indeed been plentiful. They'd get out while the going was good. One last time they made love, drank a bottle of red, strolled in the sprawling park beside the hostel. Next day Simon accompanied Sandra to the bus station. He deposited her on the bus, bowed to her and immediately headed into town. The air was fresh, the sky clear. He felt that his lungs were cleansing and a new life was beginning, not a variant of the previous one, but something wide, expansive and unknown. A frivolous spleen took hold of him, a hint of some sort of regret, but the kind that one can enjoy. He went into a garden restaurant, ordered a beer, and enjoyed the peace that had suddenly alighted on the world. Before long, some fellow students of his appeared in the garden; Peter was not among them, but there was a girl whom Simon knew only by sight, and that her name was Anita. On a well-meaning whim he got talking to Anita, and soon it came to light that they had an awful lot of things in common. Simon had a mild intuition that such things happened only in films and that Anita was, who knows why, making advances to him. That same day he slept with her; actually, for the remainder of that week he never emerged from her room, or indeed from her bed. He told himself he was boundlessly happy and he didn't even need food, it was enough to have water and wine. A new semester began in the autumn and Sandra appeared on the scene. Her friends had kindly informed her of Simon's summer adventures. All Sandra needed to do was flash her eyes, shake her red mane, snap her fingers, and Simon ran to her like a little pinscher. When he caught the scent of Sandra, his knees gave way and it was decided: from that moment Anita was simply air. He thought, ah, how simple it is, everything goes right in the end. Bar, ten vodkas, cinema. Simon to the station and home, Sandra to the hostel, they'd see each other again tomorrow, let their newly revived relationship blossom. But that night Simon was wakened by his mother and told he had a telephone call. Sandra's horrified voice in the earpiece: Anita had attempted suicide, they had to call an ambulance, right then they were pumping out her stomach. Simon feigned cold-bloodedness, *calm down, I'll come by the first morning train* (He absolutely did not plan to take the first morning train—*the 9.30 will do*; he thought it wouldn't be that bad with Anita, she had a theatrical disposition). Where were you dossing all this time? Sandra said, making some comment about his cynicism. Then she sent him off, he had better go and console Anita. By some odious metaphysical contingency, they both lived on the same passageway in the hostel: it was just going out one door and in another door beside it. Anita truly disgusted Simon then. Although he did not have any experience of girls attempting suicide, in this instance he clearly felt that it amounted to hysterical blackmail. He was well enough acquainted with female hysteria, from his mother in childhood; hysteria took hold of him too when he felt it in others. But Simon was also disgusted with himself. His own instinctual drives and insatiability were disgusting, and it disgusted him that he got together with women who saw him as prey. Sandra had triumphed over Anita, because she had lured Simon back, and Anita again had triumphed over Simon, because with her hysterical suicide attempt she had properly sugared the *revived* old love affair. In less than a month Peter got involved in the story. After a few vodkas, he confided to Simon that one Saturday he'd boarded a bus for the village where Anita lived, to ask for her hand. Simon's jaw dropped, but he didn't let on. He simply asked in an indifferent tone: Why did you do that? But Peter said nothing. He didn't need to. Simon worked it out. He reckoned that Peter had seized an opportunity, literally a *research* opportunity, to enable him to carry out a further experiment. Evidently, he believes (Simon thought then) that by *steeping* himself in such situations he'll become a second Dostoyevsky; surreptitiously, Peter is surely at work on a novel whose main character will be him, Simon Blef. Well, and one must intervene in the fates of the characters, not only those that are already written in detail but also those whose immortalization on paper still awaits them, while in the meantime, sensing nothing, they run round the world; one must prepare bizarre situations for them and observe their mimes and poses. Peter is quite like Justin: because Justin too can ruthlessly observe how people around him toss and twitch, how emotions tug at them, how the past agonizes inside them. Simon, then, again asked Peter why he had done it. Peter tossed back another tot of vodka and said: *Because I wanted to save her, that's why.* Simon knew that was a lie. A lie so enormous that Peter wasn't even capable of apprehending it. So, he could not hate Peter. He could hate the world in which such things happen, but even that was too much for him. He was weakened by the knowledge that Peter, this intelligent, educated and pious youth, was incapable of being aware that he was governed by hatred, which then took on words like *humility, penitence, rescue, salvation,* as its masks. Afterwards many years went by, and when the revived relationship between Simon and Sandra once again foundered, again came Peter and asked Sandra for her hand. As before, maybe purely so that at the end of the *story* he could write a novel and thus immortalize Simon's crimes.

You'll burn in Hell. No, Peter wouldn't use such words. He looked at the Catholic 'value' system from a philosophical standpoint. More precisely: from a standpoint closer to metaphysics and mathematics. Simone Weil? Of course: *Perfectly clear attention is prayer.* Whether Peter's *attention* was *perfectly clear* is not known, but certainly it was at least *prayer.* Prayer: at the outset of their friendship Simon and Peter had understood it differently. Simon laid emphasis on fervour and words, Peter on attention and silence. Which is why Simon was so naively astonished when he heard Peter, who was still located in the world of his grandparents' little prayerbooks, in a world of words, indubitable doctrines, pathetic stories, church canopies, organ music and the lilac perfume of May altars. But now, at least according to the reports that reach him, things have flipped about; now he himself is silent and Peter drives his children to church and teaches them to pray—in words. Simon has turned into something like Peter, and Peter into something like the one-time Simon. Today, perhaps, Peter might after all use the words: *You'll burn in Hell.*

He'd do better to go over there, that way. Not follow the routes in the guidebooks, routes along which helpless knots and pairs of tourists stand, with more guidebooks clutched in their hands. He should walk the lanes and narrow passageways fringed with crooked, undulant and stooping facades, along a sticky pavement smelling of rot. One day the houses of this city will fade like flowers in a vase and without a single sound of reproach will sink in the swelling mud, amid tens of thousands of rusted bicycles.

69. 'I'll tell you how it is.

Many times I thought about leaving. From over there, that country. Many times. You know how it is, Eddie. You left too. Since childhood I've had the feeling that I don't fit in there. It's like I don't understand how it functions, on what lines. Well, not that I've any better grasp of the methods here. Where do I fit in, I honestly have no idea. My mother was constantly nagging me to stop dithering and go. I'm dragging her in here again. She fostered a feeling in me that I was living in a country overwhelmed by some frightful catastrophe, which made everyone go mad. And those that didn't go mad progressively became stupid. So in spirit I was prepared for the fact that one day I would leave. But there's no possible way to prepare for something like that. So I was just deluding myself. I never thought about where I should go. Where. I imagined it would be something special. Something unusual. I don't know why I fancied that nothing bad could happen to me. For example, I imagined I would become a musician or a composer, and I'd have an assured living forever. My granny, would you believe, had a concert piano with angels, so said her son Tomi, a fantasist, he said that angels watched over that instrument, well, and this woman told me that she'd read many biographies of famous people and a fair number of famous artists had gone hungry. Doesn't matter, I said, I too will put up with some hunger. I'm talented, sooner or later I'll make a breakthrough, already I've appeared in the regional cultural centre and everyone liked my stuff. Definitely I'll break through, nothing bad can happen to me. I'll live in a cosy villa in a quiet place, on the outskirts of some capital city. That's how I envisaged myself, and I continued paying no attention when grand-dad screwed and mounted and hammered things. And so I never learnt anything properly. I could not pay attention to what my father was doing, because he'd moved out from us early on and he taught all the useful boyish things to his other son, by his second wife. I don't know what exactly he could have taught him, because my father too is just a *dromer*, even to this day, like me, and he too never learnt any-thing properly in life, he just swindled people, I think he himself didn't know if it was deliberate, and sometimes he did sport, he brought up his second son as a sportsman. And I just dreamt and dreamt. How one day I'd be gone out of there. That country. The country my father loved so much that he stopped speaking to me. I'm not surprised at him. He was able to love that country so limit-lessly. He's a great comic actor. If you ask me, all the fathers who show their parental love to the world are comedians. Just that they're not all funny. But most of them would kill a stranger child without bat-ting an eye. Eddie, believe it or not, I'm no idler here. I'm ceaselessly concerned with how to find work. I examine the environment where I happen to be, where I must somehow invent myself, somehow sur-vive. Stop me when you've had enough of this. You asked why I'm not seeking work. I am seeking it, *geloof me*, but I don't want to be pushy. Shall I go somewhere and say: Give me work? Or shall I stand on the street and hassle the first passer-by, whether he knows of something? At home I was lucky. *At home!* I keep forgetting that I'm not at home any longer. And I never was. In the time that I lived there, I never managed to grasp what matters to those people. *There. Ik begrijp niks.* But my father, I call him Old Blef, my surname too is Blef, stupid name, anyhow, my father loves that country. He lives merrily in his land of dreams. Actually, even Justin, one day I'll introduce you to him, as he ages, more and more he begins to love that country. *Ongelooflijk.* But I'm not going to laugh at him for that. I try to understand him. I ponder this manifestation in him: expressing resignation, or victory? Victory over what? I admire him. Sometimes, though, I can't stand it. Then I train myself in indifference. Maybe it's old age that makes a person aware that he need not see everything. And so, all the more easily he shuts his eyes to degeneration, corruption, brutality, dirty deeds. I do not want to be the judge of this world, but it doesn't help me when I shut my eyes. I still see the dirty deeds. They do not vanish just like that from before my eyes. Justin perhaps is not conscious of this, but he genuinely loves that country. Unconditionally, despite its defects. In his youth he was not so courageous.'

70. Dead mother,

everyone has a dead mother. Even those whose mothers have not died yet. Those especially have to imagine that she is dead. To imagine what kind of world it will be when she is no longer there. And then they must further imagine that the language she speaks in is likewise dead. The language of mothers cannot be assimilated. It is like an acid that corrodes every certainty. Despite which, yes, obviously, no mother wishes ill to her child. Estrella had transcribed in her notebook this, from Simone de Beauvoir's *A Very Easy Death*:

> *She did not allow us to learn to swim, and forbade our father to buy us a bicycle: she would not have been able to share those joys with us and we would have escaped from her . . . She was incapable of self-control and at times she was like a Fury, but when she cooled down, her humility went to the verge of self-abasement . . . She did not wish us evil, she just needed to prove that she had power.*

(Yes, Estrella too has a notebook, though she is far from being a notorious recorder. Simon imagines that if he were to write a novel and if a female figure similar to Estrella were to appear in this novel and were to have a notebook, the editor editing this novel would surely be surprised at Estrella having a notebook too. So yes: she has one, and maybe she keeps it only because of Simon, to be able to give him quotations from books that perhaps he will never read.)

Everyone has some corpse—de Beauvoir: *the corpse that was lying in the bed instead of Mum*—Estrella's father died; Sandra's mother died; both of Peter's parents; Justin's mother; Eddie's mother (he'd never known his father). For Kees Visser and Jan van der Vlucht, apart from parents, their wives had died. The carers' role had devolved on both of them. We care for skeletons while they are supports for quivering flesh. Afterwards we lay them in the earth or burn them; they interest us no longer. And yet they are 'more lasting' than the life from which we cast them out: they live in our memory, they evoke the eternal law. If Simon Blef wrote a novel, he would certainly mention caskets and forgotten skeletons inside them. He would drag them out from there, in that novel of his; he'd colour them and dress them nicely, giving them tailcoats, hats, skirts, veils and flounces. Stunning yellow, orange, purple, pink and azure skeletons with false pearls instead of teeth.

The death of Sandra's mother had affected Simon, he didn't know why. He learnt about it on the day when Sandra with her pram caught up with him at the tram stop. They went to the nearest cafe and there, in the middle of conversation, Sandra told him her mother had passed away. Breast cancer. Sandra's mother had been one of those aggressive and domineering beings whom Simon had feared most. He might do anything, he could behave however courteously and spin words however beautiful: in her eyes he was ragamuffin, riff-raff and clown. After all, he didn't have any proper trade, just those scribblings of his, ephemeral ambitions and plans. And who cared about those? When Sandra said that her mother had died, Simon for a moment felt overwhelmed, yet somehow, he could not express the mighty shock. After all those years that had passed since his separation from Sandra (he thought at that moment), he should not be so shocked by the death of a person whom he'd never been able to get on with. But the shock matured, it grew slowly; it returned weeks, even months after the encounter with Sandra. One day he admitted to himself that it was *unnatural* for that woman to die. Such a powerful, such an authoritative and explosive woman, an indestructible fighter: such a woman could not begin just like that to languish, grow feeble, diminish and finally become immobile like a wooden statue in the village church. At moments it seemed to Simon that he'd only imagined her death; the meeting with Sandra could only have occurred in some sort of hallucination. Eventually he ceased to be certain whether Sandra's mother really had died or not. He thought it was odd that the death of those with whom we are unable to coexist in peace for one moment, left behind it a much greater void than the death of near relatives.

In each corpse there is something eternal, and death lurks in every mother. Women give birth, so that in this very way, soullessly and mechanically, they may protest against death. Mothers, however, do nothing else, merely bring up (or neglect) in the path to death. *I am not thinking of death; you still have plenty of time for such things, sonny.*

The woman who once inhabited the body of Simone de Beauvoir wrote: *Death is not natural. Nothing that befalls the human being is natural, because his presence poses questions for the world.* In a few hours' time, in one of the bars at Schiphol, when Estrella reads these sentences to Simon, he will realise that nothing further needs to be written about death. Yes, but a novel that isn't about death, about the threat of death, about the incessant waning of life and coming nearer to death, is not a *real* novel, so that it makes no sense for him ever to set about writing one. And novels that pose *questions for the world*, or seek answers, are just common calculated frauds. Which is however no obstacle, because: *Nothing that befalls the human being is natural.* Maybe that's how it'll happen, maybe Simon will have just this realization. If Estrella pulls out the notebook. If she travels to Amsterdam at all.

The plane is for now in the air, still plenty of time, he may allow himself one or two snifters plus. But certainly not more. He has the journey to the station before him. Get going about seven, will that do? It will. Maybe even at seven thirty.

Eddie is preparing coffee, pouring beer. He's fully engaged; more guests are coming into the cafe as time passes.

Simon extracts the notebook and starts browsing there. When reading Crowley he had made a few fleeting notes, probably they'll correspond with Estrella's extracts, though who knows, maybe she hasn't made any: *the skeleton and the scythe are important Saturnian symbols . . . Death's image here represents the elementary essence of things, which does not succumb to the ordinary changes that are manifest in natural processes . . . when the skeleton raises his scythe, bubbles are produced, in which new forms surface . . . a dance of new forms . . . the letter Nun, which means 'fish', is ascribed to the symbol of death . . .*

nor is it a coincidence that St Peter was a fisherman . . . the fish, for its cold-bloodedness, swiftness and splendour, is consecrated to Mercury . . .

Eddie is back. Simon closes the notebook and pushes it away from him.

71. 'Where else can a person laugh at himself

with such relish, if not here in Amsterdam? I don't know why I think that, Eddie. This place is not grandiose, it is not impressive or monumental or cheerful. And that's actually the point. It doesn't obligate a person to anything. If you look in the display windows in these streets, you see yourself precisely as you are. When you're in Rome, you feel less mortal and somehow exceptional. In Madrid such trivialities don't interest you. Cairo is too dusty, you won't see yourself in the window. But in Amsterdam, which doesn't bind you to anything and which loves you and hates you in equal measure, you will see yourself in the window unembellished, time-worn and grey, just as you are. Look, I'm sorry, I didn't mean you personally. You're not at all grey, that's me, I'm the grey one. In Rome and Madrid, I'm motley coloured and merry, in Cairo I'm brown and yellow, but here I'm grey. Only when a person is grey right down to the depths, only then can he set off for a country such as Mexico. Tell me, Eddie, have you been to Mexico yet? I'm assuming that there, like in Amsterdam, but I don't know why I think this, I suppose I've drunk an amount of this stuff and now I'm talking off the rails—in short, I'm assuming that there too a person can laugh at himself with relish. Look at himself, at his clothes and how grimy and *worn* he is, and put the question: *What the hell am I doing here?* After such a question, all that can follow is a laugh. I'd figured out that I understood the *language* of this world less and less. A foreign land is good for that. To make someone comprehend that the world is even more incomprehensible than it seemed at home. *At home.* I can live without that phrase quite easily. Or it's the reverse, yes, now, when I think it over, my experience is more the reverse: for me, in a foreign land the world is more comprehensible than at home. And when you're on that wavelength, when you've travelled along through that *incomprehensibility*, then you cannot turn up at some employment agency and say: It appears to me that the world is ever more incomprehensible, but even so, I would like to take up employment. Or the other way round: I'd like to be employed, though the world becomes more and more incomprehensible to me. That's like saying: I know that all of you are stupid, but do allow me to pretend for a moment that I'm one of you. Allow me to join in your game, where we're playing that all of you are wise, I am the only stupid one. Just that some such sentence as this *must* be uttered. I can continue and say, for example, this: I know that you're all liars, but if you give me work, I will pretend I know nothing about all that. And with this I have to knock on the door of the Labour Office! Up until now, every superior I ever had figured that I didn't take them seriously. I don't envy them. Just imagine it, Eddie. Imagine you're a boss, and around you every day you must tolerate faces on which you see that they'd very much rather not see *you*. And now am I supposed to take an interest in some employment and pretend I will never regard my superior as a buffoon? But I want to be honourable, so I can't promise anyone anything. I cogitate too much and it prevents me from getting on with people: that's what you're thinking of me now, right? Well, OK. I'll watch myself. I'll try to think less. That won't even be so hard, because what appears in me as *thinking* is no thinking at all in reality. They didn't even teach me to think. When it seems that I'm thinking, what am I actually doing? Just raving. Ideas and memories displace one another in my head, spill about, tip over. Should I call such a state of stupefaction thinking? But tell me when you're fed up listening to me, OK? Anyhow, in a while I must be off to the airport. But first another jenever, yes, I'll have one more. Not immediately. First, I'll finish this. Sometimes I imagine how I'd set about that. Looking for some job. I suppose first of all I'd buy a newspaper. Advertisements. Or if by chance there wasn't some report on the front page, thanks to which now I needn't seek work at all. Thanks to which now I needn't do anything. Thanks to which now no one need do anything. For example, that an asteroid is colliding with Earth and we don't have the slightest chance. Pointless to run here or there. I'm in terror of such a report, but on the other hand, on the other hand, I would not be against it if something, some really big thing overturned and subverted the Earth, and from one second to another everything was different. Actually, it would be a relief. End of boredom. New beginning. So then, I'd start by buying a newspaper. Then I'd look for some quiet cafe. It's not beginning well, what? After that, I would study the job offers in detail. My father didn't have such problems. He joined the party and that was his work. Ads. If I want to solve my problem creatively, I should not study the offers but offer something directly. Place an ad. So, let's see what I can offer. How I can enrich the society which it has occurred to me to live in? I begin with the fact that I don't know its current condition. I don't know the demand. I'm not an engineer or installer. Languages. If I count the mother tongue, let's see. I can say that with greater or less difficulty I have the use of four languages. Four European. Only one of them global. Because how far will I get with my broken Italian? About from Sicily to South Tyrol. So four. If I knew Dutch better, then five. But where could I get with Dutch, apart from Holland? To Surinam. To the South African Republic. Or to Indonesia. Thus far, then, four. Without the mother tongue, three. But with those two Central European languages . . . I'm supposed to do what? In this situation? Historical ages alternate, countries appear and disappear. Pshtt, and it's gone! A country. Some countries aren't even born. Change just a little, and the country I come from need never have come into being. Except it did. But I tell you, Eddie, there's no difference. It exists, and yet as if it didn't exist. And I don't exist along with it. I know, probably it won't be that bad. Probably, despite all, I exist a little bit. At least enough to sit here and talk to you. I exist at least enough to be able to be an anonymous visitor in any bar. Customer in hundreds of bars whose names I don't remember. I remember Het Bolwerk in Enscheda. In the same town also, Café MacBerlijn. Here, in Amsterdam, I remember Corner House. Nothing special. Just location. Nearly every single nonentity tourist strays in there. To Jooske. D'you know Jooske? Well, of course not. I've a feeling they're bullying her, those Aramaeans who own the business. Jooske. Probably that's not her name. Irrelevant. That's another word I've picked up from my father, *irrelevant*. By now I've successfully rid myself of all that reminds me of him. But I've held onto this word. For some *irrelevant* reason. OK, what other pub? For example, Cafe de Postillon in Utrecht. You're goggling, what? That name amazes me too. Sounds as if it's been standing there for three hundred years. In the Hague I know a restaurant that's called Da

Sebastiano. But listen, Eddie. Today I was in a pub in Jordaan and I heard a woman looking for some Eddie. Was that you, by any chance? She was Black, the woman who asked. Couldn't she have been one of your girlfriends? Or what if she was the fourth, whom you haven't met yet? So, what am I supposed to do with my mother tongue, which is equally as *irrelevant* as the official language of the country that I came here from? The mother tongue, in which one can hurt a person the most. But as if that wasn't enough, if the mother tongue is not identical with the state language, then the state language can easily be seen as an instrument for bullying on the part of the government. On the other hand, I don't know how it would be if the mother tongue was identical with the state language: I suppose it would go sour on my tongue. To speak the language of power, the language of governmental coercion. But you probably don't see it like that. You have no such concerns; you speak English beautifully and Dutch even better. And French too? Of course, Haiti. Spanish? I'm amazed Eddie, I'm bowled over. Spanish, now that's something. That's a real-world language. From Argentina to the Philippines, you'd never be at a loss. And in Haiti you probably don't bother your heads about who understands what language, probably you don't project emotions into language like us here, in Europe. You wouldn't go out to die for your language, because probably in Haiti people die for other things. I mean, I don't know how it is, I'm just imagining. And have you been to Mexico? And besides, you have an honest profession. One day this Anglo-American world is going to collapse. And the Hispanic-Chinese civilization will take over. That'll be fun! Everywhere just carnival, samba and paper dragons. Well OK, so skills. You at least know how things go in hostelries. You have experience. I've got some too. But only with ridiculous and *useless* things. I don't even know how to pour drinks properly. According to the instructions. Are there some instructions for that? Does somebody still respect them? You see, I don't even know that. From dire need I'm a journalist, one who doesn't even have his *home* newspaper, or his language. A journalist with a notebook, but without writing. *To write.* No reason why, nothing to write about, no way how. No one to write for. But I don't despair. Because I probably couldn't go into some agency and say: I can write articles, but only in a Central European language. Guess which one. In the mother tongue or the official tongue. But you, you could open a cosy pub, something like this one, anywhere on the globe. Anywhere people speak a bit of Spanish, even if it's under some volcano.'

72. 'Once I almost became

a reporter. Investigative journalist. I applied for a position in a fairly
solid illustrated magazine for women. The editor-in-chief had previously been a TV presenter of Sunday political debates; she sized me
up and said, OK. OK, but first they'd give me a trial. Tomorrow you'll
go to the neighbouring town and you'll do an interview with the
brother of such-and-such—a politician, she said. Isn't that sensational?
Most of our citizens never have any idea that this politician has a
brother who works as an ordinary waiter. Great, but how do I find
him? All we know of him is that he works in one of the wine cellars.
Which one, you must find that out yourself. Right then, will you take
it on? Sure, I said, and strode out of the editor's office with the feeling
that there was no obstacle I wouldn't surmount. The neighbouring
town was a well-known centre of a wine-growing region, spilling over
with pubs, as you can imagine. Ominous start. I went into the first
pub that I found on my way from the railway station, and sat in a
corner. To have a good view and cover my back. When a waiter

appeared, I went straight to the point and asked him if he knew so-and-so. He didn't, he'd never even heard the name. OK, so bring me a beer, please. Nor did I make any progress in the next pub, but there I sensed that they knew the man I was looking for, just they didn't want to say anything. Hopeful sign. In the third pub (having told myself that I mustn't get blind drunk, and so I must drink non-alcoholic, because otherwise my venture would end badly, in a state of unmanageable dullness) the head waiter wrote down for me the name of the pub where I'd find my man. At the address divulged to me I found a not very sizeable pub, overgrown with ivy. I sat in a corner and waited. A waiter came, who showed no facial resemblance to any politician I knew. I asked him about my man. Yes, that man does work here, shall I call him? A minute later the lad I was looking for stood before me. White shirt, black trousers. And vaguely familiar face. Features resembling the well-known politician. Is that you? You his brother? Yes, I am, he said, and asked: What do you want? To do an interview with you, I said. Yes? And about what? About your private life, I said. Oh, well then no, he retorted. I don't wish to show the world how I live. And won't you reconsider that, I rejoined further. No, I won't reconsider. OK then, I respect your will, I said. Will you bring me a beer? Yes, that I can. When I'd drunk up, I went to the courtyard and phoned the editor-in-chief. Alas, didn't work out, I deduce that you probably won't take me on, right? You deduce correctly, the editor-in-chief responded. So, Eddie, you see, an investigative journalist no, I can't be that, actually I don't have the stomach for it, I don't miss those stresses before the deadline closes. I have my years, and maybe some self-respect. I'm not any longer going to let some ambitious editors-in-chief, some snotty-nosed kids bounce me around, or neurotic layout men, snotty-nosed likewise. That path leads me nowhere. I'd do better to sit on my arse and not have fancies.'

73. 'I always thought

that if I read a lot, one day I'd grow wise. Did I grow wise? And Granny? She that had the piano with the angels—did she grow wise? And yet, what an amount she read. I never understood her. What she was doing, or not doing, rather. Maybe she really did grow wise. But OK, let's go on. What could I be? I could place an ad that I heal people with bioenergy. My father says he has miraculous healing capacities. What if I've inherited those from him? Just that I don't have the nerves for people. My father doesn't either, but he pretends to be above it all. People, people. Limbs, skulls. All of us are dancing like paper skeletons in the wind. Do you know Anita Desai? No, she's not a model. Nor a presenter. She wrote a novel about Mexico. Well, not about Mexico, it's just set in Mexico. The background isn't important. But paper skeletons are mentioned there. I haven't finished reading it yet. It's not that gripping. My aunt made a paper skeleton like that for me. She coloured it too. And she's not even Mexican. We don't have Mexicans in the family. Well, my wife Estrella, I'll introduce her to you some time, she's half Mexican. And do you know what else I could do? I could write a really gripping book, have it translated into Dutch and get rich. But until then? Until then what can I live on? Should I go to work in a meat-packing plant like my fellow students at the evening language class? I'd get arthritis. They drudge nine hours daily at two degrees temperature. I'm over forty, I won't be talked into something like that. I'd sooner roam the city and look at shop windows. Maybe there's a saving idea lying in one of them. Any detail will do. Any triviality. And I can search in other employment agencies. Imagine that I go into one of them, and . . . What are your skills? asks the lady behind the table. I'm a teacher of language and literature. And a former journalist. I can speak these and these languages. Just now I don't have anything for you, will be her reply. Fill in this form, I'll put you on our list. When something turns up, we'll call you. At that moment it occurs to me that they might be looking for a storeman. I have the impression, you see, that it's fairly undemanding work. Uncle Tomi was a storeman for some time. He didn't seem to be sweating mightily. The lady asks me how I am with figures. Sums. *Wiskunde*. And there I finish. Let's imagine another situation. I'm going along a street, the one not far from here that has so many restaurants, one after the other, somewhere near Leidseplein. I'm walking along it and I have a plan. If I see a chef standing in front of some restaurant, immediately I will ask him if. Certainly he'll be a powerful fellow. Silently he will take my measure and either invite me inside or turn away from me. I envisage it something like this: I'll go to him and: May I have a word? Mr Chef, do you happen to need help in your kitchen? Chef is silent. Casual help? Untrained. Chef silent. Hallo, do you understand me? Waving before his eyes. I'm asking whether you don't need an industrious dishwasher. Chef silent, or shrugs shoulders. Chefs make a living, they never remain without work. How could I have been such a dunce that it never occurred to me to train as a chef? Secure, unshakeable, safe profession. Wartime or peacetime, chefs are always needed. Everywhere. If he asks me inside, soon it will come to light that I can't even slice an onion. And a fellow who can't slice even an onion, what does he want from the world? To wash dishes? I won't say, an auspicious beginning of a career abroad. Especially on the threshold of forty. Am I boring you? Let's talk about women. Or another thought that struck me, that I should ask the church for help. My granny, not the one that had a piano with angels, but the other one, used to tell me, Son, whenever you're in need, you can always rely on the church. OK, but this country's full of Calvinists. Suppose I found a Catholic Church. I go in and what next? I tap on a confession box, dear father, can I have a word? Certainly, my son, go ahead, I'm listening to you. Father, I'm looking for work, and my granny told me I could always rely on the Church. And what would you want to do, son? Anything, I don't know. I can sweep the church, water the flowers, light the candles and quench them. Ah, my unfortunate son, we have a sexton. Well, OK, so I could stand in front of the church beside a container and collect used clothing from people. I'd get involved in charity. Or you might help me, Father, to fill in some forms and I could go on the missions to some tropical country. I think, in the Brazilian jungle, at the source of the Amazon I would not be out of place. Even better though would be Mexico. I understand, son. But in Mexico there are Catholics enough, they could make up numbers. We've already brought the whole of Mexico to the true faith. Even the state of Chiapas? I would ask. And the priest would say: not just anyone can go on the missions. A missionary has to have a clean past. Since when? I'd ask, astonished. That's the rule now, the priest would say. Supposing you're a paedophile? And supposing your father was an atheist and a bitter opponent of the Holy Church? What was your father? And that would finish me off, Eddie. If I told him the truth, namely, that my father was an apparatchik and detested the Church, probably he'd regard me as crazy and throw me out on the street. If I invented things, he would check and find out what the truth was. No, I'm not paranoid. I know something by now about the Catholic Church's information channels. The very word *katholikos* means that nothing remains hidden from Rome: everything is known, everything is net-worked with everything. OK then, certainly they know not only what my father was doing in the past but also what he's doing now. Certainly, they know about his charlatan seances. You're from Haiti, Eddie, for you that's not charlatanism, but I can't see it any other way. My father thinks he has supernatural capacities. OK, so maybe he does. If he really does have them, maybe I have them too. I could open an oracle, since for the moment I've no interest in healing peo-ple. So I could practise something like what my father does. But what to call that profession? I call it *simony*. You don't know what that means, right? Nor do I. Or I don't know exactly. But I have the feeling that what my father's engaged in, and what I myself could engage in, can't be called anything else but *simony*. Maybe he himself is aware that he's involved in simony. Subconsciously, maybe he knew it ages back. That he'd end up like this. And that's why he gave me (needless to say, subconsciously) the name Simon. If indeed it was he that gave me the name. Maybe it was his mother, his pious and hardworking mother, who when she saw that she could not have a priest among her sons, transferred her desire to her grandchild, to me, and hoped that if I were called Simon, one day I'd turn into an apostle Peter. Let's assume that they'd take me on the missions after all. What about

Estrella? I'd never persuade her to do any church work, not her! But let that be. Nothing actually bothers me, Eddie. I'm happy, I tremble, I dance in the draught of freedom. It blows me where it will. I'm light as paper. In a while I must be off *naar Schiphol.*'

Simon tensed to retch, but he suppressed the rush of nausea. Poxy Jonge Jenever! He slithered off the barstool and planted himself on his feet. For a moment he remained standing, holding on to the bar counter. Saying 'Sorry' to Eddie, he moved in the direction of the toilet.

74. No gurgling,

no subterranean burble. No darkness, only lights and metal, a trough instead of pissoirs. An unfriendly urinal, a metal receptacle the length of the wall, with a trickle of water at the bottom. Nothing so mournfully cosy as the toilet in Gravenstraat.

Malevolent, jabbing little stars dance before his eyes. He hears water, but doesn't know if it's flowing already or just preparing. Drops, he grimaces. One after the other, a barely audible waterfall. Tiny and feeble as the urine stream of a timid, ageing man. Falling to the bottom of the metal urinal. Trough in a torture chamber. What is a trough doing in a torture chamber? And a torture chamber? What is that doing in a cafe? What secret do they want to get out of him? The secret of the bladder, of course. Secret of the bowels. He'd retched, so he came here. Didn't tarry. Here one may also puke. But only in whispers. But how is he to stand to that elongated trough? He grimaces. No way, the pissing can wait. In sequence it comes after the Roman ceremony. Psst! Let's wait, let's calmly wait, until something moves. Trough, over it a mirror. Opportunity to ask. But how long it is! And all along the wall. For what? Aha, the mug! Swollen, purple. Are you happy? Estrella would ask, if she saw Simon now. Are you happy that you've got in such a state? His whole life is swelling, it's turning violet, the hopeful apostle Peter. He thinks he's becoming beautiful. Quite like his friend Justin. That one also thinks he gets more and more beautiful. No, he doesn't really think that. All he thinks is that he isn't changing. That he's thin, weak, sinister. Like when he was young.

Roman festivities . . . It happened once in his old homeland, in a reddish-brown pub in the reddish-brown homeland. Simon had drunk enough wine for three; he'd been drinking all afternoon, and in the editorial office he announced that he had to go out on a job. He called a taxi and had himself carried to the centre, to Kamenné Square, with his favourite cafe just a step beyond. He was enjoying himself, toping at a rate of knots. Two hours later he felt an oppression in his stomach and knew immediately that if he wanted to continue, he must throw up some of what he had put down. So, he shut himself in the toilet cubicle and there, to the accompaniment of ghastly sounds like cattle bawling, he puked and he puked and he puked. Someone knocked on the door: Don't you need help? Aren't you ill?

On the contrary, my dear Miss. On the contrary. Probably you haven't yet heard about the ancient Romans and how they relieved themselves after a feast?

No, I haven't heard that. But how do you know I'm a Miss?

Simon knew who that voice belonged to: a certain squinty-eyed frustrated artist, and probably also ecological activist, with thick glasses and repulsive blond dreadlocks.

He continues checking his face in the mirror. When he met Justin not long ago, Justin had said simply: You're puffy. Justin knew how to situate himself in this world, all respect. A smart being. Evaluated his position, his capacities and opportunities, and got situated. Secure chair, secure table, spacious office in a branch of an international insurance firm. Life according to rules and agreements. Quite like Peter. Except that Peter with age had become a more and more fervent Catholic, and Justin had become a more and more obdurate atheist. Or not. Years had passed; maybe everything had turned right round again. Peter as an atheist? Who'd renounce Simone Weil? All the one. The main thing is that both are useful members of society. For which they've resolved to live and die. No con men. Men, standing firmly on the earth. On those the world's course depends. They are useful: they do not care to what purposes *this* world uses their *talent* and *love of order*. A world like this. In which officials officiate, stamp documents and compile tables, managers manage, financial jugglers juggle and finance, advisers advise, insurers conclude insurance deals, political analysts analyse, human resources experts look for human resources, visual artists visualize theories about visual art, university dozents write longwinded tractates that nobody reads, but without which the world would probably collapse. And footballers football, golfers golf, tennis players tennis, developers develop, and they don't at all feel useless. They do not doubt the meaning of their existence. The momentousness. Each works hard. Each works hard at pretending to do hard work. Simon works hard at pretending idleness. He had begun pretending this before he read, in a novella by Cervantes, the narrator saying that to be useless in such a world is actually a virtue. But a virtue for what? All have respect before virtue. Even criminals, though they do not admit this. No one doubts that it's virtuous to be useful; but whether virtue itself is useful? Simon needn't let that trouble him; he knows it's both unprofitable and non-virtuous. Certainly, though, it's not pointless. Oh, indeed it isn't; he will not lower himself to the level of certain heroes in Russian novels. That's why he doesn't write novels. One day the cosmic mischief-maker that invented and bungled all this will pull the cable from the socket and this whole cabaret will suddenly be extinguished. And then it will become evident that no one knows how to change a light bulb, no one knows how to hammer a nail, no one knows how to bake bread, construct a chair, mend a roof, grow vegetables, slice an onion, cook onion soup.

Time for the digestive tract, by which all higher animals are distinguished, to manifest its defensive reflex fully! The gullet and the oral cavity will provide an exit for harmful stomach contents and also for harmful contents of the mind. Simon moves into a cubicle. He bends over the bowl and closes his eyes. Tears begin to trickle from under his eyelids. He opens his eyes. Closes them. Opens them again. He feels a faint dizziness. It'll pass instantly, instant.

Justin deserves admiration. Finally, he managed to extricate himself from his mother's despotic claws. It seems that non-despotic mothers do not exist. Justin had successfully escaped *from the galleys*, but evidently not because his mother had died, no. Justin had liberated himself earlier. But first he'd had to live through hell, when he allowed a certain excessively caring woman to move in with him. And she, thinking it was to Justin's benefit, controlled him from morning till night: don't smoke so much, don't drink so much, educate yourself. She took any amount of ancillary drudgery upon herself, simply so that Justin could have still more comfort. And Justin simply wasted away. In vain, Simon warned him that he needed to get rid of that woman. Justin had to serve his full time in that comedy, so that he himself might arrive at insight. Himself, without Simon's analytical remarks, he needed to get the fact the right way up in his head, that he had gone from the frying pan into the fire: freed himself from the mother's claws and fallen into the trap of a loving tyrant. Finally, he got rid of her also, and now he stands on his own feet. Today he knows his own capacities and limits—can a man wish for more? Justin knows clearly in which situations panic and faintness would overpower him, so he avoids them. He knows that travelling would cause him nervous stomach upsets, sociophobic fits and vertigo, so he doesn't travel. Rightly so. Once a man reckons his limits, he can live a quite normal, to all appearances healthy, ordered life. If he providently avoids certain situations, he need not fear that at certain moments he will lose control and be distressed, and the world will see his inadequacies. He who knows how to manoeuvre in life, how not to distress himself, how always to *play* the competent, thorough and just person: of such a man one may say that he has grown up and is standing on his own feet. So there's no point analysing Justin any farther. A character that stands on his own feet and always has resources to hand is unsuitable for a novel.

Simon stretches, again leans forward, retches.

Nothing. He does a couple of quick knee-bends. Again stretches. Leans forward. Retches.

Scenes go hurtling through his mind: two shaven-headed lesbians in medieval costumes; drunk Dutch pensioners on a train, terrorizing their fellow passengers with their whooping; greasy red faces, spittle blobs, expectoration, snots, a red-headed dozent of mathematics chewing his nose pickings; hulking pensioners in beige-coloured balloon shirts stumbling over chairs in a cafe; obese girls sweating as they caper to the marching rhythm of a Netherpop hit song—enough, enough! Now something from the land over yonder: the rust-eaten, weed-bestrewn old homeland crammed with dilapidated apartment blocks and fissured footpaths, a carcass with its guts hanging out; the native town and its inhabitants, fettered by centuries-old grotesque rituals of ordinary life; spit-spattered pubs; devastated, shit-coated toilets with swarms of flies; battered bald-headed creatures; politicians' suits; the lascivious language of Anton Blef. Political slogans, post-election financial affairs, blocked toilets of suburban pubs, life's wisdom of celebrities. And something Netherlandish now: squares covered in shards of glass and plastic cups and a white foam that football fans have pissed and vomited out; the sticky pavements in the red-light district, where pungent perfumes mix with the odour of sweaty bodies and the urine of drunken customers; and Marjon, as she runs into the bar after her child. Marjon, Marjon. Simon imagines her copulating with her husband, imagines her enormous yeasty thighs, imagines the smell of her underwear, the pong of dried menstrual blood. Analis, he imagines Analis, her name, as spelled correctly, imagines her utterances, imagines how she behaves when she gets drunk, imagines her coarse voice, her blokeish guffaw, her armpit. Then he remembers the verbal collocation *girl's fart*—Estrella categorizes farts and among them is a *girl's fart*; Simon doesn't know why, but the combination of the words *girl's fart* always gets to him, every time it turns his stomach: *girl's fart* is the ultimate, that conjunction of innocence and bestiality, silkiness and sadism, cosmetics and intestinal flora—say what you will, it must shake absolutely anyone.

And now and now and now! Now it's rolling. GRRRRRRRRRR-CHCHCHCH . . . BLÉÉÉÉÉÉOOOOOOUUUFF!!! CHRRR-RRRRRRCHHHH. Translucent mass. Spittle, phlegm, blood. Altogether nothing dense, nothing serious. Just a sort of froth, so once more:

GRRRRRR, well OK, let's go, one more time, hey rup and: BUÁÁÁÁÁÁ. Lace the cocktail, press, flush. Flush again. And toilet paper. Simon, blinded with tears, gropes for the toilet-paper holder. Spits leak from the corners of his mouth. He wants to wipe them off with the back of his hand, but the hand somehow oddly flies away; he'd smile wryly at that if he didn't see that his legs too are flying away, as if escaping from some ragged buffoon. He hears a dull banging. Immediately it turns dark. And silent. No gurgling. Nothing. Not even space. Not even a hint of thought.

75. Where was all this brought from?

This furniture, chairs, kitchen unit, plates, knife. Simon has no idea where they came from, or how they were fitted in here, into this little narrow room. How? When? Why in here? He doesn't want to, isn't able to think about that. He has a pleasant, easy feeling, it's a sunny morning. They're sitting in the kitchen, having breakfast. Talking. Estrella: And that rare bookseller in Deventer, you know the one I mean. What did he say to you? (Estrella crosses to the kitchen unit and puts slices of bread in the toaster.)

I don't feel like talking about him now.

Something unpleasant? (Estrella goes to the fridge, opens it and takes out a green pepper.)

No, not at all. Just nothing special.

You were bored. Will you have some pepper?

No, I wasn't bored, I'm never bored, but I don't want to talk about it now. I mean, look at me. My eyes are not yet properly unglued. I'm looking for a grammar book. (Simon rises, opens the fridge door, takes out the smoked cheese, places it on the table, looks at it for a moment, then picks it up, opens the fridge door, puts back the cheese and takes out the butter.)

I understand. Will you have onion too? (Estrella approaches the fridge, opens the door, and looks at Simon. Waits.)

I don't know. Do you want to slice it? (Simon begins to spread butter on bread.)

Do you want it or not?

I don't know. Are you slicing?

So you do. (Estrella takes an onion from the fridge and the smoked cheese that Simon a moment ago put back.)

And are you having some?

Probably not, but I'll slice it for you. Will you have tomatoes too?

But slice them only in the event that you're also going to slice the onion. (The toaster clinks. Estrella takes a knife from the drawer.)

I will, gladly. (From behind a cooking pot she fishes out a plastic board for chopping vegetables.)

Do you know what I've discovered?

What now?

That now I'm not shitting such big heaps as before.

So we're at this again. (Estrella is cutting tomatoes.)

Do you think I've got bowel cancer?

Is something hurting? Have you got bloody stools? (Estrella opens the cupboard over the unit and takes out a small plate, on which she lays the sliced tomatoes.)

No.

So there's nothing wrong with you. (Simon spreads butter on a further, third slice of bread and waits for Estrella to sit down.)

Well, so what? Hypochondria is as hard to live with as any other illness.

Why is it that every time when we're eating you start talking about shit?

Me? If you only knew how often you begin talking about shit yourself! Do you think it interests me? You're not wrong, it really does interest me. After all, we're living together, we must have precise information on the state of our digestion.

I'm disgusting, I know. (Estrella takes the toasted bread slices from the toaster and puts them on the plate which she had laid on the table at the very beginning of the breakfast ceremony.)

No, not at all. Who else could you talk to about shit, if not me? We took a vow, didn't we: in joy and in sorrow . . .

Shit is not actually a bad thing . . .

Obviously not, it's important, we must have a view of what's happening inside us, and shit is a messenger that doesn't tell lies.

Simon, do you think the cow that married us in the wedding hall was drunk?

It was weird, how she garbled her words. But we controlled ourselves, we didn't roar laughing.

Not right away.

But almost right away, just not there. Behind the door.

Do you think she heard us?

Who cares?

We didn't want a wedding march, but she got them to play one for us anyhow. She forced us to listen to it.

They played it all wrong.

And now we're sitting here and talking about who has what kind of shit.

That expresses the height of our mutual trust. Trust that can be generated only between spouses. (Simon reaches for the chair on which he has thrown a heap of newspapers. He fishes out the weekend edition of *NRC Handelsblad*.)

Depth. (Estrella places the little plate with sliced onion and tomatoes on the table.)

Height or depth. No difference.

So are you now *descending*? (Estrella sits opposite Simon and fingers the toast to see if it's still scorching hot.)

I'm descending to your depths. (Simon is riffling pages.)

To mine? It's your own shit you're talking about. Don't forget to take some onion.

It will not escape an attentive person that he isn't producing such large heaps as before. When I moved here, I shat a kilo at least every day. Although in a magazine on health and diet they wrote that a person produces a quarter of a kilo of excrement daily. Maximum. So probably it wasn't a kilo. Though why not? Maybe I'm an exception, maybe I cack more of it than others. And besides: who knows what kind of sample they studied in that project? Maybe just some desiccated nullities.

And couldn't we talk about something else?

Why are you so annoyed?

I'm not annoyed. I'm listening to you. (Estrella takes *Hollands Diep* from the pile of newspapers.)

You *are* annoyed. But besides that, I have to listen patiently to your dietological commentaries. And endlessly answer your questions: 'Don't I have a big belly?' 'Don't I have a fat arse?' Does it ever occur to you how many times you ask me these things?

Are we quarrelling now? (Estrella rises, takes the smoked cheese, opens the fridge door, places it inside and takes out the sliced cheese.)

According to me, no.

According to me too, no. (Estrella puts sliced cheese on the bread.)

I shouldn't have gone to Deventer. It did me no good. I thought it would bring me relief, my anxiety would recede. But no. The weather was vile, a merry-go-round had been installed in the square and I had nothing to say to that fellow in the rare bookshop. I didn't want to. Should I ask him right out of the blue if he'd employ me? He didn't look like he needed a helper. And what kind of helper would I be? When I can't even slice onions properly.

Don't worry, you'll learn. When the cooking fit comes on you again, I'll give you an onion to slice.

I don't know if I'll ever again want to cook.

If not, you'll find another amusement.

This is not about amusement, Estrella. Don't you understand? I ought to learn some regular craft. I probably don't have the makings of a professional cook. I don't know if I'm capable of preparing lovely aromatic foods. And yet I'd like to.

You're impatient. In other words, in reality you wouldn't like to.

The reason human shit stinks so unbearably is because of stinking foods. When will human beings finally realize that? No animal's shit stinks so disgustingly as man's.

Well, cow dung too can smell quite unbearably.

It doesn't bother me. When that smell wafts in on the wind from the fields, it brings me my childhood, my grandparents' garden.

You had a happy childhood?

There was nothing I lacked. Well, something was lacking, but to this day I can't put a name on it.

Would you like to go *home* to look?

No, I think. We don't have time for such things. But what if we went to Rome this autumn? (Simon takes another slice of bread from the bag.)

Once more? Remember Campo de' Fiori.

What about it? (Simon begins to spread butter on the bread.)

D'you remember that *meisje* with the beret and the notebook?

Mhm.

Do you want to savour more such scenes? Rome is swarming with them. American girls. In Rome they give themselves up to melancholy reverie. They nest in some godforsaken cafe, say in Campo de' Fiori, unsheathe the notebook and peck out complete novels. Or Skype the boyfriend in Boston: hi, howdy, right now I'm sitting in Campo de' Fiori, flower market in front of me, there's a flower seller, can you imagine, looks like she's Lollobrigida's twin. We know them. Disgusting.

Lollofrigida.

Quite so. Lollofrigida. Have some of that onion. Why did I cut it?

OK. What if we went to Seville again?

You think there are no Lollofrigidas sitting in the cafes there? Lollolitas?

We don't have to notice them. (Simon gnaws a bit off the bread.)

They will notice you. Us. They'll invent a story about us. Go chase them. Aha, look what they're writing about in *Hollands Diep*: *Brooklyn has streets full of writers*. Look at this photo. Would you like to be sitting there? *Mnam, mnam*, hey? Behind every table a writer. Before every writer a notebook. Read.

Volle bak in schrijverscafé Building on Bond. And so what?

On the previous page you've got a map with other cafes. Farrels. Perch Cafe. Atlas Cafe. Lucky Cat. Can you imagine all these wretches with notebooks ensconced in the Bolwerk?

And what if they were? At least there'd be quiet. (Simon again bites from the bread.)

And Mexico? You did want to go to Mexico. (Estrella planks a slice of hard yellow cheese on fresh toast.)

Mexico will wait. Mexico is a life's goal.

And what's in Seville?

When we were there, something eluded us. Something we never looked at, because we didn't know about it then. (Simon rises, goes to the kitchen unit, takes the small saucepan, pours the water from it, runs new water into it and places it on the cooker, switching that on.)

I don't want to go through memories.

But this is important. Something that could be connected with your father. (Simon opens the cupboard above the kitchen unit and selects a box of Moroccan tea.)

And how so?

Posada's graphic sheets. (Simon puts a tea bag in a cup that he'd put on the kitchen unit the previous evening.)

And what about them?

Do you know what skeletons Juan Valdés de Leal was able to paint? *Finis Gloriae Mundi* and *In Ictu Oculi*. Both paintings are in Hospital de la Caridad. (Simon pours the tea and sits again at the table.)

And you want to go only because of that?

And?

Let's go somewhere we haven't been yet. (Estrella rises and puts away the sliced cheese in the fridge.)

We haven't yet been to Hospital de la Caridad.

We've time yet to think about that. Instead, let's consider what we're going to cook on Saturday.

Nothing, we're slimming, aren't we? Needn't cook anything.

And do you know that all those detox cures are pure nonsense? They were talking about it on television. They tested people. One group got unhealthy foods to eat, another group healthy foods. Results were the same in both groups.

That's been clear to me for ages. Nothing at all surprises me. The world is a fuck-up. No point philosophizing about it.

And have you heard that according to some feminists, a woman who has never in her life tasted her menstrual blood cannot be considered emancipated? Can I take out the tea bag?

Leave it in a while longer. I hadn't heard this condition for a woman to be emancipated, but about menstrual blood being consumed, yes. It's a common event in magic. Witches. But that won't stop these women, inspired by who-knows-what, from pretending that they've just discovered it. Everything repeats in a cycle. One generation matures, another dies off, and information is uncovered that's already been uncovered a thousand times. But today, when living is faster, the generations don't even get to mature properly, and in the course of their lives they several times present facts that have long ago been explained, refined and discriminately analysed, as if they were some earthshaking sensation. Even journals that claim to be on a certain so-called intellectual level keep that same information circulating. There is no continuity with what has already been said; simply, always only those things are said that have been said already. In the course of two or three years, young enthusiastic article spouters will repeat to young enthusiastic article guzzlers numerous times, who such-and-such was and what they did and how. Always round and round. Always we get bogged down at the level of introductions and presentations. And when the moment of reflection should come, we compile. This happens with information, this is what we do with it; we don't think much about the mainsprings. Anyone who thinks about it quickly comes to the conclusion that the repetition and the recycling serve only one purpose: stupefaction. Anyone who thinks, soon loses their job. But what use is stupefaction? A wiseacre will say that the ground is prepared for further manipulations. Certainly. The ground is prepared for those also. Some kind of ground is prepared always. It is certain that the repetition of information forces the human being to repeat certain thought processes, and their repetition leads to repetition of emotions, and *their* repetition leads to repeated outbursts of instinctual and herd activity. I'm afraid. Everything that has been hitherto, all that disgusting brutality, will be repeated. Maybe in a more sophisticated form. There's nothing at all on which I could base myself, our common existence, plans. Estrella, don't you feel that we're living in a vacuum? And that's why I'd rather be with Valdés de Leal and his skeletons. When I look at them, like at the prints of your Posada, for a moment I feel relief. But I don't stop being afraid. I fear that someone will injure you. Will beat you, will torture you, and I will not be able to do anything to stop it. I know, I know what you want to say: hidden behind my fear for you is only a fear for myself. That may be, but even so, the fear remains.

When those refrains and repetitions become unbearable, we have a solution, but you know that. (Estrella rises and puts the plates in the sink.)

Yes, I know.

76. The legend of Simon Magus

says that. Irrelevant. Simon Blef opened his eyes. He had been a minute unconscious, at most. He rose, dusted down his trousers and left the cubicle. He splashed cold water on his face and looked in the mirror.

We have a solution always.

According to legend, Simon Magus envied the apostle Peter his spiritual power. He wanted the apostle to call it up in him, Simon, also. He offered silver pieces for this, but Peter did not condescend to trading in sacred things and said: 'May you and your silver be lost together!' Who would not have felt annoyed at such an attitude? Legend may say what it likes, but Simon will not believe that an ordinary uneducated fisherman, who originally also was called Simon, turned the screws on such a well-shod intellectual as Simon Magus. The poet Apollinairis de Kostrowicki, who (not that this has any relevance) was born in Rome, understood that something in this legend does not ring true. He solved the contention between apostle and magician in a distinctive way that enchanted but also properly appalled Simon Blef. Apollinaire's Simon Magus says: '*Simon Peter, I am none other than the man that you are, and our names are identical.*' Well . . . A fine rock that the Church rests on! A rock that did not trust its Teacher, when he called upon it to come to him by water. And afterwards too he betrayed his master. At the end of Apollinaire's story Simon Magus, in face similar to Peter, approaches the executioner seeking to purchase the body of the dying martyr. The executioner says: '*Once this man dies, you will carry away his corpse so that believers may reverence it . . . But until then, to shorten the long while, let's play dice: my silence against your azure sandals, adorned at the instep by a quadruple golden triangle.*'

The legend of St Peter says that before his execution the apostle asked to be crucified head down, because he did not feel worthy of dying in a similar manner to his Teacher. Christians admire the apostle's martyrdom, without noticing that the inversion of the cross—or at least that of the follower of Him who died on Golgotha—is a traditional sign of Satanism, and if not that, then certainly of denial of the Christian teaching. Saint Peter was accordingly the first Satanist. Or was it that they crucified Simon, that lord of a legion of demons? Or was it Peter after all who, in the moment of martyrdom, changed back in essence to Simon the fisherman, down-to-earth fellow, desiring in his last hour to have his head closer to *Earth*, or more precisely to what is underneath Earth? Or like this: the apostle Peter, after all, died on the cross. But since he still was not certain whether he was not more Simon than *the rock* of the Church, then (so as to kill two birds with the one stone) he had himself crucified head down, wanting thus to dissuade Simon from committing *theft of sacred things*. Kind soul. Peter, however uneducated and retarded he may have been, knew that Simon, the experimenter and first among heretics, would have monetized the stolen 'spiritual value' of the martyr's death without hesitation and would thus have *traded in sacred things*. Incidentally, Simon had turned up in Rome with Peter. They knew Simon by the name Faustus, which means favourite. Evidently he could do break-neck acts, because in the sight of the apostle, naturally with the help of demons, he rose high into the air. Peter launched into prayer and caused Simon to fall. The fall did not kill him. According to another source, Simon continued to live an active life thereafter: he sat under a tree and lectured to his pupils. He died on the day when he pro-posed to show his immortality by having himself buried alive.

According to Simon's teaching, the world was created not by God but by a female emanation named Ennoia. The angels who rebelled rose up out of that emanation. This confused Ennoia so much that she forgot her true essence and *fell* into material existence. There she passed through a number of reincarnations, eventually being reborn as the prostitute Helena. If Helena is to embody *soul*, everything is OK; Simon's followers used a truly captivating image: *the soul impris-oned in matter as in a brothel*. God resolved to save Ennoia, and he therefore incarnated himself in Simon, who had to play the role of saviour. This saviour married Helena and introduced baptism by fire, part of which was to enter water. Their wedding is, allegedly, once again only a parable. According to Simon's teaching, an androgynous divinity exists who is called Man. His 'lower essence', which is formed by *the spiritual person*, is splintered into the many human beings.

We have a solution always: he hears Estrella's voice in his ears. We don't have to search for it. Sufficient to reach for it. Unceasingly avail-able and quick. It would be enough to leave this cafe, cross through Rembrandtplein, then through Thorbeckeplein to Herengracht, and there try *walking* on water. Is he mad? In such an exposed place? Well, so what? Even Simon Magus needed a public. But he, Blef, can wait until it gets dark. And then jump into one of the circles of this *mockup of Dante's Hell*, as the skirt-chaser from Algeria called Amsterdam.

If, instead of founding an ideology, Simon Magus had written novels, he wouldn't have had much trouble finding a theme; there was one obvious choice. Simply, he would write the story of the unfortunate apostle Peter. He'd write it, maybe afterwards read what he'd written and then destroy it. Suddenly he would feel it was odious to write the story of the man who most attracted and simultaneously most repelled him. Simon Magus, if he were a real magician, would not be satisfied with the role of writer; he would not see anything attractive, beneficial, or indeed uplifting in feeding off so-called *true life stories*. He would rather make the energy of his unwritten, alternatively destroyed or thoroughly concealed (enciphered?) novel dependent on the atmosphere of centuries yet to come.

Again, he splashed his face and again he looked in the mirror. Just to make sure he wasn't beginning to look like anyone else. A moment ago, he had lain unconscious in a truly uninviting spot, but somehow it did not trouble him in the least. The one thing that seemed out of place was the excursus into the history of religion. That was simply not appropriate here, in Amsterdam. Otherwise, he felt light and clean. Stomach empty, but also composed: he therefore decided to have one more snifter. He must somehow

77. get a grip on himself.

He'd been saying this for quite a few years. Rising in the morning, he'd begin: I must get a grip. This morning, really and truly. Today I must finally get a grip. So what am I going to do first? I'll go to the bathroom, splash down. Then I'll go to the toilet. Then I'll put water on for tea. If I remember the rituals and if I remember them in the right order, I'll survive. I'll survive if I can remember what I should daily call to mind. I must get up, I must go, I must put water on for tea, I must brush my teeth, I must decide what I'll wear.

But now I'm not at home and I must get a grip. I'll go and have the last shot of gin.

'Everything OK?' Eddie asks.

Simon smiles and says: 'Nog een keer!'

'What? Jenever?'

'Yes, sir,' Simon nods. 'And water, please.'

Eddie places the tot in front of Simon with a half-pint glass of iced water, and leans on the bar counter.

'Listen, Eddie. Have you ever given a woman a few slaps? No? Because I have. My father too, yes, he too. My mother. She was the closest. We slap the ones who're closest, right? My father is able to control himself, but he didn't control himself then. Only seldom that he loses control. He beat me too. As a five-year-old, when I was asked, *what do you want to be when you grow up?* and I replied, *a philosopher.* That annoyed him dreadfully. Instantly he lost his self-control, he gave me two or three slaps. I don't know what it was about *philosopher* that annoyed him so much. Maybe he thought I was sneering at him. That I was mocking his university graduate's title. You know, Eddie, originally he wanted to be a gym coach, but it didn't work out. A pity. His intelligence would have been enough for PT teaching, certainly. He became ill, so they directed him elsewhere. Not to philosophy, no, but to some similar pseudoscience. So he beat my mother. And not once. But all I remember is the beating when he drew blood from her nose. Maybe he beat his second wife too, I don't know. He took me to their place a few times, to the capital city. I saw that she had red eyes. From crying. I don't know, I never discovered, why should I have discovered, why she was crying. Whether they were quarrelling, or just some rushes of melancholia. Or whether slaps were flying. And yet my grandmother, the mother of my father, was the embodiment of Catholic goodness. Maybe that pious woman suppressed her dark side so much that it grew over into her son. And he afterwards battered my mother. Maybe he battered other women too. I remember that he trained a women's football team. Maybe he used to whack some disobedient girl from time to time. In sport that's normal. In our country battering women is usual. The previous regime gave them so much by way of equal rights that we thought the feminism you have here was a joke. In the country I come from, no one may stand up for men, therefore it is permitted to batter women. You don't believe me, do you? And yet, yet sometimes with women there's no other option. I'm not saying they're all stupid. No. Just that somehow, I can't properly understand their mental processes. Once, I myself used to think that women should not be battered. But afterwards I discovered that they are, presumably by nature, in some ways stronger than men. One woman, in the course of her single human life, will manage to liquidate crowds of men. To be sure, most men are unfaithful, but just consider: the man does his rutting and moves on. But the woman, the woman, she comprehensively savages her victim, draining one dry and then finding another. And all the time pretending that the victim is herself. Well, nothing. You, I believe you've never in your life slapped a woman even lightly. My father used to give me proper wallops. His patience ran out. Which doesn't surprise me. I myself lose patience pretty quickly, as I know too well. So I wouldn't have patience with children. I'm dreadfully sensitive to noise. Especially high, wailing sounds. Shrill whistles. I can't stand dogs. Even the bitches unnerve me. The whining of pups. Dizzying nauseating clamouring for attention. Convulsions and helplessness of the material universe. So I smacked her. A few times I kicked her too. You don't believe? And yet it happened not far from here. Right by the statue of Thorbecke. Some junkie woman harassed me. She hung onto me, so I shoved her away. I can't stand Amsterdam at night. That's the time when all have done their sweating, pissing and puking, they've released all possible excretions, and now they're just staggering along by the ghastly canals. Who am I telling, you know Amsterdam better than me. She was harassing me and I was afraid she'd knock me over. Besides which, I wasn't in good humour. I shoved her, and naturally she fell. She all but hit her head on the plinth of that statue.

You don't believe me, what? And yet you ought to. She fell and stopped moving. Just whined. I hunkered down to her, to see if she'd injured her head. Apparently not. She whined and at moments burst into drunken laughs. That annoyed me. I gave her a slap. Mentally I excused my slapping by the need to wake up that poor slut, so that she wouldn't fall asleep and choke on her own vomit. So I hit her a second time. She began whining. That high note. I ceased being in control. No longer counted the slaps. I didn't know what I was doing. A boundless desperate fury took hold of me. I drowned in that fury. It flooded me from all sides, that rage was like if you fell drunk into a canal and began sweeping your arms out left and right. And she just whimpered and whimpered. It never occurred to me that I might cause her internal bleeding. I cannot stand drunken females. I can't stand it when my mother gets steamed. Eddie, don't be angry, but you've been lucky in your own way. You don't have to look at your drunken mother. At her boozing and ageing. I envy you. And I envy all my friends whose mothers have died. I envy Sandra, I envy the way that her mother died so quickly. Why are you laughing? You don't believe I battered that wretched woman? I understand, you want to be polite. But I have no doubt you've got knowledge of your own, by now you've lived some life. How do the Dutch put it: *Je bent niet van gisteren*? You weren't born yesterday. She shouldn't have harassed me. She shouldn't even have spoken to me. She shouldn't have fallen. I understand she was in a desperate frame of mind. Who knows what happened to her that night, where she woke up and who did what to her? But I was caught up in it likewise. Night in Amsterdam, that's no paradise. Paradise! How could it be paradise, in the middle of those circles of Hell? Listen, Eddie, why don't you rename the pub as, for example, *Mexico City*? Do you know there's a book, it was written by a fellow who liked women and fast cars, the book is called *The Fall,* it's set in Amsterdam and it mentions a pub there called *Mexico City?* Do you know such a pub? No? In the novel someone throws herself in the water, some woman, but the main character, the narrator, doesn't save her. Do you think that slut who clung onto me by the statue of Thorbecke, she also was seeking rescue? Because I don't think so. A woman always feels *at home* in herself, whether she's a mother, or boozing, or getting battered. She always has the ascendancy. She's indestructible. She dominates the globe, ruins it, fills it with the swinishness of more and more human young, who devastate everything like locusts. The mother is the most murderous and most ruthless variant of woman. And an even worse variant is the non-mother who destroys the people around her, purely because she cannot become a mother. And this slut whom I slapped and kicked that night, guaranteed she was such a woman. She dopes herself and begs because she couldn't be a mother. But even in such a state, she attempts to dominate her surroundings. That night her surroundings was me, a chance pedestrian, a potential host. What troubles me is not that I battered her, but that I can't forget it. Do you think it would be better if I was troubled by things that I can't remember, or that whatever doesn't emerge from the mind wouldn't bother me? You don't understand? Nor me. I'm drunk. But I've got an idea. What if I didn't go to meet Estrella at Schiphol, what if I phoned her to come here? It would be an opportunity to get acquainted. What do you say, a first-class idea, isn't it?'

78. 'I remember

that my mother once took me to a place,' Eddie said. 'I was small, I might have been just seven or eight, and I didn't understand what kind of place it was and what was done there. Don't think, even today I'm not the wiser, but out of that atmosphere something attached itself to me that I've never got rid of since.'

'Was it a ritual place?' Simon asked.

'Yes. She took me to a place where the *loa* are invoked . . . '

'And something happened . . . '

'According to how it's taken. *You* wouldn't have seen anything strange there, certainly. You'd have thought we were dimwits, leaping and jerking in front of an altar that's nothing more than a heap of all sorts of motley-coloured junk. But for me, coming face-to-face with the magician and the cult members made a deep impression. OK, I was a small child, I saw everything differently, and today I know that the *loa* are nonsense, even if I don't know whether that's really so. Someone may say that the *loa* function only in Haiti and the Dominican Republic, or in the Caribbean region, but not anywhere else. But how is it, for example, with Haitians who are living in another country? Do the *loa* go with them? I'm a Haitian, I've been years living in Amsterdam, nearly my whole life. If I were to meet some Haitian sorcerer in this city, do you think that the *loa* could be revived here?'

Eddie laughed with relish.

'Well OK, I was joking.'

'But why? This happens to interest me a lot.'

'It's silly stuff. But even so, it would interest me how things are with the dead, whether I could still meet them. Whether I could still some time see my mother. I can't say that I miss her; she was with me too briefly for a real bond to be formed. Even so. Even so, there is something in a person that tells him everything might have been different. Something tells me that it's right if I have a feeling that I miss my mother. I didn't know her very thoroughly, and today I'm an old dog and maybe she wasn't even a good woman. Even so, I miss her.'

'The mother is probably only an inadequate symbol of something more powerful.'

'You think? And what could that be?'

'I could say all sorts of things, but I won't, because it would sound like lies.'

Eddie chuckled.

'You're a spoofer, Simon. You and that slut. The story of yours, that you battered her—I almost believed it. For sure, you had me entertained.'

'Well you see, it makes no sense for me to tell you about *mysterious* or *incredible* things. But that's OK. My father says all that is OK. *The world wants to be deceived.* And my mother confirmed that much. You can say anything whatever, but even so, people will imagine something else, something so astounding that you would keel over. Worse still is the fact that I can say anything whatever to my mother, but mostly she understands it entirely differently and believes only in her own fantasies. And she lives in that fantasy world of hers; she lives in it but does not live well, you get me? If only she at least felt well. But now she will never find peace of soul and I cannot help her even if I wanted to. Because, by now I don't want to.'

'How can you speak like that about your mother, Simon?'

'Why? How should I speak about her? You seem to know how a mother should be spoken of. And actually: it's not *how* that's important in this question, but *why*. Why must a mother be spoken of only in *a certain* way and everything else is immediately regarded as blasphemy? What do you think, Eddie: those two *meisjes* over there, if they sometimes talk about their mothers, how do they speak of them? How does one speak of mothers, and generally of other women, in the *women's* world?'

Eddie was silent.

'But we can speak of my father. You know, in his old age he devoted himself to charlatanism. I don't know what else to call it. Maybe it's just simony, but I can't call it anything else. In Haiti he'd surely find his place, Black priest that he is. Lately he's saying that in some preceding life he lived in Atlantis and he remembers well what people told him there. My father is a lady-killer and he hasn't ceased to attract women even in his pension age. If he can hook some sixty-year-old *lekker ding* on his fables about Atlantis, why wouldn't he do it? I don't know what your sorcerers are like in Haiti. They surely don't have such a problem with it as I do now, do they? Moral dilemmas, our speciality. Except that I have not moral but *aesthetic* dilemmas. My father sees it as proof of his once having lived in Atlantis, that he has a recurring dream where he's standing on the seashore with his mother, out of which a hundred-metre-high wave suddenly rises. Some other wise charlatan told my father that that's how Atlantis disappeared. To my mind, this is just tacky twaddle. And what crowns the whole thing is that after all that he'd brought upon his mother, he wanted to meet her after death, to ask her advice in a difficult moment.'

'What had he brought upon her?' Eddie asked.

'Lots of things. He'd upended his marriage consecrated by the Catholic Church, which his pious mother never fully recovered from. Then he didn't come to the funeral, because he was worried about his function and his second family. But above all he inflicted this upon her—that he did not become what his mother would have wished him. That is the worst thing a man can do to his mother: when he does not evolve according to her ideas. My father, then, did not become a Catholic priest, as his mother secretly wished. Afterwards she transferred this unfulfilled desire onto me, her grandson, and thereby made me a submissive and impotent ruin.'

'You're exaggerating, Simon. That's not fair of you.'

'I'm not exaggerating. That's how it was. Above all else, he inflicted on her his not becoming what she wanted him to be, and then I came along and even I ultimately did not become what my father should have been. But maybe soon I will do the same as he did to his mother: I will not come to my mother's funeral. You know, I can't say which I'm most afraid of: that my mother may one day die, or that I won't want to come to her funeral.'

'And how did your father try to make contact with his dead mother?'

'Through a magic mirror. Eddie, just imagine it! A magic mirror. He set up a mirror in front of him, lit a candle, and gazed fixedly at his image. After a while he had a sense that something was flickering in the mirror, some indistinct face, and it scared him so much that he had a fit of the shakes and immediately he ceased his experiment. He actually believes that the mirror is a gateway, a passage into the otherworld dimension, and thought he could take himself off there just like that, without any experience or knowledge. Typical Anton Blef. I've inherited some of that arrogance, and honestly, I tell you, I'm afraid of what I may do.'

Eddie laughed. At seven, another employee would take over from him and he could run along to Rembrandtplein to another cafe which was also owned by his father and exact an advance from him, part of which he would spend this evening, devil-only-knows with whom, or in what district of Amsterdam.

'Yes,' Eddie began. 'I'd like to know what's *there*, in the other world, or however it's called. Just to look in there for a while, and then quickly return. And go on living just like I've lived till now. Three girlfriends, booze, the odd joint and a quiet life. I don't think they'd punish anyone *there*. After my mother died, for a while my grandmother raised me. She too used to go to the sorcerers, to those meetings. Actually, I don't even know if those ceremonies were conducted by a man or a woman. Maybe my grandmother conducted them.'

Eddie pulled out a handkerchief, wiped his sweaty forehead and continued:

'She used to tell me there's a *guardian*. In Haiti they call him Papa Legba. He's the Lord of the Crossroads, actually the most important divinity. At least, that's how I see him. Legend tells that Papa Legba was once a man of flesh and blood like you or me. He was a Black slave who ran away. He was so skilful that always he was able to find shortcuts and open any gate. I think he was a genuine *jokerman*.'

'Like Hermes,' Simon muttered.

'Like who?'

'No matter. Carry on, Eddie.'

'In short, Papa Legba was always able to slip away from his pursuers. Once, though, it happened that they caught up with him. But Papa Legba stood at the crossroads and told his pursuers: Enough, because I have control of forces that you do not know! As soon as he said this, he vanished. You know, what Papa Legba discovered within him is something even he himself hadn't known. Therefore it deserves respect. Us too, you and me, we have something in us that we don't know about, and probably just for that reason we're worthy of respect, who knows. That something is maybe also visible in us, but we never see it. I don't know how it is. Papa Legba, since they say he is Lord of the Crossroads in Haiti, knows the passageways to the other worlds. Without him and his keys we are not capable of connecting with the *loa*, you understand? I know a story about a Catholic priest who went to Haiti to consecrate the Church of Saint Peter. He was hugely surprised to see the crowds of natives coming in from all sides, on land and on water. He thought there were lots of pious Catholics in Haiti. But an older colleague put him right: the Haitians regard a statue that has a staff in one hand and a key in the other, as a likeness of Papa Legba. Saint Peter and Papa Legba, they are one and the same.'

Eddie looked seriously at Simon and suddenly burst out laughing.

'You made that up.'

'No,' Eddie said. 'It's really so. Papa Legba and St Peter are one in Haiti. Both have some connection with a gate. And both came from below, they're no scholars. But wait, I'm going to play something for you.'

Eddie hurried over to the CD player and after a brief search inserted a CD.

Beats on some sort of metal percussion instrument spread out through the room. It sounded like the beginning of the Peking Opera.

'Do you know it?' he asked Simon.

Simon listened awhile.

'I can't place it. What is it?'

'The song is called 'Papa Legba'. Talking Heads recorded it sometime in the 1980s.'

'I've heard of Talking Heads, but I don't know this song.'

Eddie raised his index finger: 'Listen to the refrain'.

Rompiendo la monotonía del tiempo
Rompiendo la monotonía del tiempo
Papa Legba,
Come and open the gate.

'Impressive,' Simon observed.

'I think there's something I can reveal to you,' Eddie bent towards Simon. 'Here, on the upper floor, I have built a little altar. I consecrated it to Papa Legba. Would you like to see it?'

79. He was not mistaken.

Eddie really was not mistaken when he didn't believe Simon saying he had beaten up a woman. Simon Blef had never battered and kicked any woman in Amsterdam. He had not slapped any unknown woman, but rather the woman who was closest to him: he had slapped Estrella. In the summer, coming from a Greek pub, which as it turned out was run by some Aramaeans.

Simon had chosen Eddie, in order to explain to him that Estrella . . . that after Estrella . . . that the airport . . . He chose Eddie because, by some purely alcoholic fancy, he imagined that he had never yet confided in a Black man. To say something to a Black man, especially if he has appeared on the scene by chance, is like whispering in the darkness. In a windless darkness. He opted therefore for Eddie, who reminded him of Nekrotzar in Ligeti's opera, an alchemical maroon emerging from the sea, though actually the devil knows if it's a true sea, because after all *Moor, maroon, marine, mare,* are so close that maybe even *marine* designates something black; maybe when the Black man emerges from the sea, he is actually only emerging from himself, *maroon* from *Moor*, or more precisely *Moor* from *Mauro*. By making a confidant of Eddie, Simon sent back the *devil's deed* he had committed that stifling summer's night a year ago, to where it belonged: to the *black earth*. The shocking experience, the memory of the repeatedly slapped, drunken Estrella rolling about on the pavement in alcoholic intoxication at night on a street in Enscheda became an entertaining story, something one could *unsheathe* in the pub to grip someone's attention.

Simon slapped Estrella: he wouldn't have beaten some unknown street walker, since after all he had compassion for fallen women. For Estrella too, whom the Greek aniseed liquor had so thoroughly overpowered that her legs gave way and she fell, he had felt compassion. At least in the first moment. Then rage ensued. No, rage followed after fear. First, he was seized by fear that Estrella would lapse into unconsciousness. That she would fall asleep on the pavement and choke on her own vomit. So that it was not compassion but fear, first of all it was fear, or more precisely a deadly danger, that compelled him to act, act quickly, rashly, frenziedly. He bent down to her and gave her two light slaps. Estrella murmured something, but she did not open her eyes. He hit her twice more, harder. She began to sob. That enraged him. Whimpering of women. He roared at her to pull herself together immediately. He caught her under the armpits and tried to make her stand. But Estrella's legs buckled again, she fell on her knees; then she sat on her heels, which must have amused her, because she began laughing loudly; and immediately she sprawled in a heap on the pavement. Simon rushed to her and began hitting her. He still believed he was doing this in her interest. He still believed he must *physically* shock her, so as to awaken her, to sober her up. Estrella, however, alternately whimpered and giggled. Simon stopped battering her and sat on the little stone wall that ran alongside the pavement. He covered his face with his hands. Chaotic thoughts rushed upon him at hurricane speed. He did not know what he should do, what the next step should be.

Beloved Cervantes, writer of all writers, no *notorious recorder*, writes easily, entertainingly and above all instructively about the beating of women. In the novella *Rinconete and Cortadillo* Simon read (alas, about a year after Estrella's *fall*) the dialogue of two benefactresses:

> —*Because—said she—I want you to know, sister Cariharta, if you don't know already, that the one we love is the one we lash; and when those confounded ruffians beat us, whip us and kick us, that's when they love us; confess now, was there ever a time when Repolido after beating and abusing you didn't caress you at least once?*
>
> —*Once isn't the word!—she replied, in tears.—A hundred thousand times he fondled me, and he'd have cut off a finger just to get me to go to his dwelling; in fact I had the impression that after beating me so badly, he had tears welling in his eyes.*

Tears? There was no laughing and no weeping that night for Simon. And he wasn't able to caress Estrella for several days afterwards. He was afraid that something in her had broken. He didn't want to be obtrusive. He didn't understand, actually he doesn't understand to this day, why that happened. There, then, at that moment, on that nocturnal street he felt the presence of some unknown force. Today he calls it *a devil's deed*. Then he had actually seemed to be possessed by red devils who did not allow him to stay his hand. He had a feeling of coming out of his body, rising above himself and looking from a height on the whining Estrella, who with her last remnants of strength was trying to protect her face from his blows. It seemed to him, really it seemed, he would swear to it anywhere, that at that instant he was not present in himself: some bloodthirsty astral force had come to inhabit him and there was nothing he could do. All kinds of things were mashed together in his head: he saw his mother in front of him with blood streaming from her nose after Anton Blef beat her; he saw the graveyard with his granny's grave, and he saw the blade of the knife that she meant to stab Old Blef's Blef with; he imagined Estrella when she was still small and her father Ernesto rolled in home drunk, grabbed his wife and began to thump her. But especially at that moment, in the stuffy and humid silence of that June night, he remembered Sandra and how once he grabbed her roughly by the elbow and he all but gave her a fatherly whack for provoking him. Yes, he remembered Sandra: they left the pub when it was already dark, and Sandra, well-fortified with alcohol, began running about, howling and shrieking, cavorting and hiding behind the bushes in the vicinity. Simon then flew into an enormous rage, chased and caught her, grabbed her elbow, and began to shake her. Simon kept shaking her and shouting something about his fears: how irresponsible she was, because what if there were maniacs lurking behind the bushes, waiting to rape her and cut her throat? Among all of these images, however, what Simon found strangest was a consoling, supraterrestrial indifference. He sat on the little wall, observed the blinddrunk Estrella as she rolled about on the pavement and felt indifference. Indifference and boredom. Boredom, and simultaneously hope of liberation from boredom. Why had he so cruelly slapped his beloved wife, the most important being in his life? The answer was clear, that night, as he sat on the little wall and observed the moaning Estrella, the answer shone for him as brightly as a neon sign: from curiosity. He'd beaten her from curiosity. And curiosity had possessed him because he was bored. Where is this rhythmically organized life leading, morning breakfast, midday lunch, evening supper, television, at night sleep, morning breakfast, and always round in circles and always just a silent, foxy-sly waiting for some event, be it catastrophic. Where is all that leading? So he battered her. To know what it's like. When he was still a stripling, he'd avoided boyish brawls. He never had broken bones, he never took any considerable punch or smack from his peers. Not that he couldn't imagine what being beaten was like, because old Blef had boxed him a few times and his mother occasionally slapped him; but now he wanted to see what it's like to dish out the slaps, what it's like when the beloved person groans. All that remained, then, was to sit on the little wall, and although there were moments when he felt a boundless despair from the deed he had just committed, what prevailed was the knowledge that he actually was enjoying the situation, that he was *above* the thing, that he was observing not only the beaten, whimpering Estrella, but himself as Estrella's *observer*. And at that moment he suddenly understood Justin, how he could so detachedly and with *objective* interest look on the emotional suffering of others. Motif of the battered wife: one must remember this well. At all events, it will be *rewarding material*, which may be used to excellent effect in the potential novel.

This is how he would probably handle the passions accompanying the beating of the beloved wife in the novel: he was furious because the woman he lived with was behaving irresponsibly. His slaps were only meant to wake her and help her to sober up, though at the same time he also wanted to educate, warn, and express disagreement with all frivolity. But this minor nocturnal *tuition* somehow slipped out of his hands. He was possessed by red devils who'd locked onto him from the hate-filled Aramaean owners of the Greek restaurant, and he didn't know if Estrella had something broken. Not just spiritually: for a few days more he was trembling at the thought that he might have damaged something in her fragile body. He remembered that most of the time he spent with Estrella he was tormented by distress, fear of violence, visions in which he saw Estrella bloody, abused, and helplessly stumbling in a circle of her torturers. He would go mad if anything happened to her, if he had to be a witness of anything like that, it would derange him. He'd be capable of killing anyone that hurt her; a monster would awaken in him. And now that someone, that torturer, was himself. He was the one whom he had most feared hitherto, against whom by all possible means he had wished to protect Estrella. Now he is that someone. Someone who does not avoid indifference; someone who by his own indifference is not only horrified but also flattered. He would not be surprised if Estrella did not return today, if she stayed in Madrid, if she resolved to have a different life. He would not be surprised.

—*What, marry me, you brute?—Cariharta retorted.—Hear what a string this fellow strums for me! That would be fine and dandy for you if I married you, but I'd sooner marry a skeleton than you!*

And now, after all that had happened between them, should he walk the world as the greatest criminal? Should he feel *dirtier* than the next, when he has no way of knowing whether that person hasn't committed a hundred even more disgusting crimes? One June night, a few minutes' loss of control. Who hasn't had that experience? To be sure, he does not wish to cleanse himself with questions, he has no illusions that he can ever again in his life be clean; but to desire to be clean—perhaps he still may, must do that . . . or not? And perhaps he may keep in mind that worse people have lived and are living still: mass murderers, sadistic manipulators, designers of pain-bringing social orders and treaties . . . May he reckon with the fact that much worse things are happening in this world than once-off violence committed in an alcoholic transport? May he rely on the huge numbers of evildoers? May he rely on the *evil-doing* essence of this entire cosmic theatre? Can one think anything else of the relations that prevail in forests, in deserts, under the surface of the ocean, and even on ice floes? Monsieur Verdoux, marriage fraudster and murderer of rich women, pointed out that there were crimes of global scale ('*One murder makes a villain, millions a hero*'); he accused society, but he should equally have accused the entire universe. There is still minimal harm from mankind and its wars, when compared with the pain that screams from countless jungle thickets, under rock faces and peaks, from molecules, cells and planets. And where then is he, Simon Blef, with his few slaps?

The red devils possessed him, using his open hands, his face. They overpowered him, but only for a moment. They slipped his face on over theirs, as Simon Magus slipped on the face of the Apostle Peter. If only Simon could have changed that night to Peter, who so loved to help *fallen* women. He too, Peter, had once taken slaps from Simon. He'd drunk himself senseless and keeled over on the pavement, like Estrella some years later. Simon could not hesitate, he had to slap Peter out of it. The *fallen* Peter. But he wasn't able to lift him; three more companions had to take a hand. With Estrella, though, he was on his own. Unable to count on any help, he had to cope by himself. Presumably it was this very isolation that gave his slaps such hysterical urgency.

Chaplin in the role of Monsieur Verdoux, with bushy eyebrows and an engine driver's smile, leans forward out of memories, lifts his hat, and says:

'*I shall see you all very soon . . . very soon.*'

80. Kees and Jan

are going to make a trip to Amsterdam, one of many. Needless to say, they will sleep over in Janneke's apartment in Jordaan. Whether they'll come to Amsterdam by train, or Janneke will bring them in her car—Simon hasn't decided that yet, or indeed, whether he will really portray this trio in his planned novel.

Kees, since he moved from Amsterdam over thirty years ago, has woken up in the capital city possibly four times. No traveller or adventurer, he: everything that a *shaman* needs, he will find in his dwelling place. Insofar as he is a shaman. Insofar as he isn't, he must go and search. Kees does not need anything, that's what he says, so he doesn't even need to be a shaman; but Janneke knows him like old money and sees exactly how to lure him out of his den. Kees, like Debussy, is a collector of oriental antiquities (Simon: Why don't you get an alarm installed?), and Janneke knows an out-of-the-way antique dealer in Jordaan.

Jan van der Vlucht is different, you don't have to persuade him twice to set off somewhere. Maybe this has to do with the fact that he is in far better physical condition than the dumpy Kees Visser. And Jan is not merely interested in music but even plays in a local string quartet. So then Janneke, music teacher and organizer of concerts, has a ready-to-hand Amsterdam programme for Jan also: a unique concert, musicians from Britain. But Kees too wants to go to the concert; he's a little bit jealous, though it's rather Jan van der Vlucht that he accuses of jealousy. He has seen him at night, after all, with tears coursing down his cheeks. Janneke deliberately draws both men into embarrassing situations. She coquettes with both, fanning a boyish, non-routine competitiveness in them, though mentally she has long ago decided. Kees is not stupid, and he is aware that Janneke plays with the two of them. But he lets that go without comment. Such trivialities do not trouble him when he can look at this splendid, almost seventy-year-old, fiery woman.

A few hours before the concert. Kees and Jan are sitting in the Hoppe Cafe in Spui Square. Kees is enthusing about the lovely sunny weather, the lively bustle of the square, and the provocatively dressed girls sitting on the benches opposite the cafe. Jan merely smiles; he'd prefer to talk about football, but he knows that's not possible with Kees. Any mention of sport makes Kees respond with annoyance, as according to him all sporting fans are apes. In turn, he regards supporters and representatives of political parties as extraterrestrials (with relish he uses the English expression *aliens*). Cheered by two glasses of red wine, Kees looks roguishly at Jan and says:

'I didn't see anything last night, have no worries.'

'And what was there to see?'

'You were crying.'

'That was just your impression.'

'You like Janneke, don't you? She has to decide.'

'That's an impressive woman.'

'You know I don't read much, but a long time ago I read some-where that in true friendship you should also see the friend when he sleeps.'

'Nietzsche writes about that.'

'Nietzsche? I thought it was in some Buddhist book.'

'He says, or he asks: *Have you ever seen your friend sleep, so as to learn how he looks? Otherwise, what is the friend's face? Your own face in a rough and imperfect mirror.*'

'You have some memory!'

'Maybe I haven't cited it exactly.'

'Even so. You don't understand much about art, but you do have a memory.'

'What don't I understand? I surely picked up something from my wife, while she lived. And she understood art, you must acknowledge that. How else could she run a gallery?'

'You know yourself, the paintings in that gallery of hers weren't worth much. I mean, what sort of artists exhibited there? Out-and-out apes.'

Jan van der Vlucht smiles. Typical Kees: the old grouch. Not a single thing exists in the whole wide world that would content him. Maybe those Indonesian sculptures of his are all that he can't find fault with.

'Listen, Kees. Aren't you hungry? I could do with something to eat. I'll ask for a menu.'

'I'll pass. I'm not hungry.'

Jan calls a waiter and asks for a menu.

'I wanted to add something to the Nietzsche piece,' he said. 'The part on friendship continues like this: *Have you ever seen your friend sleep? Didn't it horrify you, how he looked?* Kees, haven't you ever been horrified by yourself?'

'No. Why should I?'

If Simon had been sitting with them then, he'd have pulled out his notebook where he had quotes from Cervantes, to declaim in stilted Dutch:

Sleep, and in sleep you will be the equal of him whom you envy.

He can imagine that Kees and Jan would look at him in bewilderment and at first might not catch his drift. That wouldn't matter, at least it would launch a debate about meanings. And Kees, as always when they met, would ask once again:

'Simon, in the novel you're planning to write, will we be appearing too?'

Simon would nod and hasten to say that he need not fear: the core of the novel was in Amsterdam and the Amsterdam pubs, and Ernesto Varegas besides. But Kees would enquire further:

'And will Janneke be there?'

She will, Simon would answer, and again he'd assure Kees that Janneke, naturally under a different name, would be portrayed in the best light. She would appear in the story as the woman who fundamentally changed Kees's life, managed to get him drinking less and moving more, coaxed him to work in the garden and return to fine art and playing the flute. And Jan van der Vlucht would just mutely smile and nod as someone who knows these matters well, though perhaps he would silently nod because he's a little hard of hearing and has not understood all that Simon is saying. And Simon would weigh how best to smuggle a Cervantes quotation into the novel. And mentally he would pose questions: What do I know about Justin if I haven't yet seen him in sleep? Would I wish to see him in such a state so that we might be equals? Do I want to compare myself with Justin, or does he want to compare himself with me? And is there any reason why that should matter? Peter, yes, he'd already seen him in sleep, no need for comparison with him. And it appalled him, how the sleeping Peter looked. That was why he had to slap him quickly. Peter drunk to insensibility, repulsive in his unconsciousness, despising gravitation, responsibility and elegance, and the fears of others, from on high. Whoever can't hold his drink had better be slapped quickly.

81. If Simon were to write a novel and have Estrella's father Ernesto

appearing there, in the pub in an intimate conversation with his daughter, one of a few that took place shortly before his death, Ernesto would have roughly the following things to say:

'You know? Don't know? So pull my little finger.' Heard that one? A favourite trick of your uncle's. Drinking with him was pure joy. He knew how to listen to a man. He'd nod, but not just an absent nod. He never concerned himself with why I'd left Mexico. For me it's important that I should never cease to remember the reason I left it, but I don't want anyone else making that his business. I'm chattering on, what? Just that I always wanted to live as far as possible from the parents. From early on. When I was little, I couldn't put a name on what it was at home that repelled me, actually I can't name it even now, I can only chatter about it. About that loving atmosphere of the family home. About parental kindness, that annihilates every attempt at independence. Mexico too, is such a loving country. It stifles you, chokes you. In Mexico the only people who breathe easily are the foreigners, and they only manage it for a couple of weeks, while their holiday lasts. And yet I'd return there. Not today or tomorrow, but certainly some time. Why? I can't answer that, any more than I can say why I left it. I left my parents, my sister, my aunts and girl cousins, who stifled me with their kindness, and now and again with their improving lectures, I left them because I discovered that I was beginning to waste away, and where did I come to? To this noisy and misty country, to the embrace of your mother, who ruins me just the same as my Mexican relatives. Mexico tortures a man slowly, with relish, painfully. Mexico compels a man to feel like a murderer from morning till night, a Judas, prodigal son, disobedient child. Mexico will say one thing to your face and do another behind your back. Mexico will injure you, show you that you are good for nothing, and then in the middle of your greatest suffering will tell you it was only a joke and a test. A joke, and a special kind of test of how you behave. Mexico is fervent, falls in swoons, thrashes about in ecstasy, but you know that it's only theatre, a theatre you don't believe in, but which nonetheless moves you by its childishness. Mexico doesn't allow you to believe in anyone: Mexico is like a mother who'll tell you: Son, be careful, all women are beasts, even the one you've got, just that you're such an idiot, you haven't noticed it so far. As it happens, Mexico wasn't wrong about that. Your mother's greatest fault, Estrella, is that she cannot fly. She cannot relax and throw her schemes overboard; she ascribes importance to things that are of no consequence, she sweats to ensure that the order she mindlessly adopted from her parents will be upheld to the last dot and comma. She cannot fly, and yet she flies all day from shop to shop, from room to room, and then she tumbles onto the couch like a zapatero who's been shot. What's oppressive isn't the things of life: what's oppressive is the meanings we ascribe to them, probably over a long while. Your mother has finally found the kind of partner that she wanted to have in me. Jaap doesn't talk back, his life flows by in the quiet dusk of the garage. That's not me. And you are not like that. We wouldn't endure such a life. Guanajuato. Would you like to have a look at it some time? You ought to. You won't regret it. A splendid city. But I didn't last the course there. Everything there *stabbed* me, if you know what I'm trying to say. Houses, walls, furniture, people, everything had stabbing points, everything seemed to be draped over cactuses. And that's what I felt with your mother too. Maybe I should have returned to Guanajuato and discovered where it *stabs* most, there or in the Netherlands. Maybe life is better in Guanajuato today than when I was young. Maybe today it's a city for people of my age. But then, then it was unbearable. My mother, hysterical, crazy about the colour white. And Guanajuato is so many-coloured! My mother would have preferred to be born in Greece. She dressed me in white trousers and suits. And that white stabbed me. And the words of the people stabbed me, their customs, the tedium, their appearance, all places, every street, every corner, every single stone of that city. My body itched unceasingly, I wanted to scratch off my skin. And with that skin, to tear off from me all those Masses I had to go to, all the Sunday lunches that the entire family attended, all those apathetic afternoons. I wanted to slough off all the fears and the persecution complex that my mother tried to transmit to me. My sister Aldonza, who's still alive, in every way she imitated her grandmother. Aldonza may have inherited hysteria from her mother, maybe and maybe not, certainly she gives the impression of a calm and judicious woman. She took prudishness and generosity from our grandmother, and I'm assuming that in her old age she has also become a bigoted Catholic. Our Mum can't stand *her*

Mum. She suspects her of envy towards herself. What exactly she envies, no one knows. Youth? Beauty? But Aldonza is forbearing towards our mother: she no longer regards her as an authority, only as a kind of distant relative, who can't help the fact that her mind is clouded by hysteria. Aldonza has the gift of excision. She doesn't see, doesn't hear, doesn't concern herself with anything that she thinks could disorder her. She supposes that she only excises what's bad. Big mistake, she also cuts out what gives juice and sparkle to life. According to her, a person has three possibilities: take on the likeness of one's parents, fight those likenesses with all one's might, or combine the new with the inherited. Aldonza thinks she has successfully taken the third path. I don't know the truth, how far she's been successful or not, but I probably wouldn't even be able to talk to her. Aldonza's a monster. A teacher who goes on holidays with her colleagues! I suppose there's nothing abnormal about such holidays, but listen, Estrella, tell me, would you go on such a holiday? Can you imagine a healthy man who wouldn't feel bothered if his wife went on holidays with old schoolmarms? No man ever wanted Aldonza. Maybe some man did want her, I mean, she wasn't a bad-looking girl, but something radiated from her that drove men away. I think that an anti-male repellent force took possession of her because in every way she resembled her bigoted grandmother, who deeply despised men. But maybe everything's different, maybe Aldonza has changed. Old age may have pruned away everything I remember from our youth. But I wouldn't have high expectations. Your mother is like that too, Estrella. She too, like Aldonza, hates men. She only keeps Jaap to have somebody to insult. That's how she saw things in her native *dorpje*. Men are unnecessary, one must persecute and torture them. But that's not the worst thing about your mother, Estrella. Do you know what's most appalling in her? *Excision*. Yes, precisely the same excision as your aunt Aldonza practises. On the one hand she'll tell you that you must be an optimist, not think of the flowing of time, of expiry, death and catastrophes, but on the other hand—what does she exude? Isn't it an oppressive, grey, sticky mist? Estrella, your mother has forgotten that life can also be enjoyed. She goes through life like one of those mechanical toys that you wind up with a key. She no longer has any desires, nothing holds her attention now, the one thing that remains to her and still binds her to the world is anger, which she metes out to that unfortunate Jaap. Your mother would never say out loud that she no longer enjoys life. She wasn't enjoying it even when she married me; something in her must have broken long ago, or maybe she was born with it broken. Life for her is boredom, duty, something that doesn't allow her to sleep even longer. Living with her is like letting yourself be buried alive. Actually, do you know that this happens in Mexico? I read in a newspaper some time back that somewhere near Cancun they abducted a woman and buried her alive in a hole with three corpses, and she survived! She survived in that hole for ten days! Women are indestructible, just as indestructible as Mexico's *tristeza*. Just look how many words Spanish has for sadness: *tristura, cabaña, desolación, duelo, funebridad, noche, flato, luto* . . . Those women, all those women, mother, Aldonza, my aunts Caridad and Catalina, all of them were the wisest, all of them knew best how Ernesto Varegas should behave, how he should dress and what words he ought to choose. Society of women, atmosphere of the morgue. Estrella, I know I can say it to you, you'll understand: in every phase of life, be it young, be it shrivelled, there's something ghastly and repulsive, every time there's a kind of ravenousness and ruthlessness. And one must try to flee from that ruthlessness, that ruthless ruinous love. You too, you must try to flee from what hides within you as a woman. Woman is harnessed to the skeleton. Look at a skeleton's pelvis and you'll understand everything. Look at Posada's graphics. Look at those skeletons in women's clothes. Those richly pleated skirts, tremendous hats, veils, parasols. Among those skeletons I felt free. But when I looked at your aunts, especially Caridad, she's a teacher too, who thought that death is something morbid and disgusting and so one must pretend it doesn't exist, but simultaneously she declared that Mexico is the most wonderful country in the world and Mexicans are the wisest people. Caridad, poor creature, didn't grasp the fact that whoever does not understand death will not understand Mexico either. Catalina, again, used to drill everyone. She regarded men as draught animals, unable to think independently. One must therefore give them a detailed daily programme, actually a schedule for the entire year. Catalina thought of herself as a stunning cook, but what emerged from her hands was brown gelatine masses of unknown composition; however, no one wanted to insult her, so we all had to force it down our throats. Just imagine it: the hideous square in Guanajuato baking in the afternoon heatwave, fear of going out, all of us indoors in the cool dimness, and Aunt Catalina's 'specialities' on the table. You won't escape Hell whether you go out or stay in. When you think that the name Catalina means pure . . . You won't escape Hell. Mexico will stretch out its bony hand to you and strew you with reproaches. I managed to escape from all of those Mexican mummers, and then I fell into the snares of your mother. I fell into them willingly; I suppose I'd been searching for them. I was searching in a country whose language I didn't know. Today I speak that language, a language that belongs more to you, my only daughter, than to me. I'm conversing with you in a language that will always be foreign to me, though it's the mother tongue to you. Estrella, I'm talking to you and I'm aware that in my native tongue I was unable to reach understanding with those closest to me, and now I'm speaking a language that I'll never be at home in, never. But this feeling of foreignness is somehow closer to me than any homeland, do you understand that? Estrella, do you remember how once I threw the saucepan out of the window? I was expressing my opinion of Dutch cooking, I didn't need words. Your mother thought I was drunk. Well, I was. But not so much that I didn't sense what a *mythological* deed I had just committed. I threw out that shit, because it was shit, what are we to call it, the same shit as my whole life. As the life your mother prepared for me, a life of repeating mindless rituals. So that then I threw out my life hitherto. Actually, for the second time. We were not yet divorced, but that saucepan prefigured the further fate of our marriage. But we weren't yet aware of this at the time. I threw the saucepan out the window and I don't know how your mother reacted to that, but I have an idea that after a few seconds of silence all three of us burst into uproarious laughter. Do you remember? We don't have a lot of time. In the figurative and non-figurative senses of the words. Always there's something to escape from and one must escape, but you won't escape Hell. And in my view at least, the greatest hell is the society of women. The society of those women who, for whatever reason, imagine that they are capable of sober thinking. Such a woman has never yet been born. Estrella, you as a woman, if you want to save yourself, avoid them, avoid those cackling and scratching hens. Avoid them, as far as you can. Always remember Posada's graphics, and what this whole thing, this entire life is about. Each one of us is only a skeleton; flesh covers us during life, but after death we are revealed in our full beauty. Mind you, not every person is beautiful, but a skeleton is something that is beautiful pure and simple, no clods and hillocks of flesh, no piercing gaze, no tyrannizing and wounding words. Skeletons are a lot better to look at than people. We are just skeletons, all our lives we dance, shiver, tremble, we are shaken by desires, plans, thoughts, duties and feelings that others have inserted in us, and either we dance to the tune that others whistle, or we whistle to other skeletons. The body encumbers skeletons: they dance, they want to be rid of the flesh, cleansed. They dance while they live, but in vain: peace will not come about even after death. We will dance on further like those *calaveras* of paper or plastic in the draughts of wind, when La Noche de los Muertos comes and the gates open between this and that other world, gates that actually no one ever locks, only our imagination. It doesn't matter very much which world I'm sitting in; there is always enough space for me. Some figures are moving behind the windows, but I don't know if they really are alive. Whoever isn't sitting with me in this pub, behind this table, that person for me is dead.

Passages cited

Short passages in English translation or the English original have been taken from the following books:

Albert Camus, *The Fall* (Justin O'Brien trans.). London: Hamish Hamilton, 1957.

Anita Desai, *The Zigzag Way*. London: Vintage, 2005.

Guillaume Apollinaire, 'Simon Mage' in *L'hérésiarque et Cie*. Paris: P.-V. Stock, 1910.

Malcolm Lowry, *Under the Volcano*. London: Jonathan Cape, 1947.

Miguel de Cervantes Saavedra, *The Exemplary Novels of Cervantes* (Walter Kelly trans.). London: G. Bell & Sons, 1881. (Some passages modified, others retranslated.)

Simone de Beauvoir, *A Very Easy Death* (Patrick O'Brian trans.). New York: Pantheon Books, 1985.